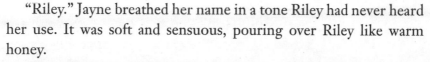
"Riley." Jayne breathed her name in a tone Riley had never heard her use. It was soft and sensuous, pouring over Riley like warm honey.

Riley's blood raced through her veins, her nerve endings on alert, gathering in such a surge of hot desire she moaned deep in her throat.

At the low sound Jayne's lashes fell to shield the expression in her eyes, and her tongue tip nervously dampened her lips.

"I've read in books," she said softly, brokenly, "about people saying they'd die from wanting someone. Now I—" She swallowed, the pulse at the base of her throat beating a wild, erotic tattoo. "Now I know what they mean."

Visit

Bella Books

at

BellaBooks.com

or call our toll-free number
1-800-729-4992

DREAMS
FOUND

LYN DENISON

Bella
BOOKS
2004

Bella Books, Inc.
P.O. Box 10543
Tallahassee, FL 32302

Printed in the United States of America on acid-free paper
First Edition

Editor: Christi Cassidy
Cover designer: Bonnie Liss (Phoenix Graphics)

ISBN 1-931513-58-9

For Glenda, my LT

And for Leona K, who will always be remembered

ABOUT THE AUTHOR

Lyn Denison was born in Brisbane, the capital of Queensland, Australia's Sunshine State. She was a librarian before she retired to become a fulltime writer. Lyn's partner is also a librarian, which only goes to prove that tidying books is not all that goes on between library shelves. Apart from writing, Lyn loves reading, talking about books, cross-stitching, genealogy and scrapbooking. She lives with her partner in a historic suburb a few kilometers from Brisbane's city center.

CHAPTER ONE

"I think it's the most ridiculous idea I've ever heard and I'm not the only one who thinks so."

"You've talked to other people about this?" Riley James turned to face her friend. "It's not something I want bandied around, Lisa. Just who did you tell?"

Lisa looked a little disconcerted. "Only Cathy and Brenna. They won't repeat it." Lisa shrugged. "I was simply worried about how all this was going to affect you."

"I appreciate your concern but I'm afraid this is something I've decided I need to do." Riley turned back to the bed and the pile of clothes she was sorting.

"That you need to do? Since when? How come I've never heard you mention it before?"

"I just don't talk about it." Riley frowned. "I don't think about it constantly. I just—oh, Lisa, it's hard to explain. Let's just say it's something I've always wanted to do."

"Well, it must fill your mother with great happiness and joy," Lisa commented dryly. "I take it you have told Mrs J. about your intentions? Tell me you're not going to up and spring this on her out of the blue, are you?"

"That's unfair, Lisa, and I think you know that. I'd never do such a thing. Mum and Dad know how I feel about them, and they know I've never regretted being a part of our family."

"So you say!" Lisa walked across Riley's room and half stretched out on the bed in amongst the clothes. "But don't you think it's being a bit, kind of, ungrateful of you, after all you say they've done for you?"

Riley raised her chin. "No, I don't. And they don't think so either."

"Yeah, right!" Lisa sat up and picked up one of Riley's T-shirts, and Riley took it from her and put it down again.

"You don't understand, Lisa," she said earnestly. "Somewhere out there is a woman who carried me inside her for nine months, who gave birth to me. I'd just like to talk to her, maybe get to know her."

"And ask her why she gave you away?"

Riley stiffened, then gathered up a pile of underclothes, smoothed them and put them into the open suitcase.

Lisa stood up and walked around the bed. "I'm sorry!" She took a step closer. "I am, Riley. I shouldn't have said that. Okay?"

With a sigh Riley leaned back against the bed. "I suppose you're right," she said softly. "My birth mother did give me up for adoption but I don't know the circumstances. Is it too difficult to understand that I would like to know what happened?"

"That's all very well, Riley, but I'm worried about you. I don't want to see you get hurt. You know, getting pregnant and giving up that child is rarely movie stuff, all fluffy and romantic. It's bad news and I mean, this woman, your birth mother, she could be really awful. Have you considered that?"

"Yes, I have thought about that." Riley ran a hand through her short dark hair. With a sigh she shoved her hands into the pockets of her denim cutoffs. "She also might be very nice. I won't know until I find her."

"Yeah, well, keep your ideals about her, that's what I'd do. I wouldn't go searching for someone I'm very likely to hate."

"Lisa, I have to know." Riley shook her head. "No, that's not strictly true. I don't *have* to know what she's like, but I'd *like* to know."

"A lot of people who find their birth parents aren't happy with the outcome and wish they never made the effort."

"I know that, too. I've read all the literature. I've considered it from every angle and I know all the pros and cons by heart. But I am going to do this, Lisa."

There was a moment's heavy silence. Riley continued to pack her clothes and she felt the weight of Lisa's censorious gaze on her.

"So what are you going to say to her if you do find her?" Lisa asked at last. "Are you just going to come straight out and ask her why she didn't want you?"

"What if wanting or not wanting me had nothing to do with it?" It was a question Riley had asked herself many times. "We are talking twenty-five years ago. It wasn't as easy back then, being a single parent. My mother simply may not have been able to keep me. Maybe she wasn't well."

"Or maybe some bastard just got her pregnant and ran out on her. Maybe she had a broken heart and didn't want any reminders of him staring her in the face every day. And that very probably hasn't changed over the years," Lisa retorted.

Riley turned and slammed the lid of her suitcase closed with a decisive click. "Nothing you can say will talk me out of this, Lisa," she said quietly, and they stood facing each other in silence again.

"All right!" Lisa conceded exasperatedly. "So you want to find your mother. But why do you have to go down to Brisbane to do it? Why not just use the telephone?"

"We've been through all this before. I feel I need to get away for a while, have a holiday, if you like, and with the housing industry in a bit of the slump, Dad and Martin can get along without me for a month or so. It fits in well."

"Then let me come down to Brisbane with you," Lisa said. "I could use a break, too. We could go together. I have a couple of weeks leave due."

Riley pulled the suitcase off her bed and set it in the corner. "This is something I need to do on my own. And besides, I don't know how long I'll be away."

Lisa swore under her breath. "So what do I do while you're on this mission? Sit around twiddling my thumbs?"

"I just want to do it alone," Riley stated firmly.

"It could take months, even years. What makes you think you're just going to find her straightaway? If ever?" Lisa stalked across the bedroom and back again. "I've heard of people searching for families for fifty years and with no results. This woman may not want to be found."

"I know where she is."

"You what?" Lisa spun on her heel and stood looking at Riley in amazement.

"I said I know where she is," Riley repeated.

"Since when?"

"Since last week."

"And you didn't tell me?" Lisa raised her hands and let them fall. "Well, thanks for that!"

"I didn't tell anyone. Except Mum."

"For fuck's sake, Riley. Think about this rationally. You haven't got a clue what you're getting yourself into. Your mother, your real mother, the woman who raised you, she can't want you to do this, surely? If I was her I'd be dead against it. I sure as hell wouldn't be too happy about bringing this unknown woman on the scene."

"Mum knows I have to do this and she knows it won't change the way I feel about her and Dad. She understands."

"Well, she's a saint, because I don't understand it at all. If I couldn't find my mother we'd both be happy to leave it that way."

"I'm sorry you feel like that but—" Riley shrugged. She knew Lisa had had a less than happy childhood.

"Yeah, well, you're sorry. Apart from all that, you've got it so great here." Lisa waved her arm around Riley's small bedsitter. "Your own flat attached to your parents' house. You can come and go as you please. It's the best of both worlds. Who in their right mind would leave it?"

"I plan on coming back," Riley replied defensively.

"Oh, sure. But the question's when?"

Riley frowned at her. "Please don't make this any harder than it already is, Lisa. You're shifting the goal posts in the middle of the game. We've had some good times these past few months—"

"They've been the best," Lisa put in and took Riley's hand in hers. "You can't deny that, Riley."

"I'm not denying it." Riley gently removed her hand and took a step away, putting some space between them.

"Don't say it wasn't great between us. That night."

Riley shook her head. "You know that was a mistake as much as I do. I wasn't thinking. I was upset."

"But you enjoyed it," Lisa said huskily. "We both did."

"It has nothing to do with the situation now," Riley persisted.

"Oh, I think it has. Great sex is a pretty good basis to build a relationship on no matter what all the chat show psyches say."

"Lisa. You're totally missing my point. Right now I can't give anything of myself, my time or the emotional energy it takes to build a relationship. It wouldn't be fair to you or myself."

"I'm prepared to wait," Lisa said quickly. "As long as it takes."

"I don't want you to, Lisa. And I'm not asking you to hang around waiting for me to come back."

"And I don't think you mean that."

"I assure you, I do. I can't be any plainer." Riley raised her hands and let them fall. "You've known how I felt right from the beginning. And at this particular time in my life I can't handle building a relationship with anyone, not on top of this search for my birth parents. Please say you understand."

"I can't say that, Riley."

"Then I'm sorry. I've been honest with you right from the start and I thought you were with me, too."

"What if I said I was in love with you?"

Riley shook her head. "You aren't in love with me, Lisa. You simply enjoy the chase. If you recall, you admitted as much when we first met."

"I think it might be different with you."

Riley turned and leaned against the doorjamb, gazing unseeingly at the neatly clipped lawn, her mother's wonderful flower gardens. "I don't want to discuss this anymore, Lisa. And you'll be late for work."

"Riley, I—" Lisa ran a hand down Riley's bare arm. "I'm worried you'll get down to Brisbane and meet someone else."

"Believe me, I have no intention of looking about in Brisbane for anyone except my mother. While I'm away I'm just going to get some part-time work to tide me over, and I hope I can talk to my birth parents. That's the sum of it. I don't need any extra complications in my life at the moment."

"So now I'm a complication?"

"Don't put words in my mouth. Look, Lisa, can't we just stay friends? I really want to do that."

"So do I." Lisa sighed. "I guess I'll have to settle for that. For the moment." She put her finger on Riley's lips when Riley would have protested. "Okay. Okay. Friends." She glanced at her wristwatch and pulled a face. "And you're right, I do have to get to work." She pulled Riley against her and kissed her on the cheek when Riley moved her head. Lisa frowned and then shrugged, clearly resigned. "When are you leaving?" she asked, holding Riley in the circle of her arms.

"In a couple of days probably."

Lisa nodded and sighed again. "Will I see you before you leave?"

"I have a lot to do but, well, maybe lunch tomorrow."

"I'd like that." Lisa smiled crookedly and stepped outside, picking up her motorcycle helmet from the step where she'd left it. She turned back to Riley as she settled the crash helmet on her head. "But I should warn you, I'm not going to give up on you, Riley James."

The back door was open and Riley could hear her mother moving about in the kitchen. The delicious aroma of fresh, homemade cookies drifted outside as Riley crossed the back deck. She rapped lightly on the closed screen door and clicked it open.

"Hello, love." Lenore James looked up with a smile as she slid a tray of freshly baked Anzac biscuits onto a rack to cool. "I've just brewed a pot of tea and you're just in time to try out this new recipe."

"They look like your famous Anzacs," Riley said as she reached for a cup and saucer from the old-fashioned dresser.

"These are Anzacs. I meant the others." Lenore placed a few cookies onto a plate. "Mavis George gave me the recipe at bingo the other night. Apricot and macadamia."

Riley poured herself a cup of hot tea and added a slice of lemon. "Want your cup topped up, Mum?"

Lenore nodded and they both sat down at the table. Riley absently took a cookie from the plate her mother passed her and took a bite.

"What do you think? About the biscuits?" Lenore added when Riley raised an inquiring eyebrow.

"Oh. They're great. Delicious as usual," she said honestly, savoring the tart apricot and nutty taste. She smiled at her mother. "The Cookie Queen of Rockhampton still reigns supreme."

Her mother chuckled. "Your Dad should like them. You know macadamias are his favorites. He collected a bag of nuts from the tree and cracked them for me last night. Ate more than he left, I might add."

Riley sipped her tea. "Mum, about my going away for a while. You're sure it's all right workwise? I know Dad said it was but—"

"Of course. It's fine. Martin's back from his break so I see no reason why you can't take a holiday, too. And things are slow right now."

"But Dad *will* tell me when things pick up and they need me, won't he?" Riley persisted. "Because I'll come straight home."

"I know, love." Lenore patted Riley's hand. "And I'll see he lets you know, so stop worrying. Your Dad and Martin will manage."

"And what about you? I know you said you understood but—" She paused. "Are you okay? With why I'm going?"

Her mother sighed. "You know your father and I have never kept your adoption a secret from you. When we made that decision we both realized it would only be natural for you to show some curiosity about your birth parents." She gave a quick smile. "I suppose you could say we've been preparing ourselves for this day from the moment we brought you home with us. Our only concern is that you don't, well . . ." She sighed again.

"Get my hopes up too much?

"Partly that, I guess. We don't want to see you get hurt in any way by this."

Riley nodded. "I know, and I am prepared to face all possibilities. Really I am."

They both took a sip of tea.

"Lisa said my birth parents could turn out to be awful. Or maybe not want to have anything to do with me. She thinks I should just let it go. And maybe she's right. Perhaps I should just forget it, let sleeping dogs lie."

Riley's mother set her teacup down on its saucer with a firm clack. "I thought I heard that motorbike."

Riley knew her mother had never liked Lisa Markham. Although Lenore had never said as much, Riley had sensed her mother's reticence about Lisa when she'd introduced them a couple of months ago. And she knew the feeling was mutual on Lisa's part.

Lisa just wasn't into family, she'd told Riley. And Riley knew Lisa's upbringing had been poles apart from her own. Lisa's parents had been through a messy divorce, and Lisa and her three siblings had spent their childhood years swinging between an alcoholic father and his latest partner and their manic-depressive mother. Lisa had left home as soon as she was able and she'd never gone back. She hadn't seen either of her parents for years and was happy to maintain that particular status quo.

Riley's sense of family had been a source of tension between them on a couple of occasions. Lisa couldn't or wouldn't recognize Riley's closeness to her family, the respect and love she had for her parents and her older brother.

"Certainly Lisa is entitled to her opinion," her mother continued, "but you've put a lot of emotional time and energy into this, Riley. I know how long you've agonized over your decision to try to find your birth parents and, for the most part, I've let you make those decisions yourself. I'll admit sometimes that's been a little difficult."

"Mum, if you don't want me to do this, I won't," Riley said quickly and her mother shook her head.

"No, Riley. I'd never try to stop you from doing this. But it's been hard for me not to interfere, I'll give you that." She smiled. "According to all those magazine articles you read these days I'm something of a control freak."

Riley laughed. "Well, if you are, you hardly control with an iron glove, maybe a soft woolen one."

"Oh, the worst kind of control freak, apparently." Her mother sobered. "As I see this, love," she continued, "the most important thing is whether or not you want to contact your birth parents. You've done all the research and now you have a name. I know it's not too late to change your mind, but do you really want to?"

"But what if Lisa *is* right?" Riley asked. "What if my birth mother doesn't want to see me? What if I contact her and she doesn't want me complicating her life?" Riley twisted her teacup in her hands. "I'm not sure how I'd feel about that."

"If your birth mother felt that way, if she didn't want to hear from you, she wouldn't have made her name available to you, don't you think?" said her mother rationally.

Riley nodded slowly. "I suppose she wouldn't have, wouldn't she? But what if she doesn't like me?"

Her mother laughed. "I know I'd hardly be considered unbiased but I don't think you need to worry about that, love."

"I'm not exactly, well, I'm hardly your typical daughter figure," Riley said dryly. "I'm a carpenter, a lesbian—"

Lenore James shook her head in disbelief. "What utter nonsense, Riley James. You're attractive, generous and loving, and besides, what's wrong with being a carpenter? You're a very good one. Your father's seen to that."

"And the other thing?" Riley prompted.

Her mother sighed. "So you prefer women. I don't really understand that, Riley, but I accept that you feel that way. Although how you can when that dishy-looking Mac Bradford has been making eyes at you for years, I don't know." She glanced at Riley. "His mother and I still hold that small shred of hope for you two."

"If Mac was a woman he'd be perfect," Riley said, and they both laughed.

"Being a lesbian is part of you, Riley, and your father and I love you. I can't say I didn't wish you, well, weren't a lesbian." Lenore pulled a face. "I even hoped it was just a phase you were going through. But that wasn't for any reason other than I didn't want your life to be any more difficult for you than life already is. I just want you to be happy."

Riley reached across and covered her mother's hand with her own. "Oh, Mum." She blinked back tears. "I love you so much. There are so many of my friends whose families disowned them when they came out." Riley shook her head. "But what if my birth parents aren't as accepting as you and Dad?"

"What if they are?" Lenore smiled. "If you keep putting pitfalls in front of yourself you'll never go forward with this."

Riley sighed. "I suppose I won't. And there is this small part of me that needs to find them if I can. But I feel so guilty, Mum, for wanting to do this, for taking the chance on hurting you and Dad."

"Riley!" Her mother stood up and walked around the table. She reached out and put her arms around Riley and hugged her, then pulled back to look at her. "Stop torturing yourself about us. Your father and I understand. Look for your birth parents, talk to them, then you might be able to fit the missing piece you need."

"Yes, but—"

"Riley, we love you and we know you love us. But no matter how this turns out I want you to know that if your father and I had had our own biological daughter we would have wanted her to be just like you."

"Oh, Mum." Riley hugged her mother. They both wiped away tears and then laughed together.

"Tsk tsk!" said Lenore. "These tears will be doing nothing for our complexions."

Riley laughed again and her mother patted her arm.

"But there is one thing I'd like you to do, Riley. If you're leaving on Thursday as you plan to, I think you should phone your birth mother. I've never been happy with the idea of you heading down to Brisbane without contacting her before you go."

"I thought maybe I'd get settled and then ring her."

"Just think about it from her point of view, love. She obviously wants to meet you but we don't know her situation. She may have married and she may have a family. There may be people she wants to tell before, well, before you arrive on the scene."

Riley glanced at her mother. "I have thought about that, that I might have other siblings. It feels sort of strange."

Lenore nodded. "It may not be convenient to tell her family just now," she said gently.

"I take your point, Mum." Riley bit her lip. "Maybe the time to meet my birth parents, well, maybe it will never be the right time," she finished dejectedly.

"Come on now, love. I don't think that will be the case at all. But I don't think you should expect she'll want to meet straightaway. I'd feel happier about your going down to Brisbane if I knew you'd already made contact with her."

"I guess you're right, Mum. I could ring her tonight."

"There's no time like the present," her mother said lightly, and Riley rubbed at her bottom lip with her finger.

"But what if she works?"

"Then keep trying."

"I'm just, well, nervous." Riley gave a quick laugh. "Make that petrified. What if she does have a family and she doesn't want them to know about me? I just don't know how I'd feel about that."

"I'm sure she would have considered all that, Riley, so I don't see that as an issue. No, my concern is you, knowing you're safe. And don't forget that she's had twenty-five years to think about this, too, love."

"I guess she has," Riley agreed reluctantly.

"Riley." Lenore took her daughter's hand. "You can put forward any number of positives and negatives for any time you might call her. But do this one thing for me. I'd feel better letting you go off to face this on your own if I knew you'd at least spoken to her before you left."

Riley nodded and stood up. She drew a much-folded piece of paper out of the pocket of her shorts. "I guess—" Riley took a deep, steadying breath. "I'm so nervous." She looked at the paper and glanced at her mother. "I have absolutely no idea what I'm going to say. I've thought and thought but I—" She raised her hands and let them fall.

"Just tell the truth. Chances are she's waiting for your call, and has been for some time."

Riley took her mobile phone from her pocket and turned it over in her hand. "It would be cheaper if I rang this evening."

Lenore put her hands on her hips and pursed her lips in exasperation.

Riley grinned. "Okay. I'll do it now. But I think I'll . . . Mum, do you mind if I go into the living room to make the call?"

"Of course not. It's your private call, love. And I'm sure you'll be more relaxed if you're on your own when you call her."

Riley nodded and went through to the living room. She stared nervously at the phone and then took a deep breath. With shaking fingers she pushed the buttons in sequence. The phone rang hollowly, seemed to echo through her body, and her knuckles whitened where she held the receiver. Maybe no one was home.

"Hello. Hellsgate Monastery. Father Jacobi speaking."

She nearly dropped the phone. "Oh. I think I must have the wrong number."

"No. No. Sorry." The young voice rose a little. "I thought it would be my Dad. Who did you want to speak to?"

"I'm looking for Margaret." *Margaret*. The name sounded strange when she said it out loud. "Margaret Easton."

"Margaret? Oh. Okay. Just a minute and I'll get her for you." The phone clunked onto what sounded like a wooden countertop. "Mum! It's for you. It's not Dad."

Then came the sound of muffled footsteps approaching.

"I'm off to Brett's. Okay?"

"All right. But you be sure to be back by five-thirty. You still have your homework to do."

"Sure, Mum. See you."

A door banged and the phone was picked up. "Hello."

Riley moistened her dry lips. "I was looking for—Is this Margaret Easton?"

There was a slight pause. "Well, yes, I'm Margaret Easton."

"Oh." She swallowed. "They gave me your name and phone number. I was born on September twenty-fourth."

"September—Oh, my God!" There was complete silence and then a muffled sob reverberated over the line. "My baby," whispered in a choked voice. "My baby girl."

CHAPTER TWO

Twenty minutes later Riley came back into the kitchen and sank down onto a seat at the table.

Her mother turned from the kitchen sink and dried her hands on her apron. "You spoke to her then, love?"

Riley nodded. "She said she'd been waiting for my call." Her throat closed and tears trickled down her cheeks.

Her mother crossed the room and wrapped her arms around her daughter.

"She does want to meet me, Mum." Riley's breath caught on a sob and she drew back and looked up at her mother. "She sounded so nice."

Lenore nodded. "And did you make arrangements to meet?"

"Yes. She wants me to ring her as soon as I get to Brisbane. She took my phone number and she said she'd ring back tonight. She wants to talk to you, too."

"Well." Lenore squeezed Riley's hands. "That will be good." She gave a soft laugh. "Though I think I'll be as nervous as you were."

"She did sound really nice, Mum."

And she was nice, Riley reflected three weeks later as she sat down on an empty paint can and felt a sense of accomplishment at the sight of the room she'd just finished painting.

She pushed back one sleeve of the oversized overalls she was wearing and glanced at her wristwatch. She had plenty of time to get herself cleaned up and dressed before heading off for dinner with Maggie Easton. With her birth mother.

Riley sighed and rested her chin on her hand, wrinkling her nose at the smell of paint. The past three weeks, since she'd made that phone call, had been unbelievable. She couldn't have imagined how things would have turned out.

First, she hadn't had to drive down to Brisbane on her own, something that had pleased her mother immensely. Mac Bradford, their neighbor's son and Riley's best friend, had accompanied her.

Mac's uncle was recovering from minor surgery and wanted to drive up to Rockhampton from Brisbane to visit Mac's parents, so Mac's mother had arranged for Mac to go down to Brisbane to share the driving with his uncle on the 600-kilometer trip north. With these arrangements in place, Lenore and Mac's mother had decided the most sensible thing was for Mac to hitch a lift down with Riley. Quite honestly, Riley had been happy to have Mac do some of the driving and she had to admit she was grateful for Mac's undemanding company.

After she'd dropped Mac at his aunt and uncle's she'd continued on to a motel on the other side of the city. Riley's brother had recommended the motel and Riley had prebooked to dispel her mother's concern about where Riley would stay. She planned on finding a small flat while she was in Brisbane. Of course, how long she decided to stay in the state capital would depend on how her meeting with her birth mother went.

As soon as she'd settled into her motel room Riley had picked up the telephone, listening to the dial tone as her fingers paused over the numbers. What if her birth mother had had second thoughts about their meeting? It was a big step for a woman to take, especially a woman who had apparently moved on with her life, kept her pregnancy a secret. Riley could hardly blame her if she had changed her mind. What would Riley do then?

What was the worst scenario? That her birth mother would have decided not to meet Riley. Well, Riley told herself, she could always have a short holiday and then simply go home.

It had taken Riley three attempts to dial Maggie's number but she needn't have worried. Maggie Easton had been excited, seemed eager to make a time and place to meet the daughter she'd never known.

Maggie suggested they meet in a little park near where she lived and not too far from the motel where Riley was staying. By meeting in the park Maggie said their first meeting wouldn't be on such public display as it would if they'd met in a restaurant. And besides, across the street from the historic park was a small bookshop with a café where they could have a coffee after the initial meeting. Riley thought this was a great idea.

So Riley had driven the short distance to Paddington, a trendy historical suburb not far from the city center, and parked her truck. She'd been incredibly nervous as she walked up the footpath, past the quaint, beautifully restored workers' cottages that were indicative of the area. And there was the small park on the ridge with its commanding views over the city and suburbs, its mosaic posts bearing the sign *Trammie's Corner*.

Riley had a quarter of an hour to spare and she stood reading the historical plaque, not really taking in the fact that the park was a tribute to the bygone era of the trams. At the beginning of the twentieth century this section of Paddington had been a very busy and very social area of the suburb, the tramway running from the inner city to a terminus just around the corner. The trammies, their families, local businesspeople and residents of the working-class neighborhood helped to shape the area into the popular suburb it was today.

Even as Riley read the information her eyes darted back and forth looking for the woman who had given her life. Eventually she told herself she couldn't stand lurking by the plaque forever, so she walked over and sat down on a bench beneath the open shelter, nervously trying to concentrate on the magnificent view.

Part of her recognized that the sun was shining, that the sky was a clear Australian blue, that the soft breeze carried the aroma of newly mown grass. The sound of a mechanical buzz rose from below her as a group of orange-shirted council workers cut the lawn and trimmed the hedges in the lower part of the park. Yet Riley's whole body seemed to hold itself poised, all her senses simply waiting.

And she sensed rather than heard Maggie Easton's approach. When Riley slowly turned around, a woman of about her own height was walking toward her. She wore a neat skirt and blouse and, in the sunshine, her softly curling hair burned with auburn highlights.

She has the same color hair as I do, Riley thought inanely.

The woman's step faltered when she caught sight of Riley, but as Riley stood up the woman seemed to gather herself and she continued forward.

"Riley?" she asked. "Riley James?" Her voice was low and Riley knew Maggie Easton was as nervous as she was.

"Yes, I'm Riley James." Somehow Riley found her own voice while her whirling mind tried to take in the other woman. Maggie Easton. Her mother. A million thoughts skittered about inside her. She's beautiful. But she's so young. Too young surely to be the mother of a twenty-five-year-old? There must be some mistake, Riley decided as the woman stopped in front of her.

"Riley." Maggie Easton swallowed convulsively and her lips trembled into a tentative smile. "You're so beautiful."

Riley barely caught the words as tears welled in Maggie's eyes, then rolled down her cheeks, the teardrops glistening in the sunlight.

Then they were in each other's arms and Maggie drew Riley close, held Riley's head into her shoulder, murmuring her name over and over. Eventually they parted and Riley brushed her own tears away as Maggie Easton fumbled for tissues in the bag slung over her shoulder.

"I promised myself I wasn't going to do this," she said at last. "But—" She shrugged slightly and her lips trembled again. "It has been twenty-five years since I've had the chance to put my arms around you."

"I won't ask if you recognize me," Riley said with a shaky laugh.

Maggie Easton's gaze moved over her face, taking in each feature, and then she nodded. "You have my family's coloring but you look—I can see your father. I don't know. You have his eyes and maybe the shape of his chin." She continued to study Riley. "You're so beautiful," she repeated.

Riley blushed. "I wouldn't go that far. But thank you. Must be genetic."

They had smiled at each other and sat down side-by-side on the bench. And then they began talking.

Now, here she was in Brisbane with a place to stay, a job, and she'd met her birth mother.

Maggie was—Riley paused. Maggie Easton *was* a very nice person, as she'd told her mother when she phoned her after they'd met. And Riley genuinely liked her. The only sad note was that Riley had learned that her natural father had died before she was born.

Physically, Maggie was just a little shorter than Riley, but she had the same darkish brown hair with a hint of auburn, and she looked much younger than her forty-two years. She'd been just seventeen when Riley was born. A woman in a child's body, Maggie had described herself.

Riley sighed. Although her birth mother had glossed over a lot of the details of Riley's birth, Riley knew Maggie had had a difficult time. But she had also assured Riley that her life had turned around when she met her husband. Riley had yet to meet Maggie's family, but as far as Riley was concerned, if they were anything like Maggie they'd be fine.

The day before Riley had arrived in Brisbane, however, Maggie's husband had been called away on business. There was a problem within a company his law firm was representing and he'd left immediately for the States. He didn't think he'd be back for at least a month. Maggie had wanted to tell her husband about Riley before she told the rest of her family, but with the suddenness of his departure she felt the time wasn't right for such a revelation. Riley could understand that.

Her birth mother had apologized for this initial secrecy, assuring Riley she had every intention of telling her family about Riley, but she said she wanted her husband to be the first to know. As he was overseas on business until the end of the month Maggie had asked Riley if she minded that they wait until Andrew Easton's return. Of course, Riley agreed, assuring her birth mother it was her call. Perhaps they need never know, Riley had suggested, but Maggie was adamant she wanted no secrets.

They decided to spend the time getting to know each other. When her husband returned Maggie would tell him the secret she'd kept for twenty-five years, and then together they'd tell Maggie's stepdaughter and two sons.

Of course Riley would have preferred not having to keep her relationship to Maggie a secret, but she had to acknowledge it was up to her birth mother. But at least tonight she was going to meet the younger of her two half brothers. Maggie's elder son was attending university in the north of the state and her stepdaughter was working in Melbourne for a few weeks.

Riley leaned down and gathered up the drop sheet she'd folded earlier. Time to tidy away the rest of the gear.

When Maggie discovered Riley was a carpenter she'd introduced her to a couple of her friends who needed odd jobs done about their houses. Then, Maggie's stepdaughter's painters had had to leave the job unfinished, so Riley had offered to take over the job of painting the magnificent old house. And here she was.

"My God! Joe, you're a genius!"

Riley jumped at the sound of the voice behind her. She pushed herself to her feet and spun around. Her heart seemed to leap into her chest and she gulped a steadying breath. And it wasn't simply the fact that she'd been startled by the unexpected voice that had her heart racing. As she stood there gaping, Riley realized that before her stood the most beautiful woman she had ever seen.

CHAPTER THREE

The woman, immaculately dressed in a pale green jacket and matching short, tailored skirt, was surveying the finished living room. She was tall, a couple of inches taller than Riley, and her fairish hair, shoulder-length, shimmered in the light from the door behind her.

Riley swallowed convulsively again as she tried to steady her wildly beating heart.

"You were right about the color of the dado, Joe," the woman continued. "It looks great. Absolutely great."

She turned slightly and glanced at Riley then, and the smile on her face faltered. Her dark eyebrows arched in surprise. "You're not Joe Camilleri!"

Riley swallowed again and shook her head.

"Ah." The woman relaxed a little. "You must be his brother. Joe said his brother would be coming down from Townsville to help him." She walked across the room toward Riley, her stockinged feet making no sound on the highly polished wooden floor. Only then did Riley notice the pair of high heels the woman held in her hand. "I'm Jayne Easton," she said and held out her other hand toward Riley. "Tony, wasn't it? The other half of Camilleri Brothers, Painters and Decorators."

Riley automatically took the offered hand and as her fingers closed about the warmth, felt the softness of the fair skin, her throat closed again. She coughed, forced words out of her dry throat. "Um. No. Not exactly. You see, your painters had to return home. To Townsville. There was a family crisis. I'm not sure what. Their father, I think." Riley stopped, realizing she was babbling. "So your mother—Maggie asked me to finish the job they had to leave."

Riley realized she was still holding Jayne Easton's hand and she flushed, reluctantly letting it go.

The other woman looked just as disconcerted but she seemed to pull herself together. She nervously pushed her hair back behind her ear and took a step away from Riley. "I see. When did this happen?"

"Just this week, I think." Riley told her. "I've only done this room. The outside was finished." Riley waved a hand vaguely toward the veranda through the open French doors.

"You did this room?"

"Yes."

Jayne Easton walked closer to the wall, inspected the paintwork, the vintage peach-toned cream walls, the darker trim.

"I am experienced," Riley said hurriedly. "I have references. Qualifications. Well, actually, I'm a qualified carpenter, but I have done lots of painting and decorating. I worked with my father and brother. We have a building company in Rockhampton. Mostly houses, but we do everything." She finished in a rush.

The woman turned back to Riley. "I know Maggie wouldn't have hired you without checking your references." She tapped her forehead with her hand. "Now I realize what her cryptic message meant. That solves that mystery. I think she did tell me all this but her mes-

21

sage only now makes sense." She gave a wry grin. "Let's start again. I'm Jayne Easton, the owner of this place."

"I'm Riley. Riley James." Riley smiled back. She tossed the drop sheet she'd been clutching onto the floor. Taking the cap from her head she set it on a can of paint before ruffling her flattened hair. Then she pulled at the press-studs on her paint-smeared overalls, shrugged out of the arms, slipped the top down to her waist and over her hips. Hopping from one leg to the other, she shed the baggy garment.

Jayne Easton's gaze ran quickly over Riley's cotton shorts, settled on the rise of her breasts beneath her old T-shirt. Riley watched a tinge of color wash the other woman's face. A chuckle bubbled from her lips and Jayne Easton started.

"That's what I get for borrowing Joe Camilleri's overalls," Riley said, her grin broadening at the stricken look on Jayne's face. "It was an honest mistake," she said easily. "You expected Joe, or at the very least his brother Tony."

Jayne gave a faint laugh. "And that's what I get for, well—" She grimaced. "I'm sorry. I seem to have settled for a preconceived idea. But I left a very handsome young man painting my house so I just assumed you, in painting regalia, would be his brother." She shrugged. "In my defense could I say that you make a very handsome young man and those overalls were an extremely heavy disguise. Apart from that, members of the jury—" Jayne raised one hand, palm upwards—"Riley is a very interesting name for a woman."

"My mother's maiden name," Riley explained.

"I'm glad my mother didn't think of that." Jayne's lips fought a smile. "Grayson Easton would have been something of a cross for me to bear I think."

Riley laughed delightedly. "Doesn't flow at all."

"So. How far did Joe get with the painting?"

"Practically all the exterior." Riley walked over to the open back doors and Jayne Easton followed her out onto the veranda.

Riley thought the house, built on the side of a ridge in the early 1880s, was magnificent. It was a typical Queenslander, featuring a steeply pitched roof and wide, open verandas on three sides, in deference to the hot climate. Consisting of three levels, the middle floor where they were standing fronted the top of the ridge. This floor contained the living room Riley had just finished painting, a formal dining room, a kitchen with a walk-in pantry Riley's mother would love, a study and a small powder room. Upstairs under the gabled roof was a huge main bedroom and en suite. Downstairs there were four more bedrooms and bathrooms.

At the front of the house, facing the road that ran along the top of the ridge, was a three-berth garage built in the colonial style to match the house. Behind the garages, and at the end of the side veranda, was a small flat that used to be the house's separate kitchen. Back in the days when the house was built the kitchen was usually separated from the main house to prevent any fire starting in the kitchen from spreading to the rest of the wooden building.

The small self-contained flat was where Maggie had suggested Riley stay while she finished painting the house. It was an arrangement Jayne Easton had apparently made with Joe Camilleri.

All three levels of the house had uninterrupted views across the inner city suburb to the central business district of Brisbane. Riley never tired of the spectacular view and usually sat out on the veranda at night gazing at the city lights.

"Joe did the exterior except for the railings," Riley continued. "I finished those before I started inside. Just the burgundy on the handrails fortunately. I'm not so sure I could handle the heights here to do the rest." Riley looked over the railings and down about twenty feet to the sloping back garden with its tangle of native bushland. Two scrub turkeys were pecking nonchalantly in the undergrowth. "It's hard to imagine this is only a mile or so from the city center."

Jayne nodded, bending to rest her elbows on the top rail, her gaze on the city skyline. "I really miss this when I'm away."

"Maggie said you own a computer software company," Riley prompted, surreptitiously studying the other woman's profile, her small, straight nose, her well-defined lips, her firm chin. A flutter of

23

awareness warmed the pit of her stomach, surprising and disconcerting her.

"Not quite." Jayne gave a derisive laugh. "Half of one. And the ownership bit is a moot point. I'm not sure the company doesn't own me."

"Maggie said you were away a lot."

"My stepmother seems to have said a great deal."

"Oh, not at all," Riley put in quickly. "She just said that you and a friend started a software company, that you're renovating this house that belonged to your grandparents and that you work too hard." Riley shrugged. "That's about it."

"I'd say that about covers it." Jayne smiled tiredly and Riley's heartbeats faltered again.

What Maggie had failed to mention was the fact that her stepdaughter was extremely attractive. Riley fought the urge to reach out, run a finger down the curve of Jayne's cheek. Make that mega-attractive, Riley decided, as a small part inside her begged for caution.

It had been a long time since she'd felt this nerve-jangling *frisson* of attraction. For so long she had been all-consumed by thoughts of finding her birth parents and, as she'd informed Lisa, she had no inclination to begin a relationship with anyone.

And that she should be attracted to this particular woman was totally ironic. Jayne Easton was way out of bounds. She was Maggie's stepdaughter and, although she was not related to Riley by blood, there was no reason to suppose Jayne Easton was anything but straight.

"Actually, Maggie's right," Jayne was saying. "And it does cover it. My fiancé and I . . ." Jayne paused and a faint shadow crossed her face. "Darren and I started our company five years ago and we've both worked hard to make a go of it. However, there are changes in sight." She bit her lip. "I've decided I'm going to stay home for a while."

Riley only barely heard the end of Jayne's statement. Only then did Riley notice the ring on Jayne's left hand. She had a fiancé? That was something else Maggie hadn't mentioned. Friend, Maggie had said. But fiancé? This gorgeous woman was engaged to be married?

A surge of disappointment washed over Riley and she chastised herself. She'd known the odds were that Jayne Easton was straight, so finding out a straight woman had a fiancé was no big deal, was it? After all, Riley told herself derisively, the woman standing looking at the scenery was heterosexuality personified. Wasn't she?

Riley glanced at the other woman again. If you were going to categorize on face value you'd say, tall, well-groomed, tailored suit, high heels. A lesbian? Maybe. Add a diamond engagement ring. Straight.

Deep inside, Riley sighed ruefully. But Jayne was certainly oh, so attractive. Regret welled up within her. Riley knew exactly what Lisa, what a few of her friends, would say. In fact, Riley could almost hear Lisa's jibe: *Too high-maintenance. Undoubtedly straight. But what a waste.* For once Riley could echo Lisa's sentiments.

Jayne Easton sighed, oblivious of Riley's tortured thoughts, and Riley pulled her attention back on track.

She drew a steadying breath. "There's no point in working so hard if you don't have time to enjoy life," she said as noncommittally as she could.

"No. You're right." Jayne turned away from the view and leaned back against the veranda post, and Riley was again aware of the weariness in her stance. "Trying not to work too hard has been a battle I've been fighting with myself for some time. At the moment I guess you'd say there's a stand-off."

"Right about now I feel I should say something along the lines of 'all work and no play,'" Riley put in and Jayne smiled.

"And I'd have to admit to being a dull girl. But enough of that. I believe, from what I remember from Maggie's garbled message last week about what I now know to be Joe's departure, that you've done some work for my stepmother."

Riley realized she should have expected Jayne to quiz her about her qualifications, and she hurried to reassure her. "No, not for

Maggie," she said quickly. "For a couple of Maggie's friends. I did some repairs, replaced some decking timber on one patio, rehung some doors, general stuff."

Jayne's fine eyebrows went up. "I see."

Riley shrugged. "As I said, my father has a building company and my brother and I grew up with and into the company. I am qualified. I have all my tickets and a builder's Gold Card."

Jayne raised her hand. "It's okay. I didn't mean to imply—" She stopped and shook her head. "I meant you don't look like my idea of what a builder, painter, whatever, looks like. At least, when you're not wearing overalls."

"What is your idea of a builder?" Riley asked with a grin.

Jayne pulled a face. "All I can think of is Bob the Builder?"

Riley laughed out loud. "Bob the Builder. 'Can he fix it? Yes, he can.'" She quoted the popular children's cartoon character.

Jayne smiled. "In this case, yes, *she* can, wouldn't you say?"

"Well, you don't look like a computer nerd either. Well, not my idea of one anyway," Riley teased her. "All pale-faced thick black-rimmed glasses, not-quite-of-this-world expression."

Jayne held Riley's gaze and burst out laughing. "Touché. I suppose I should be grateful for that. Let's agree that although things may not appear to be what they seem, they most certainly are. Or words to that effect."

"If you say so." Riley laughed.

"I do." Jayne drew in a deep breath and exhaled slowly. "It's so good to be home."

They stood in silence for a moment.

"Well, I need to get my bags upstairs and unpacked." Jayne started back inside.

Riley followed her into the house. "Do you need a hand with those?"

"Thanks, but no." She indicated her luggage standing by the door. "I only have one bag and a carry-on. I'm back and forth so much I've just about mastered the art of traveling light." She slung the smaller bag over her shoulder and lifted the suitcase. "Well, the spa's calling me and I need to make a few phone calls. Joe and I were supposed to go over the color schemes for the rest of the house, so perhaps you and I could get together in the morning to talk about the painting."

"Sure," Riley agreed.

"Till tomorrow then." Jayne paused on the bottom step and glanced at her wristwatch. "I'm sorry if I've kept you."

"Oh, no. No worries," Riley assured her. "I still have a few things to tidy up before I finish."

Jayne nodded. "All right. I'll see you tomorrow then."

Riley stood looking after her as she disappeared up the stairs, still aware of the faint waft of her perfume, a soft light musk, and once again she fought to quell her rising regret. Irritated, she turned back to the living room and started folding and stacking the remaining drop sheets.

She could hear the faint sound of water running and she surmised Jayne Easton would be filling the spa upstairs. Maggie had shown Riley through the house, and Riley had exclaimed in delight at the wonderful bathroom off the main bedroom. The tiles were an antique cream with burgundy features and, besides the large, glassed-in shower unit, there was an opulent corner spa.

Before she realized it Riley's imagination had conjured up a picture of a tall, lithe body slipping out of her tailored suit and into the sweet-smelling bubbles of the spa. The naked body immersed herself in the delicately perfumed suds and Riley felt her entire body grow hot as she thought about the whole scenario. Jayne Easton naked, her skin smooth against Riley's . . .The spa was more than big enough for two and Riley wished she could—

Could what? She asked herself derisively. Offer to wash Jayne Easton's back? Kiss the curve of her long, delicious neck? Erotically nibble her tiny earlobe? Slide her hands sensuously around to cup her breasts? Riley was sure Jayne Easton's fiancé would be absolutely wild about that.

The thought of Jayne Easton's fiancé brought Riley back to earth with a painful thud. What had Jayne said his name was? Darryl? No, Darren. That was it. Darren. Darren Wardell. Maggie had mentioned him, but only as Jayne's friend.

She frowned slightly, thinking over what Maggie had actually said about him. Jayne had met him at university and later, they'd worked for a short time for the same company before deciding to strike out on their own. According to Maggie they'd been extremely successful, although Riley knew Maggie thought Jayne worked far too hard. Riley had also sensed that Maggie didn't care all that much for Jayne's business partner. That Maggie had failed to mention he was also Jayne's fiancé seemed to Riley to indicate the depth of her birth mother's dislike.

Riley leaned back against the small trestle table covered in painting paraphernalia. There was no doubting the fact that Jayne was an extremely attractive woman, but allowing herself to even contemplate making a move on this particular woman would be asking for complications she knew she could do without.

Telling Maggie she was a lesbian, if Riley ever did tell her, was going to be difficult enough without having to add that she was attracted to her birth mother's stepdaughter. Riley suppressed a giggle. Talk about food for soap operas.

But the bottom line here was that Jayne Easton, tall, willowy and drop-dead gorgeous, *was* straight, so there was definitely no future along that road for Riley.

At that moment Riley heard the faint burble of the spa starting up and she sighed, disappointed. Emotional quicksand of the highest order.

After stacking the last of the drop sheets Riley headed around the side veranda and into the flat, closing the door decisively behind her. She needed a shower herself and she ignored that same inner voice that suggested a cold shower might be in order.

Riley pulled a bottle of vanilla Coke from the refrigerator and took a gulp of the cold liquid. She picked up the framed family photograph she'd set on top of the kitchen counter. Her parents, their arms around each other. Her brother and his wife and son. And herself.

A swell of homesickness threatened to overwhelm her. She missed her family, her friends, the safety, the familiarity of home. She'd spoken to her parents on the phone a couple of times since her arrival in Brisbane but that wasn't quite the same.

She sat down on the sofa and put her feet on the small coffee table. She'd had these bouts of homesickness before and she knew it was expected. She'd never lived away from her hometown. It was only natural that she should miss the security of home. Add to that the emotional turmoil of meeting her birth mother for the first time and, well, if she wasn't susceptible to being overwrought occasionally she'd be a pretty unfeeling sort of person.

And that would certainly account for her overreaction to Jayne Easton. Her feelings were already under a sensitive overload. Was it any wonder the attractive woman had hit her for six, shaken her equilibrium. She was usually so together and now she felt as though her prized self-possession had taken a major blow.

Do you really believe that, Riley James? She asked herself and shifted uncomfortably, knowing she didn't care to address that particular question just at the moment.

She finished her drink, knowing she should be getting ready for her first dinner at Maggie's home.

With a sigh Riley made herself move. She slipped out of her work clothes and headed for the tiny bathroom. Catching sight of her reflection in the mirrored wardrobe door, she paused. Medium height. Muscular body. Rounded hips. Breasts she'd always wished were perhaps a little larger. Short dark hair. Unremarkable features. Nothing spectacular.

Yet Riley knew some women thought she was passably attractive. Lisa Markham did. Gem, her first love, the object of her most painful romantic angst, had. Until she'd decided she'd only been experimenting with Riley and had married her boss, breaking Riley's heart.

But would Jayne Easton think she was attractive? The thought slipped into Riley's consciousness before she could prevent it, and she admonished herself. *Jayne Easton equals straight.* "Repeat it over and over till you get it right, Riley James," she said aloud, softly but firmly. And she'd do well to remember it.

It was such a pity though. It had been a long time since she'd been even slightly interested in anyone. Another time, another place . . .

Riley slipped beneath the shower. Straight women were off-limits, she reminded herself. It was a lesbian code of honor. She'd painfully learned that lesson years ago and she had no inclination to repeat the experience. Yet, try as she may, she couldn't seem to get the picture of Jayne Easton reclining in her spa out of her mind.

It was hormones, she told herself, simply her hormones.

Oh, yes? An inner voice reminded her that only moments ago she was blaming the emotional turmoil of the past few weeks, of meeting and getting to know her birth mother.

Hormones and emotions, she decided. Both were raw and vulnerable. And that was a dangerous mix. She'd call it a table card. It had happened and now she would get on with her life. Being aware of her own vulnerability was half the battle.

Using more than usual vigor Riley toweled herself dry and pulled on clean underwear. She peered into the mirror again to ensure she'd removed all the paint splatters from her face. Now came the decision on what to wear tonight.

This was her first visit to Maggie's home since they'd met. Their conversations had occurred on the telephone and in coffee shops or here at Jayne's house while Riley painted. Then yesterday, Maggie had asked Riley to dinner to meet Jake, the younger of her two half brothers.

Riley leafed through her sparse wardrobe. Not much to choose from. She frowned. She'd have to ask her mother to send down another suitcase of her clothes.

She pulled out her best black jeans and a tailored white short-sleeved shirt. Summer was almost upon them and the spring evenings were warming up.

Dressing quickly, Riley tucked her shirt into the waistband of her jeans before shrugging into her favorite black and burgundy waistcoat. She brushed her short hair back from her face, grimacing as the front fell forward onto her forehead. Hands on hips, she regarded herself critically in the mirror. Very dyke about town.

Should she change? Play down her real self? What was more to the point, did she have anything else she could wear? Something a little more, well, feminine? Not a thing. Maybe she could borrow one of Jayne Easton's dresses? Riley decided Jayne was sure to have one. Probably more than one.

She bit off a laugh and then felt a little contrite. It was no business of hers what Jayne Easton chose to wear. Whatever she wore would no doubt look sensational. But Riley in a dress, well, she grinned as she reached for her boots. She could almost hear her brother's favorite saying, "Now that I'd like to see."

Although Riley had talked to her birth mother about much of her life she hadn't told Maggie she was a lesbian. She had absolutely no idea how Maggie would take this revelation. She'd given Riley no indication of her feelings on any sensitive subjects. They hadn't seemed to have reached that level yet. And, quite honestly, Riley knew she hadn't pushed it. Part of her was loath to take the chance on spoiling the fledgling relationship she was building with her natural mother.

Riley pulled the leg of her jeans down over her boot and paused, her mind going back to that first meeting with Maggie Easton. She'd treasure those first moments for the rest of her life. And she was so grateful things had turned out so well.

Now it was time to visit Maggie in her own home. Just down the road and around the corner. Riley left the flat and, with one final glance back at the house where Jayne Easton was still enjoying her spa bath, she began the short walk to Maggie's house.

"Jake's off at his mate's place but he'll be back soon," Maggie said as she led Riley into the house.

"I'm looking forward to meeting him." Riley glanced around her curiously. "You've told me so much about him."

The house was obviously of the same era as Jayne Easton's, and although the furniture was antique it wasn't overpowering. Riley recognized the quiet opulence of it but also saw it was a functional home and not a showplace. A pair of sneakers had been kicked off behind the door and a couple of magazines spilled from a side table onto the floor.

"This is wonderful," Riley said reverently, touching the smooth surface of a silky oak sideboard.

"Yes. Most of the furniture belonged to Andrew's family but a couple of pieces were my parents'. The house itself was built by Andrew's great-grandparents." Maggie laughed. "There are a lot of homes like this around here and quite a few are still in the same families. Come on and I'll show you the rest of the house."

Riley followed Maggie from room to room, stopping to gaze in awe when they reached a wonderful room of desks and easy chairs, shelves of books and a working fireplace.

"Officially, this is Andrew's study but we all use it, especially in the winter with the fire going," Maggie said.

The room did have a homey feel, one Riley recognized from her own family home. The rumpus room, her father called theirs, with its pool table and her father's "bar," and a table for board games. Riley had spent many happy hours there with her family. This room had the same comfortable ambience about it.

"This is Andrew's book collection. I think I told you he loves books. He's so proud of it," Maggie was saying. "Although he's a little concerned about his bookshelves."

Riley went over for a closer look. Maggie's husband certainly was a collector, his books a mixture of old and relatively new, first editions, anything unusual. Maggie said it was a passion of his.

The rarer editions were kept in a glass-fronted case while the others were displayed on open shelves. But Maggie's husband had reason for concern. His bookshelves were sagging because the spans of the shelves were too wide.

"Andrew's father and uncle built the shelving as a retirement project years ago and Andrew's always been meaning to have them replaced but—" Maggie shrugged. "He never seems to have the time to do it."

"You wouldn't have to replace the shelves, just sort of adjust them. Want me to do it for you?"

"Could you?" Maggie grimaced. "Oh, Riley, I'm sorry. You're only here for a minute and I'm finding jobs for you."

"It's a fairly simple job. It would only take me a couple of hours," Riley began, but Maggie held up her hand.

"Don't be silly. You've got enough to do at Jayne's."

Riley was going to tell Maggie about Jayne's return but the phone rang and Maggie excused herself and went out into the hall to answer it. Riley gave the shelves a closer examination before pacing out the lengths, mentally tallying up what she'd need to resurrect the bookcases.

"Can you believe it? That was Jayne, my stepdaughter," Maggie said as she reentered the study.

"I was just going to tell you she had arrived home."

"And she told me she mistook you for Joe Camilleri. She's mortified." Maggie laughed delightedly. "I wish I could have been a fly on the wall so I could have seen the look on Jayne's face when she realized her mistake."

Riley laughed too. "Well, she did say Joe was handsome."

"He is. Very handsome. Well, come on into the kitchen while I check the roast." Maggie linked her arm through Riley's. "We'll be able to tease Jayne unmercifully. She's joining us for dinner."

If Riley thought Jayne Easton was attractive in a tailored suit she was devastating in a pair of fitted blue jeans and a sleeveless turquoise top that only accentuated the deep blue of her eyes. As

Maggie greeted her stepdaughter with a hug and a kiss Riley stood back, shoving her hands in the back pockets of her jeans. She tried to school the silly smile on her face, her knees suddenly decidedly weak. To add to her discomfort she had to consciously stop herself from staring at the exquisite contours of Jayne's seductive body.

Jayne's own eyes widened when she caught sight of Riley. "Riley?" she said in surprise. "Hello, again. I didn't know—I mean, I didn't expect to see you here."

"Didn't I mention I'd invited Riley over for dinner?" Maggie asked. "I thought I did. Oh, well."

At that moment the door behind Jayne burst open and a tall, gangly teenaged boy bounded into the room. He saw Jayne immediately and enveloped his half sister in a bear hug.

"Jaynie!" he exclaimed, giving her a noisy kiss on the cheek before lifting her bodily off the ground and spinning her around. "When did you get home?"

Jayne laughed delightedly. "This afternoon. And put me down before you do yourself an injury."

Jake laughed easily as Jayne stood back and looked at her brother. "Have you grown taller again or am I imagining it?"

"I think he's having a growth spurt," Maggie said as she drew Riley forward. "Now, Jake. Where's our manners? We have a guest. Jake, meet Riley James. She's the young woman who's painting Jayne's house. Remember I told you about her?"

"Oh, sure." Jake held out his hand. "Nice to meet you, Riley. I think we've spoken on the phone a couple of times."

"Yes, we have. Good to meet you too, Jake."

Maggie had mentioned that her elder son, Matthew, was the image of his father while Jake took after her family. Riley could see a resemblance to his mother, especially in his coloring, for he had the same auburn highlights in his dark hair.

And there was something else she couldn't quite put her finger on, but Jake was definitely his mother's son. He had his mother's firm chin and the same shape mouth as Maggie. With a shock Riley realized she shared that as well. If she stood beside Jake surely everyone would easily be able to see the resemblance.

"Did you get to that bookshop in Melbourne? The one that has all the Terry Pratchett books?" Jake was asking his sister.

She indicated a brown paper package she'd set on the sideboard. "Sure did. The three you wanted."

Jake grabbed the bag and drew out the books, turning each one over reverently. "Oh, wow. Excellent. Thanks. I tried everywhere up here to get these."

Jayne smiled at him and squeezed his shoulder. "Don't you go reading them when you should be doing your homework or your chores."

Jake gave her an angelic look. "Would I do that?"

"Of course you wouldn't," said his mother dryly. "Now, let's have dinner, shall we?" She shepherded them through to the dining room. "Otherwise my roast will be ruined."

The meal was delicious and later as they sat in the living room drinking Maggie's freshly brewed coffee, Riley sighed and thought what a wonderful family they were. And she was part of it.

Well, she reflected, maybe not officially, but she felt at home with Maggie and her family. She could also see her own parents sitting here, fitting in.

"Riley says it wouldn't take much to fix your father's bookshelves," Maggie was saying, "and I've just had a thought that perhaps I could get it done before he comes back, as a welcome home. What do you think, Jayne?"

"Dad's been talking about replacing the shelves for ages," Jayne agreed. "But it would be a fairly big job, though, wouldn't it?"

Riley shook her head. "No, not really. I could do it."

Jake looked across at Riley in admiration. "Do you do bookshelves as well as paint houses? Cool."

"Maybe you could give me an idea on how much it would cost," Maggie said as Jake stood up.

"Can I be excused, Mum? I think I'll have an early night." He held up the package of books Jayne had bought him and grinned. "I can't wait to start one of these. Nice to meet you, Riley. Are you going to be staying home for longer this time, Jayne?"

"I hope so." Jayne stood up too and stretched, her breasts thrusting against the thin material of her top. "I think I'll call it a night as well. I need to go into the office early tomorrow."

"You work too hard, Jayne." Maggie frowned. "Why don't you take a break, have some time for yourself?"

"I will. That's the first thing on my agenda. I promise." Jayne glanced at Riley and smiled.

Riley's heart flip-flopped in her chest. How could Jayne not be aware of the devastating effect of that smile?

"And I'll see you tomorrow, too," Jayne continued. "At the house."

"Didn't you say you walked over, too, Riley?" Maggie asked. "Jayne's collecting her car so she can give you a lift home. I don't like the idea of your walking alone at night."

"Of course," Jayne agreed quickly. "If you walked here you must live close by."

Jake laughed and Maggie grinned.

"You mean you don't know, Jayne?" Jake asked.

Maggie frowned at her stepdaughter's inquiring look. "But I'm sure I told you." She glanced at Riley.

"I didn't get time to mention it," Riley started to explain.

"Mention what?" Jayne asked, looking from one to the other.

"That Riley does live very close by," Jake said with a smirk, delighting in informing his sister. "Riley lives with you."

CHAPTER FOUR

"With me?" Jayne repeated in surprise. She flushed and Maggie put her arm around her stepdaughter's waist.

"Riley's from Rockhampton and she was looking for a place to stay in Brisbane," Maggie clarified. "As she'd taken over Joe's job I didn't think you'd mind if she moved into the flat when he left. I thought I'd mentioned that in the message I left for you when Joe had to return home."

"You probably did," Jayne conceded. "I mustn't have taken it in. It was a busy time just then and I—" She shrugged. "I had a lot on my mind."

"I can find somewhere else," Riley offered, her heart sinking. She'd settled into the small flat and loved it. It was ideal. Close to the job. And to Maggie.

"Of course you can stay there," Jayne said quickly. "It's the most practical arrangement. And apart from that, I like having someone at the house when I'm away."

Maggie frowned again. "Away? I thought you said you'd be staying home for a while."

"I do hope to." Jayne paused. "Darren and I just have to rearrange a few things." She squeezed Maggie's arm and smiled at her. "Don't worry. I am going to slow down."

"Well, I'd just about forgotten what you looked like," Jake accused. "Just tell Darren you're staying put and that's all there is to it. It's not like he's your boss or something. Half the company's yours anyway."

"It's not that easy, Jake. But I'll work something out with Darren." Jayne turned to Riley. "Are you ready to go?"

Riley nodded.

"Okay." Jayne hugged her brother and kissed Maggie. "See you two soon. Oh, and tell Dad to give me a call when he gets a free moment. I haven't spoken to him for a couple of weeks."

"He may be able to get home earlier than we thought he would." Maggie pulled a rueful face. "But it will still be another couple of weeks."

They were out on the veranda now and Jayne turned to Riley. "I left my car in Maggie's garage," she said. "If you wait a moment I'll drive it out and pick you up." She disappeared around the side of the house.

"And I turned quite a few heads when I drove it around town," Maggie told Riley. "I think I could get used to having an open sports car."

"Mum drove me to school in it a couple of times, so that didn't harm my image, especially with the girls." Jake grinned. "We should talk to Dad about it when he gets home, Mum."

Riley waited by the gate with Maggie and Jake while they discussed the possibility of a family sports car. When Jayne backed the racy blue BMW out onto the road Riley gave a low whistle.

"Didn't we tell you, Riley? It's wicked, isn't it?" exclaimed Jake, and Riley laughingly agreed as he opened the passenger side door for her with a creditable flourish.

"Very nice car," she said as she climbed into the passenger seat.

Jayne grinned and they said their good-byes before Jayne pulled away from the curb.

"This is my one vice," she said softly.

Riley laughed. "If you're going to have a vice then this should be it."

A few minutes later they were home. They climbed out of the car in silence and Jayne locked the garage door behind them. She stopped when they reached the veranda.

"I guess I'll see you tomorrow," she said and Riley nodded.

"I guess so. And you really don't mind that I'm using your flat?"

"Of course not. I was just surprised, although I don't know why I was. When I hired Joe we decided it was the most convenient solution for both of us. That still holds true."

"Well, thanks for letting me stay here."

"That's okay. Good night then." Jayne unlocked the front door, gave Riley a smile and then disappeared inside.

Riley continued around the side of the house to the flat and she was still smiling to herself as she changed for bed.

A week later Riley was working on the master bedroom upstairs when the sound of a male voice calling from the living room below had her straightening up and putting the paint roller in the tray.

"Jayne! Jayne! You home?"

Riley reached the bedroom door and peered over the railing as a tall dark-haired man crossed to the stairs. She was momentarily taken aback and she must have made some small sound because the man looked up.

When he caught sight of her he stopped, one foot on the bottom step, his expression one of complete surprise.

Riley was the first to move, coming down the stairs. Judging by his familiarity with Jayne's house, he would have to be Jayne's fiancé. For some reason Riley didn't want to carry on a conversation with him in Jayne's bedroom.

"Jayne's not home yet," she said when she was at eye level with him. The man stepped back and they stood facing each other.

"Who are you?" he asked suspiciously. He took in Riley's overalls. "Oh, yes. The painter." His gaze settled on the faint rise of Riley's breasts and his dark brows rose. "Jayne didn't tell me you were a woman."

"Guilty on both counts. Yes, I am a woman and I did take over the job from Jayne's original painters," Riley told him as she continued to assess him.

At least six feet tall, he had dark hair, and his glasses gave him a studious look. Quite passably good-looking, Riley thought, and she suspected he knew it. He had a certain arrogance in his stance, in the somewhat belligerent tone of his voice. There was also something else about him Riley didn't much care for. The offensive way his gaze moved over her.

Or maybe it was just plain old-fashioned jealousy, suggested a voice inside her. Riley quelled the thought. She'd known Jayne was engaged, and that meant there was a man in her life. This was, apparently, that man.

Riley's gaze met his again and he smirked, letting her know he was aware of her scrutiny. Once again Riley felt a wave of dislike and disappointment. She gave herself a mental shrug. Call it what you like, intuition perhaps, but Riley knew she couldn't like this man, whether he was Jayne's fiancé or not.

"Oh. The replacement painter. I see," he said, his tone dismissing Riley as a not-up-to-scratch second choice. "How long have you been a painter? Not the usual job for a woman, is it?"

"A dozen years or so, and no, I suppose not," Riley replied.

He adjusted his glasses on the bridge of his nose. He smiled genuinely then and Riley thought she could perhaps see what might have attracted Jayne to him. His smile added a warmth to his looks that had been missing up till now. Yes, Riley conceded, he was reasonably attractive, although certainly not in Mac Bradford's league.

"You've been a painter for twelve years? Come on. You don't look old enough," he said with an attempt at charm that he probably didn't consider would be wasted on Riley.

"My family owns a building business. I've painted houses since I was a teenager."

"I suppose I'll have to believe that," he said, and Riley stopped herself from taking umbrage once more.

Perhaps he just had a problem with social graces, she reflected. "Jayne shouldn't be long," she said stiffly, and she really hoped Jayne wouldn't be late, because she didn't care to exchange social chitchat with him.

The man glanced down at his wristwatch again, his dark brows meeting in an imperious frown. "She said she'd be here by five."

"It's not five yet." Riley wondered why he was quibbling over a few minutes. "Maybe the traffic was heavy."

What he might have said then Riley would never know because they both paused at the sound of a car door closing, followed by the hurrying tap of high heels crossing the veranda.

Jayne Easton came through the open door and glanced over to where Riley and the dark-haired man stood. She paused nearly imperceptibly and then continued toward them.

"Darren. Hi. You beat me home." She glanced at Riley. "Hello, Riley. How's the painting going?"

Riley gave her a smile. "Fine. Nearly finished the first coat upstairs." She indicated the room above them, uncomfortably aware that the man beside her had hardly given Jayne a fiancé's welcome. And would she have been thrilled if they'd embraced tenderly? asked that little voice inside her. There was no pleasing her.

"What kept you?" Darren broke in. "I expected you'd be here ages ago."

"I had to do overtime. Haven't you heard? My boss is a tyrant," Jayne said lightly enough, but Riley sensed an underlying bite to her tone. "But I see you two have met." Jayne included Riley in the conversation again.

41

Her fiancé's gaze flicked over Riley again before he turned back to Jayne.

Riley noticed the throb of the pulse at the base of Jayne's throat. The situation had obviously unsettled Jayne, but Riley wanted to tell her not to be upset on her account. Or maybe there was more to it, Riley surmised. Jayne could just as easily have had an argument with her boyfriend before they left work. Perhaps they wanted to be alone to make up. Riley just as quickly decided she didn't want to dwell on the ramifications of that thought at all.

"No. We haven't met exactly." Riley kept her voice as light as she could, doubting Jayne's fiancé had any interest in an introduction, formal or otherwise.

He moved then, slipping a proprietary arm around Jayne's waist, sliding his other arm around the front of her so she looked trapped in the circle of his arms. "And you failed to mention you had a female painter, darling."

"It didn't seem important," Jayne said easily, stepping out of his embrace. "So, Darren Wardell, meet Riley James, painter, carpenter, Jill-of-all-trades."

"Nice to meet you," Riley murmured, falling back on what her mother referred to as socially acceptable manners.

"Jill-of-all-trades?" Darren Wardell repeated with a faint smile, one hand now resting on Jayne's shoulder. "Hope that doesn't mean master of none. Or should that be mistress of none?"

Riley stiffened and Jayne looked sharply at him. "Riley is completely qualified and has impeccable references," she said. "Riley does exceptional work."

If Darren noticed the terseness in her tone it didn't seem to faze him. "Well, you know, this house, in this position, is a prime investment. But as long as you're happy with it, love, what can I say? You're paying the bill." He smiled easily at Riley. "What are you like at making coffee?"

Jayne moved then and Darren's hand fell from her shoulder. "I'll make you coffee," she said, not looking at Riley as she strode toward the kitchen.

Darren chuckled as he followed her. "I was hoping you'd say that. You still make the best coffee in Australia." He patted her affectionately on the backside.

"Would you like a cup, Riley?" Jayne asked from the kitchen.

"Thanks, but no. I'll get back to work." She went back upstairs to the bedroom. She was seething with an anger she knew was way out of proportion. She wasn't sure what had irritated her the most, Darren Wardell's condescension or his derogatory sexism. Coffee, indeed! Oh, she'd make him coffee all right. And then she would pour it over his arrogant head.

What a pill he was! Riley resumed painting the unfinished wall of the bedroom. How could a woman as attractive and intelligent as Jayne Easton obviously was be involved with a man as rude and unlikable as Darren Wardell?

The paint roller swished across the wall and Riley realized her entire body was tense with indignation. She stopped, flexed her shoulder muscles, made herself relax. The man wasn't worth the energy involved in disliking him. She put him out of her mind and lost herself in the steady motion of the paint roller dispensing its rich cream color, transforming the large room.

When she finished the back wall she set the roller aside and resealed the paint tin. She stood back and admired the room. Jayne's room. The room she would share with Darren Wardell. Would Jayne—? Riley refused to allow herself to think about that, telling herself not to go there. It was none of her business who Jayne Easton slept with.

But it was such a waste.

Riley glanced at the queen-sized brass bed covered in its protective drop sheet. She could see Jayne's long slender body sink onto the softness, turn languidly to show the rise of her breast, the smooth contours of her hip, her thigh. Riley shook her head. No, it wasn't at all prudent to go there, not even in her imagination.

Taking a deep steadying breath Riley glanced at her wristwatch. She'd finished the first coat so it was time to get herself cleaned up.

She'd have to go downstairs, risk having to see Jayne and Darren Wardell together again. She sighed. Maybe if she was very quiet she could—

She turned to find Jayne standing in the doorway. "Oh. I've just finished up," Riley said quickly. "So I'll leave you to it."

Jayne came into the bedroom and Riley realized that, thankfully, she was on her own. "It looks wonderful, doesn't it?" Jayne said as she surveyed the room. "I was concerned it would be too pale but it's not. It's just right."

"I agree. The colors are usually a little darker than they appear on the color chart. It's just the color I would have chosen, rich but also light and airy. And it will be better after the final coat," Riley added.

"It looks wonderful now," Jayne said, obviously pleased.

Riley relaxed a little. After Darren Wardell's derogatory attitude it was a relief to know Jayne was satisfied with her work. "I should be finished up here tomorrow or the next day, but I'd suggest you leave it a day or two for the paint fumes to dissipate. Then you can have your room back."

"I don't mind using the couch in the study but I do miss not waking up to that view." Jayne indicated the large glass doors that framed the panorama below.

"That I can understand." Riley smiled. The late-afternoon light from those same doors highlighted the contours of Jayne's face, and a deep yearning clutched inside Riley. She made herself breathe evenly. Jayne seemed totally unaware of her own beauty, and Riley could only hope she was as unaware of the effect she had on Riley.

A small silence stretched between them and Riley wondered if perhaps the other woman suddenly felt the heavy tension Riley sensed in the room. Of course that only made Riley more strained.

"Well, I should get cleaned up," she said, just as Jayne began speaking herself. "I'm sorry," Riley apologized.

"I was just wondering what you'd planned on doing for dinner tonight?"

Dinner with Jayne and her fiancé? Riley's heart sank. She'd have to sidestep this right away. She valiantly tried to think of an excuse to refuse.

"Oh. Well, I—I hadn't quite decided," she heard herself say. "Salad à la Riley James or baked beans on toast."

"Could I interest you in a pizza?"

"Pizza?" Riley hesitated, knowing there was nothing she'd like more than to share a meal with Jayne. But a meal that included Jayne's fiancé? The very thought gave Riley indigestion.

"I've preordered the pizza and—" Jayne shrugged. "I'll be dining alone."

Riley glanced at her and away again.

"Darren has work to do and couldn't stay."

"Oh. Well, okay. Thanks. I like pizza."

Jayne smiled faintly. "So do I. But not two large ones on my own."

Riley grinned. An evening with Jayne. Alone. She suddenly found the evening ahead looked better by the minute. "My brother Martin likes leftover pizza for breakfast." She wrinkled her nose.

Jayne laughed. "That must be a male thing. So does Jake. Ugh!"

"Ugh! All right. I much prefer it hot for dinner."

"Great." Jayne checked the time. "That gives me about fifteen minutes to shower and change before the pizzas arrive."

"And me. I'd better be off then. I have paint splatters to remove."

Jayne's gaze swept Riley's face. Their eyes met for a moment before Jayne flushed slightly and looked away. "Okay," she said. "See you in the dining room in fifteen minutes."

"Can I bring anything?" Riley asked. "Maybe something to drink?"

Jayne shook her head. "No. I have some wine. That is, if you like red wine?"

"Sure. Well, see you soon."

Riley had changed into denim cutoffs and a loose blue T-shirt and Jayne was setting the pizzas on the breakfast bar when Riley returned to the main house. She paused, watching as Jayne reached up to take a couple of plates from the cupboard on the wall.

She wore a pair of pale apricot cotton pants and a white T-shirt that molded her breasts. Her feet were bare and she'd pulled her hair back into a loose knot at the nape of her neck.

Riley's heart skipped a beat and she must have made some small sound because Jayne turned. And then she smiled. Riley felt a surge of wanting that was so strong her knees went weak.

"Just in time," Jayne said lightly. "I've made us a wholesome tossed salad to go with the unwholesome pizza."

Riley made herself move forward. "You've made it already? That was quick."

Jayne shrugged. "It's pretty basic, but I do like salad with my pizza. Makes me feel less guilty about the excess calories."

"I know what you mean." Riley had to stop herself from letting her gaze rove over the other woman's tall, slender form. She was perfect, Riley thought. "It must be all the bad press takeaway food gets. Just saying *pizza* makes you feel like your arteries are clogging, which they probably are," she added with a laugh.

"Most probably, but let's put it conveniently from our minds." Jayne looked up from tossing the crisp salad. "I thought we might eat out on the veranda." She raised her fine dark eyebrows inquiringly and Riley nodded.

"Sure. Fine by me. Shall I take the plates and cutlery outside?"

An hour later, sitting opposite Riley, Jayne wiped her fingers on her napkin. "I can't eat another bite," she said, clutching her tummy. "Whose idea was it to have that last piece of pizza?"

Riley held up her hands in surrender. "Not guilty, your Honor. And I say that piously because I didn't have an extra slice." She laughed as Jayne pulled a face.

"Coward," Jayne said with a grin.

Riley's heartbeats thudded in her chest. Jayne was completely devastating when she smiled. Her blue eyes were inky pools in the candlelight and the loose strands of her fair hair that had escaped from the tie at her nape gleamed, shot with silver.

"How about some coffee?" Jayne was saying and Riley drew herself together.

"I thought you were full?"

"I am, but I think I can fit coffee. What about you? Or would you like some more wine?"

"Coffee, thanks," Riley capitulated. "But on your head be it."

"On my hips, more likely," Jayne quipped dryly and motioned for Riley to remain seated. "No. Stay there. I'll get it. I need the exercise."

Riley watched her go inside carrying the leftover pizza and their used plates. Her cotton pants hugged the curve of her hips and Riley felt herself go warm all over. She turned quickly back to the view of the city skyline. It was far safer to look at the twinkling lights, the many facets of the dusky panorama below. Looking at Jayne just caused that trembling of want in the pit of Riley's stomach, made her yearn to get closer, run her fingers through Jayne's hair, kiss Jayne's soft lips.

Pushing herself to her feet Riley walked over and leaned her elbows on the veranda rail. She took a deep breath, recognizing the heavy scent of the neighbor's frangipani tree. This attraction she felt for Jayne was getting out of hand. And Riley didn't know what to do about it.

Back home in Rockhampton it would be so much easier. Her family and friends knew she preferred women. But down here, with her relationship with her birth mother so new, complications abounded.

If only she'd told Maggie in the beginning. But she hadn't confided that part of her life to her birth mother. Riley sighed. As to how Maggie would react when she told her, Riley sensed deep down it would make no difference to Maggie but—perhaps she was kidding herself that her birth mother would accept her no matter what, a case of wishful thinking on her part.

Riley sighed again. She had no idea how she was going to tell Maggie, let alone tell Jayne. She straightened, rubbing her elbows where she had been leaning on the railing.

"No milk. One sugar. Right?"

Riley jumped at the sound of Jayne's voice behind her. "Oh. Yes. You remembered from our dinner at Maggie's. Thanks." She carefully took the mug of coffee, her fingers tingling where Jayne's fingers touched hers. Riley pretended her hands were sensitive to the hot cup as she sat down at the small table.

"You're not cold, are you?" Jayne asked and Riley shook her head. Jayne's gaze slid over Riley's shorts and cotton shirt and Riley swallowed. "I saw you rubbing your arms just then and I thought you might be. We could go inside if you are."

"No. I'm fine. It's wonderful out here."

The candle flickered behind its protective glass and Jayne glanced at it. "I'm surprised the wind hasn't got up. It can be a little breezy when the sun goes down." She took a sip of her coffee. "It's so delightful at this time of day, not fully dark, the lights coming on."

"It's certainly beautiful," Riley agreed, deciding that Jayne Easton's face in the light from the flickering candle was every bit as attractive as the cityscape. "Maggie said this house belonged to your mother's family," Riley added, getting the topic onto a more mundane, less tantalizing subject.

"Mmm." Jayne set down her coffee mug and rested her chin on her hand. "My mother was born here. She was an only child and when she married my father they bought a house on the next hill. I was born over there."

"So you've always lived around here?"

"Yes, but Dad sold that house when my mother died. I don't think he could bear to live there afterwards. He worked and he needed someone to look after me, so we moved in here with my grandmother until Dad met Maggie. My father's parents had passed away by then and Dad had kept his family home. When Dad married Maggie we moved over there."

"That's the house he and Maggie still live in?" Riley asked.

"That's right." Jayne grimaced. "I've rambled a bit but, to finally answer your question, I inherited this house when my grandmother died five years ago." She smiled faintly. "Gran was ninety-three years old, a wonderful woman, as tough as they come."

"Do you remember your mother?" Riley asked gently and Jayne nodded.

"I was eight when she died. I remember she read me stories and smelled of roses. They were her favorite flowers." She ran her finger around the rim of her coffee mug. "Then Gran looked after me until Dad and Maggie married four years later."

"You seem to get on very well with Maggie," Riley prompted. "I mean, did you mind? When your father remarried?"

"No." Jayne shook her head. "Oh, when he first started going out with Maggie I was a little jealous. I thought Maggie might take my father away from me too. But Maggie was so nice, didn't exclude me, made us into a family again. And my father was so happy. Of course, he adored my mother and when she died he, well, it was awful. The life seemed to go out of him. Maggie changed all that. She gave my father back to me."

Jayne's fingers still played with her coffee mug and she gave a soft laugh. "I know it sounds melodramatic but it was true. And I remember the moment I knew she could do that. We were at the beach. Maggie and I dived right into the water but my father was standing up to his knees complaining about how cold the water was. Maggie teased him and splashed him and then Maggie and I were pulling him into the water. A wave caught us unawares and we all went under and came up spluttering. Maggie took hold of me so I didn't get dumped by the waves again."

She paused and smiled. "I felt, well, safe in her arms. Then Dad stood up to his waist in the water and he threw back his head and laughed. Out loud. It was the first time I'd heard my father laugh since my mother died."

Riley watched Jayne's eyes soften at the memory.

"When Dad fell in love with Maggie I realized how much he'd missed my mother. How sad he'd been. Oh, I don't know. It's hard to explain." She rolled her eyes self-derisively. "Anyway, the simple answer is that no, I didn't mind Dad marrying Maggie. She was the best thing that could have happened to the both of us."

"Maggie does seem really nice. Sort of genuine," Riley said inadequately.

"She is that." Jayne sighed. "You know she even let me talk to her about my mother and about how much I missed her."

Riley swallowed as a sudden rush of tears welled in her eyes, closing her throat. She wanted to tell Jayne that Maggie had let her talk about her adoptive mother too, had encouraged her to talk about Lenore James. She felt an almost overwhelming urge to confide in Jayne, to tell her the truth about her relationship to Maggie. But of course, she couldn't. It was Maggie's secret to tell.

"She's a wonderful person," Jayne was saying.

"Yes, she is," Riley agreed softly.

"Maggie told me you repaired her friend Jeannie's patio?"

Riley nodded, suddenly feeling decidedly uncomfortable. It wasn't strictly untrue. She had done some work for Jeannie, but only after she'd met Maggie and Maggie had recommended her.

"And you did a perfect job on Mrs. Herbertson's back windows." Jayne chuckled at Riley's expression. "Mrs. Herbertson told me that herself when I met her in the supermarket yesterday."

Riley grinned. "Oh, I get around. Don't forget Mrs. Carlotti's cupboard doors and the railing on her magnificent staircase."

"Wow!" Jayne exclaimed. "Now I am impressed. It's a high recommendation indeed if Mrs. Carlotti let you work on her prized staircase."

"That staircase is something, isn't it? It's absolutely grand. And an antique."

"Like Mrs. Carlotti," Jayne said with a laugh. "She guards her age zealously but she has to be well into her eighties. She seemed old when I was a child."

"She's ninety-one," Riley said and Jayne looked incredulous.

"She actually told you how old she was?"

Riley nodded. "She did. And she also told me the staircase was built by her great-uncle. He must have been a master craftsman. The workmanship is amazing, especially when you consider the tools they would have had back then." Riley remembered running her hands lightly over the perfectly turned railings, the balustrading. "The feel of that wonderful wood—" She stopped and grinned a little sheepishly. "Sorry. I'm told I can bore people witless when I get on my pet subject."

"Antique staircases?" Jayne asked with an arch of her fine eyebrows.

Riley laughed with her. "Yes. Among other old stuff. That's what I want to do eventually, specialize in restoring old furniture and, well, there's quite an art to it," she finished, embarrassed that she'd opened up so easily to this woman. Lisa said her eyes glazed in two seconds when Riley got started on the subject of "old junk," to use Lisa's term.

"I should imagine there would be an art to it," Jayne said, her eyes on Riley's face, and Riley held up her hand.

"It's okay. I won't bore you rambling on about it. My brother, Martin, says I can put him to sleep on the spot when I start."

"I take it your brother isn't as interested in antiques as you are?"

"No. He's a builder, too, but he likes what he calls big modern stuff, like houses. And he's building a fishing boat in his spare time. Much to his wife's disgust at what she calls the mess in the backyard."

"Do you have a large family?"

"No, not really. Just my parents, Martin and his wife, Anna, and I have a cute five-year-old nephew called Nicky. That's it."

"No grandparents? Aunts and uncles?"

Riley shook her head. "No. My parents were only children and their parents died before I was born. I remember I always wanted cousins to play with when I was a kid, like my friend Mac did." Riley smiled. "Mac lives next door to us," she explained. "He had stacks of cousins and second cousins. It seemed like hundreds. I was so jealous. But, to be fair, Mac did share his cousins with me now and then. How about you?"

"My parents were only children too, but I knew Maggie's parents. They died when I was in my teens. And, of course, Maggie has one sister."

"Oh?" Riley feigned a casual interest. Maggie had mentioned her sister very fleetingly when they'd talked about Riley's birth. From Maggie's expression Riley had suspected the sisters didn't get on very well, so she'd been hesitant about questioning Maggie about her.

"Her name's Joan," Jayne was saying. "She still lives in Maggie's hometown, Murwillumbah, over the border. She's older than Maggie by about twelve or fifteen years, I think."

"What's she like?" Riley asked as evenly as she could, hoping Maggie wouldn't mind her probing into her family life.

Jayne shrugged. "She scared the hell out of me when I first met her before Maggie and Dad got married. She reminded me of one of my teachers at school. My least favorite teacher."

Riley wanted to ask Jayne more questions about Maggie's sister, but she didn't want to appear too eager.

"Joan's retired now," Jayne continued. "She worked all her life at the Canegrowers' Association down there. As far as I know she never married, is very serious, and you'd never know she was related to Maggie, let alone that they were sisters."

"They don't look alike then?" Riley asked before she could stop herself.

"Not at all." Jayne laughed lightly. "When I was growing up I decided some guy had broken Joan's heart." She frowned. "I thought there was a mystery there, and when I asked Maggie about it Maggie didn't exactly fob me off but she went all quiet for a moment. Then she just said Joan was a shy and introverted person."

"Well, Maggie's not like that."

"No." Jayne frowned again. "I must ask Maggie how Joan is. I haven't seen her for years and can't even remember the last time

Maggie mentioned her." Jayne held up the wine bottle. "Half full or half empty. Shall we finish this off? Save its life?"

She went to top up Riley's wineglass and Riley protested half-heartedly.

"Well, we don't have to drive home." Jayne giggled as she poured more wine in her own glass.

"I do want to be able to walk a straight line to my door though," Riley said with a laugh.

"The coffee you just had will have sobered you up, don't you think?" Jayne teased.

"Very debatable. But I'm afraid I'm a cheap drunk anyway. It doesn't take much to get me tipsy."

"Ah-ha. We can't have you telling any secrets, now can we?" Jayne took a sip of her wine, her gaze meeting and steadily holding Riley's.

The candlelight flickered on the rich red of the wine, in the dark blue depths of her eyes, and Riley couldn't drag her gaze away. Her heartbeats fluttered in her chest as her lungs refused to function. Warmth crept slowly into her cheeks.

CHAPTER FIVE

"Not a lot of secrets to tell," Riley said at last. She made herself laugh as she raised her glass to her lips and took a hurried sip of wine.

"No? None?" Jayne persisted lightly. "You're an open book then?"

"Well, maybe one or two secrets that are best left not seeing the light of day. Or in this case," Riley said, indicating the sky with her wineglass, "the dark of night."

"That sounds intriguing. Now I'm curious," Jayne said softly, her tone creating havoc in the pit of Riley's stomach.

"Don't be." Riley pulled a face. "I'm really quite boring."

Jayne regarded Riley thoughtfully, her head tilted to one side. "No. I'd say you were a little reticent at times but I'd never call you boring."

"Thank you." Riley raised her glass to Jayne. "I'll take that as a compliment."

"It was a compliment. I do get the impression sometimes, that you . . ." She paused and then shrugged slightly. "You choose your words carefully."

"Oh," Riley murmured noncommittally and Jayne grinned broadly, causing Riley's heartbeats to do a triple turn.

"But I should warn you, Riley James, that I'm considered an expert at wheedling out best-kept secrets."

"Then I'll have to remember to be ever vigilant," Riley replied carefully.

Their gazes met again and the air between them suddenly grew thick and heavy. Surely Jayne had to be as aware of the growing tension between them as she was, Riley thought desperately. She looked away, focusing her attention on the wineglass in her hand.

When she'd regained some command of herself, Riley looked up again. Jayne was raising her own wineglass to her lips. Her soft, oh-so-inviting lips. Riley swallowed convulsively as she realized Jayne was watching her intently.

Jayne took a gulp of her drink and coughed. "Oops! That must have gone down the wrong way." She took a deep breath. "So, what do you do with yourself in—" She paused. "Rockhampton, wasn't it?"

"Yes, I've lived in Rocky all my life. And just the usual. Work mostly. Until just recently we've been flat out. My family owns a building company."

"No, I mean in your free time, when you're not working."

"Just the usual again." Riley replied as lightly as she could. "I like reading. Movies. Play touch football with some friends. That's about it."

"And do you have a—" Jayne glanced at Riley's ringless fingers. "Anyone special?"

"No." Riley shifted uncomfortably. "No one special."

"What about your friend who lives next door? Max, wasn't it?"

"Mac." Riley smiled. "Our respective mothers wish. But no, we're just good friends. Always have been since we were kids."

Jayne sighed. "That sounds like a great relationship."

"It is." Riley laughed softly. "Mac's adorable. A pain in the neck most of the time, but pretty adorable."

"I wish—I regret not having any close friends like that."

Riley made an exclamation of disbelief. "What? No friends. I don't believe you."

"Not close ones. I never seem to have time to keep up with people." Jayne looked down at the wine in her glass, her eyelashes dark crescents on her cheeks. "I did have a really good friend in high school. Dayna. We went on to university together but after I—well, we just seemed to drift apart." She sighed again. "Actually, it was after I met Darren. I guess Darren was a little jealous back then, possessive of my time. And Darren and Dayna didn't get on, couldn't stand each other. I often wondered what happened to her after we graduated."

"Maybe you should look her up," Riley suggested, secretly agreeing with the unknown Dayna about Jayne's fiancé.

"I suppose I could ring her mother. See if her family still lives in Brisbane," Jayne was saying. "But I still feel a little guilty though, for not making more of an effort to maintain our friendship. Then things got so hectic for me and time got away from me."

"Maggie told me you started your business after you graduated. That must have been pretty time-consuming."

"It was. Darren and I started the business a few years after we left university. We were working and trying to save money. I didn't think we were ready but—" She shrugged. "It was all long hours, uncertainty." She smiled faintly. "But it was exhilarating back then."

"Back then? Isn't it still?" Riley asked, picking up on the slight change in Jayne's tone.

She paused and then shook her head. "No, I don't think it is anymore," she said flatly.

"Maggie said you work too hard and from what I've seen, she's right. You do work long hours." Jayne left the house before Riley got up and she was rarely home before dark. "Maggie's worried you'll get rundown, make yourself ill."

Jayne pulled a face. "Maggie worries too much. Besides, I'm as healthy as a horse. But I am aware of the possibility of burnout, et cetera, so I'm thinking of taking some time off. Or at least just cutting back on all the traveling I do. I've worked out I've only been home one month in the last ten."

"And can you do that? Cut back on the traveling?" Riley asked.

"I've decided it's time Darren did some of it."

"He doesn't do any now?"

"Not much. He did at first but then he decided our clients preferred female attention. He said my pretty face would earn more orders." Jayne rolled her eyes. "I still say good products earn orders, not who peddles the products."

"You must miss each other, being apart so much." Riley watched Jayne's expression but she was giving the wine in her glass careful attention once again.

"Perhaps we used to," she said so softly Riley only just caught the words.

"You don't anymore?" Part of Riley was horrified at her probing into what must be a sensitive subject. "I'm sorry, I didn't mean to pry."

"That's okay. I really don't know what I think anymore. I thought I did." Jayne sat back in her chair and shifted her attention to the city skyline. "I've been away for the best part of five weeks but Darren couldn't change his plans to have dinner with me. And if I was honest I'd have to say I'm not all that upset that he didn't." She gave a derisive laugh. "Do you suppose the romance has gone out of our relationship?" When Riley remained silent Jayne reached over and set her wineglass on the table. "I guess that doesn't need an answer. I think we can safely say it has."

"Have you been engaged long?"

"Four years," Jayne said flatly.

Riley disguised her surprise. Darren Wardell was either a fool or a man who was very sure of his relationship. "That's a long time."

"Time is the operative word. There never seemed to be time to have the ceremony. The latest date is in the new year. January."

Riley's heart sank. "That's not too far away."

"Well, those were the plans." Jayne gave another derisive laugh. "But at the moment those same plans are on shifting sand."

Riley remained silent as she watched Jayne's profile. Was she going to call off her wedding?

Jayne turned to look at Riley. "Have you ever considered getting married, Riley?"

"No." Now was the time to tell Jayne the truth about herself. It was the opening she'd been waiting for. Riley swallowed. "I don't really think that marriage is for me," she said weakly.

"I'm beginning to think it isn't for me either," Jayne said, her fingers returning to play with her wineglass, absently turning the stem. "It's funny but I keep remembering something Maggie once said to me. I must have been about sixteen or so and I'd asked her why people bothered to get married. She said marriage between two people who loved each other was the most wonderful thing that could happen to you. Then I asked her how I'd know I loved someone enough to want to get married. Maggie said I'd just know, that I'd love someone so much I'd know I wanted to spend the rest of my life with him."

Riley knew Maggie felt like that about Andrew.

Jayne laughed softly. "Poor Maggie. I didn't let her off the hook so easily. But how would I know I was in love, I persisted. She said I'd feel that the other person was part of me, the part that would make me whole. I've always told myself Darren was that person. Now, well, we have the business in common but I'm not sure we have any more than that."

"Maybe you're just having prewedding jitters," Riley suggested. "My sister-in-law said she did. Now they've been married for nearly ten years and couldn't be happier."

"Perhaps you're right." Jayne sighed wearily. "Darren and I have hardly seen each other this year. I think we need to talk it through.

He's changed so much." She paused. "Or maybe it's me. I can't remember if we did all those romantic things like going on special dates, to the movies or dancing. When we do go out for a meal together it's more like a business meeting."

Jayne gazed out over the city scene but Riley knew she wasn't seeing the nightscape below them.

"And you know, I don't think it was ever any different back then. I mean, after we graduated our lives just seemed to revolve around working toward and then setting up the business." She was silent for a long moment and then she seemed to draw herself together. She reached across the small table and gave Riley's hand a squeeze. "I'm really sorry, Riley. I didn't intend to bore you with all this when I asked you to share the pizzas."

Riley could still feel the warmth where Jayne's fingers had touched her. "That's okay. Really."

"I just can't believe I've burdened you with my worries. Can we put it down to my tiredness? Or the wine or something?"

"I don't mind," Riley assured her. "Sometimes it helps to talk it out."

"Especially with someone not involved." Jayne finished off her wine.

Riley wished she could tell Jayne how much she wanted to be involved. With Jayne.

"The last time I broached the subject with Maggie," Jayne went on, "she got all indignant on my behalf. I complained that Darren wasn't very romantic, that he didn't seem to care if I spent time with him or not. I had to prevent Maggie from immediately pleading my cause with Darren, which was really good of her, considering she doesn't much care for him."

"Did Maggie say that she didn't like him?" Riley asked, a little surprised.

"Not in so many words, but I know my parents. Dad doesn't like him either." She sighed. "It doesn't help that Darren isn't as family-oriented as I am. His family isn't close at all."

"I guess." Riley thought about Lisa and the differences in their backgrounds.

"No matter. I'll work it out." Jayne stifled a yawn. "Oh, sorry. I really must be tired."

Riley stood up. "Come on then and I'll help you do the dishes."

"No, you won't." Jayne stood up, too. "There's only these glasses to rinse. The plates are already in the dishwasher."

"Well, at least I can carry the glasses inside."

Jayne blew out the candle and they went into the house.

"I hope I didn't ruin any plans you had for the evening," Jayne said and Riley laughed.

"Not likely. I just planned on ringing my mother, which," Riley looked at the time, "I can still do, so—"

"All right." Jayne smiled crookedly. "And thanks, Riley, for being such a good listener."

"Anytime. And thank you for dinner." Riley waved and headed out to the flat. Once inside she leaned back against the door and expelled a breath. If only—

If only nothing, she chastised herself. Jayne was way out of bounds and Riley knew she had to call a stop to her attraction before it got out of hand. She'd do better remembering what had happened before when she'd fallen for a straight woman.

With less-than-confident resolve, Riley walked across to the phone, sat down and dialed her parents' number.

A few days later Riley heard Jayne's approach down the stairs and she turned toward the door. She'd finished painting Jayne's bedroom and was now working on the downstairs bedrooms and bathrooms. She hadn't seen Jayne for a couple of days and she smiled as Jayne entered the room.

"Hi there." Jayne smiled back. "Phew. Wonder where this humidity came from? Doesn't bode well for the height of summer, does it?"

Riley wiped the thin film of perspiration from her brow. "You're not wrong there. Today's going to be a scorcher, according to the weather report last night."

"Hopefully, the air conditioning will be reconnected next week, as long as the errant part turns up. It's nearly a week since I rang the service section." Jayne frowned. "I didn't realize how attached to the aircon I was until it stopped functioning." She looked at the walls Riley had painted and shifted from one high-heeled foot to the other. "That looks great." She indicated the wall Riley was painting.

"Yes. I like it, too." If Riley didn't know better, she'd have said Jayne was nervous.

"I was—I mean, I feel like playing hooky."

"Hooky?" Riley raised her eyebrows in surprise.

"You know, like cutting classes." A small smile lifted one corner of Jayne's mouth and Riley wanted to kiss that delightful spot.

"You mean you aren't going to work?" she asked, shoving her sybaritic thoughts to the back of her mind.

Jayne wrinkled her nose. "I wish. I have a meeting I can't get out of. But I was thinking about you. Feel like putting down your paintbrush and escaping for the rest of the day?"

"Very tempting." Riley laughed. "But I'm not sure how my boss would feel about that."

"So this boss of yours is a bit of a slave-driver?" Jayne leaned casually against the doorjamb.

"Well, she does drive herself pretty hard," Riley replied as lightly as she could. What would Jayne say if she told her what she was really thinking? That her boss was attractive and desirable, and that she could drive Riley anywhere.

"Hmm." Jayne put her hands on her hips. "You sound like Maggie."

Riley smiled. "Yes, Maggie does say that."

"And she's probably right." Jayne shrugged. "Actually, she is right. So, I'm going to do what I told her I'd do. I'm taking the first step in my plan to cut down on my workload. I'm not going into the office today."

"You're not? Good for you."

"I do have an appointment down at the coast though, and I thought, well . . ." Jayne nervously played with a tendril of hair that had escaped from her chignon. "I just thought you might like a break. I could drop you off at the beach for a surf, then pick you up after my appointment. I—It's a boring drive and I'd like the company."

Her gaze met Riley's and Riley's heartbeats tripped erratically. She swallowed to steady her breathing.

"That means I have to choose between painting this room—" Riley put her finger to her cheek and feigned deep thought—"and swanning down to the Gold Coast in a racy blue sports car? Gosh, what shall I choose?"

"Is that a yes?" Jayne asked with mock seriousness.

Riley laughed excitedly. "Yes, yes, yes. Do I have time to change?" Riley began pulling off her overalls.

"Of course." Jayne made a point of looking at her watch. "Fifteen minutes long enough?"

"Sure. Are you bringing your swimsuit, too?"

Jayne nodded. "I'm wearing it under my suit just in case."

"Good. You can't wear it and not go for a swim, and there's nothing like a dip in the ocean. It's ages, far too long, since I've been down to the beach." Riley put the lid back on the paint tin and hammered it on tight. She folded her overalls, lay them on the floor, and turned back to Jayne. "I'd better get changed then."

Jayne stood back so Riley could precede her up the stairs. "Don't rush. I've got plenty of time to get to my appointment."

It didn't take Riley long to don her two-piece swimsuit and clean shorts and T-shirt. She packed a bag with her towel, clean underwear, sunscreen and various other things she thought she might need. She locked the door to her flat behind her and bounded up the steps to the garage.

Jayne was leaning against her Z3, her profile pensive, seemingly unaware of Riley's approach.

Riley paused. If Jayne was going to cut down on her work hours, Riley thought, it was none too soon. She did look exhausted. Or perhaps there was something stressful going on at work Jayne wasn't talking to Maggie about. Apart from that, Riley knew Jayne wasn't totally happy in her relationship with Darren.

At that moment Jayne turned her head and her gaze ran over Riley, making Riley feel hot all over. Her body burned, as though Jayne had physically touched her. They stood like that for what seemed to be excruciatingly long moments. Then Jayne moved to open the passenger side door for Riley to climb inside. She took Riley's bag and stowed it in the boot before joining Riley in the car. They studiously settled themselves into their seatbelts.

"Gold Coast, here we come," Jayne said lightly enough as she backed the sports car out of the garage and turned onto the road.

In no time they were through the city and out on the freeway. It was the first time Riley had been in an open sports car on the open road and she sat back ready to enjoy the experience.

"When I woke up this morning and planned my day the beach didn't feature," she said and Jayne laughed.

"It didn't feature in my plans either." She slid a sideways glance at Riley and then looked back at the road. "Darren was supposed to go down to this appointment but something came up and he asked me to take it."

Riley had the feeling Jayne was choosing her words carefully.

"We needed to see the head of the transport company we use and when Darren couldn't go down there, that left me. Not that I mind getting away from the office," she added quickly. "But I have stacks of my own work to do, something that occasionally tends to slip Darren's mind."

"Well, from a very selfish point of view, I'm glad you are getting away," Riley said, and she saw Jayne smile.

"Actually, I am too, now."

Riley tried not to read too much into those words but of course she failed miserably. She refused to admit to herself how much she wanted Jayne to take pleasure in her company.

"So," Jayne was saying, "I'm going to forget about the work waiting for me back in the office and I'm going to enjoy the day."

"Excellent idea," Riley agreed.

"I think so. So no balance sheets or paint rollers, just a day away in good company. What do you say, Riley?"

"Fine by me." Riley sighed appreciatively and looked around at the passing scenery. "The last time we were in Brisbane and came down to the Gold Coast this was under reconstruction," she said, referring to the multilane highway.

"It seemed like it had always been under construction so we were all pleased when it was technically finished." Jayne easily overtook a slower car. "I suppose having the extra lanes makes it worth the inconvenience and mess but I think it's a nothing road now. There are no landmarks and I feel like I could be anywhere."

"Well, you could tell me we *were* anywhere and I'd believe you," Riley laughed. "So I guess I'm in your hands."

Riley's mouth went dry when she realized what she'd said. How she wished she was. And quite literally.

"Then I'll try not to lead us astray," Jayne replied, only adding to Riley's discomfort.

Riley's gaze slid sideways and then she just as quickly looked away. Pulling herself together, she made herself take in the scenery, acres of trees giving way here and there to new housing estates. It was safer. Watching the way Jayne's skirt rode up over her knees, exposing a tantalizing few inches of her thigh, was disconcerting her completely.

"So where do you have to go for your appointment?" she asked, striving for normality.

"Ashmore," Jayne replied. "It shouldn't take longer than an hour, an hour and a half at the most. I could drop you at a shopping center instead if that's too long at the beach for you?"

"Oh, no. The beach will be fine," Riley assured her. It had been ages since she'd had the opportunity to feel the sand between her toes.

"How about I drop you at Surfers Paradise? Then you'll have the shops and the surf."

"Great. I take it you're going to have a swim after your appointment?" Riley asked.

"I think I might. I know when I see the water I'll want to, so why not? We are playing hooky, after all."

"Exactly," Riley agreed.

They chatted on a variety of subjects and in no time they were driving into Surfers Paradise. Jayne turned left and slipped into a convenient and, amazingly empty curbside car space on the Esplanade.

The Pacific Ocean sparkled in the sunlight, the incredible turquoise water breaking consistently on the white sand. Brightly colored umbrellas and towels dotted the beach as people sunbathed or immersed themselves in the waves.

Jayne retrieved Riley's bag from the boot and then passed her a folded beach umbrella she had had stowed behind the front seats. "You might need this for some shade. It advertises the company," she added apologetically.

Riley took the umbrella and hoisted it over her shoulder. "It's the least I can do, seeing as the owner of the company has generously given me the day off."

Jayne laughed as she slipped her sunglasses back on and climbed into the car. "And it will make it easier for me to find you when I get back."

Riley waved as Jayne pulled into the stream of traffic, and when the blue Z3 disappeared around the corner she headed down onto the beach.

Later Riley stretched out on her stomach on her beach towel, grateful for the shade thrown by Jayne's umbrella. Salty water from her surf ran in crystal droplets from her warm skin and she rested on her elbows so she could survey the scene around her.

Bodies covered in sunscreen, sand and water glistened in the sunlight. Small children built sandcastles with colorful buckets and spades. A bronzed teenaged boy tossed a surfboard on the sand and lounged back beside it. Off to her right two women sunbaked side by side, surely lying closer than mere friends would, and Riley speculated on their togetherness.

As she watched the couple she thought about herself. Although she didn't actively shout out her sexual preference she didn't consciously hide it either. The past few weeks she'd been in Brisbane was the only time she'd studiously hidden the fact that she was a lesbian.

And that had rebounded on her to some extent. In her effort to postpone telling her birth mother the truth she'd also had to keep the knowledge from Jayne Easton. Yet having Jayne know also filled her with ambivalence.

Jayne was, to all outward appearances, straight, so would she run screaming if she found out Riley was a lesbian? It happened, Riley knew. Her friend Brenna had had just such an experience. She had lost a friend of twenty years standing when she explained that her housemate, Cathy, was actually her partner.

If only Riley had an idea how Jayne and Maggie would react. While Riley hoped their reactions would be positive, she couldn't even begin to guess how they would respond when she told them.

She knew she had been extremely fortunate when she'd told her adoptive parents. They'd been initially shocked but at no time had they threatened anything negative. Their concern had always been with her happiness. Her brother had taken a little longer to come to terms with it. He'd decided she'd be fine once she met the right guy. When she'd assured him this wasn't so he'd eventually agreed it was her life to live as she chose. Her sister-in-law had never had a problem with it.

Looking back, she realized it was strange that the first person she'd come out to was her boyfriend, Mac Bradford. Not that she'd considered him to be her boyfriend but everyone else had. To Riley Mac had always been simply her best friend.

It had all started when Mac had asked Riley to be his partner for their senior year formal ball, and Riley had told him honestly why she had to refuse. When she told him she thought she preferred girls, he had stared at her as though thunderstruck, then he'd wordlessly walked away.

Riley died a thousand deaths in the next few days while Mac avoided her. Would he tell all their friends, make her the brunt of the inevitable teasing or worse? She should have known Mac better than that, and when no one said a word she felt ashamed of her mistrust. Apart from that Riley missed his company more than she realized she would.

Then one afternoon a few days later, Mac had hopped the fence when Riley was sitting under her favorite tree reading a book. He'd stretched himself out beside her on the grass as he usually did.

"I don't suppose I misheard you the other day? I mean, you didn't say you were a thespian, did you?"

Riley bit off a laugh. "No. And I'm not quite sure exactly what a thespian is."

"A lesbian with a speech impediment?"

Riley did laugh then and Mac sighed.

"Are you absolutely sure you are?"

Riley nodded. "Yes. Pretty much so."

"Have you, you know, done it?"

"Of course not." Riley felt herself flush.

"Then how do you know?"

"How do you know you're heterosexual?"

Mac gave that some thought. "Oh," he said, then he was silent for a while. "Look, it wasn't because I kissed you behind the garage when we were twelve, was it?"

"I don't think so."

"I enjoyed that kiss. It was even worth the black eye you gave me afterwards."

Riley chuckled. "It was a lucky punch and an unfair one. If it's any consolation I've felt guilty about hitting you ever since. After all, I did kiss you back, so it wasn't just your fault. So, I'm sorry."

"Apology accepted." Mac was silent for a moment. "You know, just because I asked you to go to the dance with me didn't mean I expected you to have sex with me."

"I know that." Riley knew she was blushing again.

"Not that I'd have refused if you'd put the hard word on me."

Riley grinned. "You wish."

"Oh, I do." Mac laughed. "It would have been worth the broken neck afterwards."

Riley raised her eyebrows.

"When your father and brother and probably my father caught up with me."

Riley shook her head. "You're mad, do you know that?"

"I must be because I still want you to come to the dance with me."

"You do?"

"Sure." Mac shrugged. "We dance great together. We'll have a ball at the ball."

Riley set her book aside. "Mac, wouldn't you like to ask someone, well, someone else?"

"Like who?"

"I don't know." Riley frowned. "Maybe Lexie Barton."

"Miss Up Herself."

"Georgina?"

"Too short."

"Melinda?"

"Too tall."

"Laurel likes you."

Mac rolled his eyes. "Laurel likes everybody."

Riley gave him a shove.

"Well, seeing as you can't find anyone else to go with me, you'll have to sacrifice yourself, Riley. Otherwise I'll have to tell Mum you've refused her favorite son and Mum'll tell your mother, and—"

"That's blackmail, Mac Bradford."

He raised his hands and let them fall. "I'm a desperate man."

"If I go with you, it will just be to dance."

"Fine by me. I've decided to become a monk anyway."

Riley chuckled. "They wouldn't let you. You're far too handsome."

They'd gone to the dance together and had a wonderful time, so as far as Riley was concerned she looked upon Mac as another brother and they were still best friends all these years later.

But her relationship with Mac had been another bone of contention with Lisa, who believed lesbians should be exclusive to their own. Riley disagreed. She felt friendship transcended gender, especially where Mac was concerned. Riley also knew Mac didn't care for Lisa. Although he hadn't said anything specific, his silence told Riley more than any words would have.

Riley relaxed onto her towel and closed her eyes. She knew she'd just have to continue impressing upon Lisa that they *were* just friends.

She and Lisa had drifted into a sort of unofficial coupledom. They moved in the same small lesbian community and had started sharing transport to various functions. Riley knew a lot of her friends thought the other girl was too intense, too rigid in what she saw as the responsibility of lesbians to their community. But Lisa had once confided in Riley about her dreadful family life and Riley couldn't comprehend such an upbringing. It was totally alien to her, having always had the support of her adoptive family. Riley had felt a little sorry for her.

Lisa also decried anything romantic or happy-ever-after. She had the reputation for playing the field, but as Riley wasn't interested in a relationship, she had been happy to accept Lisa's company as a friend and she'd been honest with Lisa about that. It should have worked out well since neither of them was looking for a serious or steady relationship. Lisa had been fine with that until a couple of months ago.

That evening Cathy and Brenna and Lisa and Riley had attended a party at Brenna's brother's house. Riley admitted she'd had a couple of wines, knowing they intended to get taxis home. They were enjoying themselves when suddenly, out of the crowd of people, stepped Riley's former lover, her first love.

For over six months Gem Donahue had been everything to nineteen-year-old Riley. They'd met at netball, and when Gem kissed Riley she knew she was lost. They made love every moment they could slip away together and Riley had believed it was forever.

When Gem announced her engagement to her boss, the son of a well-known local businessman, Riley was devastated. Gem told Riley she had enjoyed their fling but that Riley must have known it couldn't go on indefinitely. Now they had to get on with their lives, their normal lives. Gem had subsequently married and moved away.

So by the time Riley met Gem at the party they hadn't spoken for four years. Shocked to see her, Riley had escaped to the garden and sat on a seat in the shadows by the pool. Gem had broken her heart and, although Riley conceded she wasn't still in love with Gem, her betrayal still hurt.

Eventually Riley stood up, intending to return to the party, although she resolved to make sure she kept well away from Gem. Then suddenly Gem was there beside her, tentatively asking her how she was. Riley responded noncommittally, moving into the circle of light from the patio above them. But Gem touched her arm, drawing Riley back into the shadows, and when they were standing in the semi-darkness Gem had broken down. She told Riley she felt trapped, that her life was stifling her. She had two children, and she couldn't bear her husband touching her.

When Gem started to cry Riley put her arms around her, comforting her. Gem whispered urgently that she needed Riley, had never forgotten her. And then they were kissing in the darkness. Riley didn't know how far it would have gone that night if they hadn't been interrupted by another party-goer.

For a wild moment the four years they'd been apart had faded away and Riley could almost believe they could pick up where they'd left off. But of course they couldn't. She'd put some space between them and firmly told Gem that. But Gem pleaded with Riley. She had moved back to town so she would be able to meet Riley whenever she could get away from her husband and children. They'd be careful. No one need know. Gem said she still loved Riley and Riley had wanted to believe her.

She had been tempted, but she knew she couldn't maintain a relationship like that, built on secrecy and guilt. She tried to explain that to Gem and Gem had angrily called her a fool, striding off to leave Riley alone. Dispirited, Riley went in search of Brenna and Cathy. Other friends had joined them, drawing Riley away and for a while she'd lost sight of Gem. Then, across the room, she'd seen her dancing cheek-to-cheek with her husband. Gem had looked through Riley, pretended she didn't know her.

Riley saw this as another betrayal and she was upset and deeply hurt. When Lisa handed her a fresh drink Riley hadn't refused it.

By the time they left the party Riley had been uncharacteristically under the weather and she'd barely noticed when Lisa climbed out of their taxi and helped her up the path to her flat. Lisa unlocked the door and pulled Riley inside. And when Lisa kissed her Riley had responded, hadn't stopped Lisa when the other girl tried to take their kiss further. She'd stayed the night with Lisa.

In the cold hard light of day Riley had deeply regretted the whole thing. She'd confessed as much to Lisa and impressed on her that it couldn't happen again. Riley had made sure it didn't, but from that night on it seemed as though Lisa now saw Riley as a challenge.

Lying on the beach, Riley closed her eyes. Not her finest hour, she had to admit. But she was sure of one thing. The way she was beginning to feel about Jayne only reinforced her decision to insist she and Lisa remain just friends.

Riley thought again about her feelings for Jayne and she was overcome by a wave of regret. The whole thing was doomed from the start. But how she wished things could be different, because she knew she'd never felt quite this way before. Not even with Gem. What she felt for Jayne was so much more.

She drifted into an uneasy doze only to come awake when someone ran a light soft touch down from her shoulder to her elbow. Riley rolled over and looked up at Jayne Easton.

CHAPTER SIX

Dark glasses shielded Jayne's eyes and Riley groped for her own glasses, slipping them back on her nose. From behind the screening darkness of her sunnies she let her gaze play over Jayne's dark one-piece swimsuit, the expanse of her fair skin, the smoothness of her thighs, her enticing cleavage.

Riley closed her eyes and fought the shaft of desire that clutched at her, arrowing down between her legs.

"I didn't want to startle you," Jayne was saying as Riley's traitorous gaze settled on the upward curve of the other woman's lips. "You looked way off in dreamland."

"I wasn't fully asleep." Riley's voice sounded thin in her ears and she coughed. "Did you change in the shower block?" she heard herself ask inanely and she cringed inwardly. *Oh, really cool, Riley.* Jayne had already said she was wearing her swimsuit beneath her suit.

"Yes. But I had my suit on under my suit, so to speak." Jayne laughed. "Sorry about that." She looked toward the surf. "I'm dying to get in the water. In fact, it's been in the back of my mind since I left you here. I really had to fight to keep my mind on what I was supposed to be doing. Want to come in again?"

Riley sat up and pushed herself to her feet, stowing her sunglasses back in her bag. "Sure. Let's go. It's a bit chilly when you first get in but it's as wonderful as it looks."

They ran down to the water and Riley watched as Jayne dived into a wave and came up laughing as she wiped water from her eyes.

"Wow! You're right. Very bracing."

She'd taken down her hair and clasped it back in a ponytail, and she looked so vital and alive that Riley's heart hurt. She knew in that moment that she'd fallen in love with Jayne Easton.

Riley dived into the next wave, her mind spinning. She came up through the surf and looked about, only to find Jayne surfacing close by. Jayne put a hand on Riley's arm to steady herself but Riley could only seem to focus on the burning heat where Jayne touched her wet skin.

They stood together, close but not touching, not speaking, and for Riley they could have been totally alone. The other surfers faded into the background and only Jayne existed.

A large wave swept in and caught them both, knocking them off their feet. Riley reached out instinctively and her arm wrapped around Jayne's waist. They tumbled together, legs entwined until the waves dumped them unceremoniously on the sand.

For long moments Riley stayed where she was, her arm and leg wrapped about Jayne's long body. Then she scrambled to untangle them.

"Are you okay?" she asked as Jayne coughed. "Did I hurt you?"

"No. Of course not. It was as much my fault as yours." Jayne gave a soft laugh. "And only my pride's hurt. Let's hope none of these tourists had a video camera trained on us. They'll be able to entertain their friends for years to come."

Riley joined in Jayne's laughter and they turned and headed out to deeper water.

Eventually they left the surf and walked up the beach.

"That was wonderful. I don't know why I don't do it more often." Jayne shook out her towel and rubbed at her hair. She paused. "I used to come down here every second weekend at least. I wonder how I came to stop." She frowned. "I guess I didn't take the time." Riley watched as tiredness seemed to grip her. "All this sun, sand and surf has made me hungry. In fact, I'm starving. Can I shout you lunch?"

"No need." Jayne indicated the small icebox under the umbrella as she spread her towel in the shade next to Riley's. "I picked up a few things on my way over here. Salad. Ham off the bone. Beer. Do you like beer? I got some lemonade too, if you'd prefer a shandy. And some Coke."

"You have all that in there?"

Jayne grinned. "I told you. I travel light and pack well." They sat down and Jayne opened the icebox. "Let's eat."

And it was the most delicious meal Riley had ever tasted. Or perhaps the fact she was sharing it with Jayne had something to do with it.

She popped the last of her ham and salad roll into her mouth and licked her fingers. "That was ambrosia."

"It was good, wasn't it?" Jayne passed Riley her refilled plastic cup of lemonade and beer.

"And I think I'm getting the taste for shandies."

Jayne laughed. "A true beer aficionado would decry it but I like it on a hot day."

"I wonder if all these people—" Riley waved her cup to encompass the beach—"are playing hooky too."

"That guy definitely is." Jayne surreptitiously indicated a middle-aged man sitting beside a much younger woman.

"And do you reckon that's his secretary?"

"Of course."

Riley giggled. "I think we're falling into the stereotype trap."

Jayne grinned. "Probably."

They both surveyed the beach and Riley noticed the two women she'd been watching earlier. They were now lying closer together and one woman had her arm resting over the back of the other.

Riley glanced quickly at Jayne, who was also watching the couple. Riley held her breath but after a couple of moments Jayne looked quickly away and began to busy herself repacking the icebox.

Tell her now, an inner voice demanded of Riley. It will only get more difficult the longer you leave it. But Riley couldn't bring herself to say a word. She simply passed Jayne her empty plate and the moment was gone.

They had another short surf, then collected their gear and returned to the car for the drive home. As the high-risers of the city skyline came into view Riley heard Jayne sigh.

"Back to the salt mines, I guess," she said, sliding a quick glance at Riley. "You know you don't have to work yourself into the ground with the painting, Riley. There's no hurry."

"You mean I can play hooky whenever I like?"

"If you like." Jayne laughed.

"Only if you play hooky with me." Riley felt her breath catch in her chest as she waited for Jayne's reaction.

"Now who's tempting who?" Jayne was smiling. "I'd call today creating a precedent, so let's make a pact to do this again as soon as we can."

"Count me in." Riley said, suddenly filled with regret that their day was almost over. It was almost five o'clock.

In no time Jayne was driving into the garage. She switched off the engine and turned to face Riley. "Thanks so much for keeping me company. That was a great day."

"It was my pleasure," Riley said, and only she knew how much she meant it. "It's so much better to smell like a hot, sunny day surfing than a hot, sunny day painting."

Jayne laughed as they climbed from the car. They collected their bags and started toward the house. The front door opened and they both stopped as Darren stepped out to meet them.

His gaze went from one to the other before he took a sip from his wineglass. "Funny, I knew you'd come home eventually."

Jayne swung her bag onto her shoulder and moved forward. "Darren, this is a surprise. Have you been here long?"

He held up his glass. "About half a bottle." He looked at Riley and then back to Jayne. "My keen sense of observation tells me you two have been to the beach."

"We have," Jayne told him. "As long as I had to go down to the coast I decided I'd go for a surf. It's been such a lovely day. Riley came with me for company."

"Like you didn't know the way on your own?"

Riley glanced at Jayne. She was smiling but Riley knew her amusement was superficial. Her smile certainly didn't reach her eyes.

"Very amusing, Darren." Jayne looked around. "I didn't see your car. How did you get here?"

"Taxi. My car's getting a service. I thought you'd give me a lift over to collect it."

"You knew I was down at the coast," Jayne said.

"And I thought you'd be back about lunchtime."

"I would have been but I decided to have a surf."

"A surf?" he repeated, his gaze sliding to Riley. He looked as though he would make some comment on that but turned his attention back to Jayne. "I take it the meeting went well?" he asked a trifle dryly.

"Actually, it went very well. And you know you can always ring me on my mobile. It would have saved you the wait."

Darren smiled easily. "No worries. You know I'd wait for you anytime." He turned to Riley who had been silently watching their exchange. "You know, yours is my kind of job. Having the boss take me to the beach for the day."

She smiled at him. "Isn't it a great job, though? The best job I've had in a long time. And the best boss."

Darren's eyes narrowed but he remained silent.

Riley turned back to Jayne. "No doubt you two have business to discuss so I'll leave you to it. Thanks again, Jayne."

Riley headed around the corner of the veranda toward her flat. As she opened the door she heard Darren say, "Aren't you getting a bit familiar with the hired help?" Riley stopped but she couldn't hear Jayne's reply.

Seething, Riley dumped her bag on the floor and headed for the shower. As she stood beneath the spray she wondered for the umpteenth time what a woman like Jayne ever saw in that pompous, condescending pain in the ass.

She closed her eyes and let the water run through her salty hair. She thought about the wonderful day she'd spent with Jayne, the way she felt about her. *Let it go, Riley*, she told herself as she rubbed shampoo into her hair. No matter how much she'd prefer it was otherwise, it was a hopeless situation.

Riley rinsed her hair and climbed from the shower. She dried herself off and donned fresh clothes. With a sigh she grabbed her car keys. She couldn't stay here with Jayne and Darren next door in the main house. She strode along the veranda and as she rounded the corner the couple emerged from the front door. Riley noticed that Jayne had showered too and wore a short black cocktail dress that left her shoulders bare. She was breathtakingly beautiful.

"You can drop me at the garage," Darren was saying, "and I'll collect my car and follow you to the restaurant."

"I just wish you'd told me about the business dinner, Darren. You know I hate having this kind of thing sprung on me at the last minute."

"Just smile at them, sweetie. They'll sign on the dotted line, on the spot." Darren slung an arm around Jayne's shoulders and she shrugged him off. "Don't be like that. I haven't seen you all day. I missed you."

At that moment they saw Riley.

"Oh, Riley, hello. Are you going out too?" Jayne made a job of searching for something in her bag.

Riley held up her keys. "Thought I'd go out for a bite to eat."

Darren smiled maliciously. "Pity you hadn't changed, you could have come to the Sheraton with us."

Jayne drew a sharp breath.

"I was thinking takeaways," Riley said lightly, refusing to allow the man to get to her.

"Let's get going, Jayne." Darren took her elbow, coolly dismissing Riley. "We're late already."

Jayne stepped aside so that Darren had to drop his hand. "Takeaways sounds wonderful. Good night, Riley," she said flatly. "Have a good evening."

Riley watched them go into the garage. They did make a striking couple, Jayne as fair as Darren was dark. They climbed into Jayne's sports car, Jayne taking the driver's seat. The engine roared to life and then the blue BMW was gone.

Suddenly Riley wasn't all that hungry. She jiggled her car keys in her hand and turned back to her flat. She'd make some cheese and tomato on toast and have an early night.

And yet when Riley went to bed she couldn't sleep. Her mind kept slipping traitorously from the delightful picture of Jayne stepping from the waves, water cascading from her curvaceous body, to Jayne and Darren Wardell dining in the opulence of the high-class hotel.

Eventually Riley got up and poured herself a glass of milk. She walked out onto the veranda, padding on bare feet to the back of the house and the view.

Leaning against a veranda post she drank her milk and sighed. Go home, said the irritating voice insider her. Leave before you get hurt. And Riley had a sinking feeling she could be badly hurt here.

She turned around as the light in the living room came on.

Jayne Easton walked into the room, discarded her bag and kicked off her high heels. She pulled an ornamental comb from her chignon and shook out her hair. Her whole stance indicated tiredness.

Where was her fiancé? Riley craned her neck to see if he had gone into the kitchen. Then she stopped herself. She had no right to spy on them. She should go quietly back to her flat, leave Jayne her privacy.

As Riley turned to go Jayne opened the door. She startled when she saw Riley.

"Sorry. I didn't mean to frighten you. I was just going back to bed." Riley held up her empty glass. "I couldn't sleep."

Jayne stepped outside. "No need to go if you want to stay. I'm going to bed myself."

"You must be exhausted," Riley said gently. "All that driving, sun and surf and then a night of business."

She nodded. "I am a little. And I hope no one questions me about what was said tonight because I've been brain-dead for the last couple of hours."

Riley grinned. "Who knows what you've bought or sold."

Jayne laughed tiredly. "What indeed." She sighed. "I really did enjoy playing hooky though. We'll have to do it again."

"Anytime." Riley watched as Jayne rubbed her eyes. "Want me to make you some tea or something?" she heard herself say, but Jayne shook her head.

"No, thanks. Well, I'll say good night. I might be awake by tomorrow afternoon."

Jayne went back inside and locked the door, leaving Riley to return to her flat.

"This is some view," said Brenna, taking one of the two folding chairs Riley carried out of the flat. It was two days after Riley's day at the beach with Jayne.

Brenna looked surprisingly relaxed after the long drive down from Rockhampton. She wore black jeans and a bright print shirt and her long black hair was pulled back into its usual ponytail.

Cathy, her partner, in a neat green pantsuit, was sitting on the deck chair that Riley usually sat in. Lisa had refused the offer of a chair. She tossed her leather bomber jacket on the floor and propped herself on the railing instead.

After dinner last night Brenna rang Riley to tell her she and Cathy were coming to Brisbane for one of the Broncos' home games the next evening. She'd asked Riley if she'd like to go along. Riley had jumped at the chance, particularly when it meant she'd get to see Cathy and Brenna. She'd really missed them. So she gave Brenna directions on how to get to Paddington and invited them to call in. She'd been looking forward to showing her friends her small flat and the house where she was working.

Of course, Riley had been more than a little taken aback to see Lisa climb from Brenna's people-mover. And Cathy's telling look as she followed Brenna from the van led Riley to suspect Lisa had asked herself along. No doubt Cathy would fill Riley in at the earliest opportunity.

"Some view all right. About a multimillion-dollar one I'd say," Lisa remarked dryly. "This dame you work for must be loaded."

Riley stopped herself from rising to Lisa's bait. "I think she is reasonably well off. She and her fiancé own a software company."

"Her fiancé? You mean she's young?" Lisa fixed Riley with a level look. "I thought she was an old broad."

"I don't know where you got that idea, Lisa." Riley frowned, knowing she hadn't spoken to Lisa since she rang to tell her she'd arrived safely in Brisbane.

"Well, your mother said you were working for a businesswoman," Lisa began but Cathy interrupted her.

"Enough of this old broad stuff, Lisa," said Cathy, who at forty-five was a dozen years older than Brenna. "And it may interest you to know mature people have sex lives, too." She winked at Brenna and they exchanged smiles.

"I think she's about thirty," Riley put in quickly.

Lisa's surly look cleared. "Oh. Thirty. That's not young."

"It's not old, either." Cathy laughed exasperatedly. "She's only six years older than you are, for heaven's sake. No doubt you'll be giving me a walking stick soon."

"Don't worry, love." Brenna patted Cathy on the knee. "You'll outlive the rest of us. You've got longevity genes."

Cathy grinned and turned to Riley. "So what's she like, the woman you work for?"

Riley shifted a little uncomfortably in her chair, feeling somewhat uneasy about discussing Jayne Easton, particularly with Cathy and Brenna. Riley had known the couple for a long time and they were very astute. She knew she'd have to be on her guard if they met Jayne. Riley admitted she'd like to talk to her two friends about her feelings for Jayne but she certainly couldn't with Lisa here.

"Well, as I said, her name's Jayne Easton. She's about thirty," Riley said with studied casualness. "And she's a computer whiz."

Lisa smirked. "She's a nerdy type? All thick glasses and sensible shoes?"

"Not exactly," Riley said carefully. If Lisa only knew how far from reality her suppositions were.

"What have sensible shoes got to do with computer nerds, Lisa?" asked Cathy, her tone short. "She's not a librarian."

"It was a stroke of luck you got this job, Riley." Brenna diplomatically changed the subject and Riley turned to her with relief.

"I still can't believe it." Riley explained the series of events to her friends, about meeting Maggie, doing a few odd jobs for Maggie's friends. "And then, when Jayne's painter had to fly home because of a family crisis, Maggie asked me if I could paint as well, and here I am."

"Wait on." Cathy held up her hand. "Maggie Easton and Jayne Easton?" She slapped the side of her head and her graying curls bounced. "Jayne's Maggie's daughter and your sister?"

"Ah, no. Jayne's Maggie's husband's daughter from his previous marriage," Riley explained.

"You mean your boss is your mother's stepdaughter?" Lisa laughed. "That makes you kind of stepsisters."

"I think the butler did it," Brenna said dryly and they all laughed.

"I suppose Jayne knows her stepmother is your birth mother," Cathy said. "Finding out you have a stepsister you knew nothing about must have been a shock. How did she take it?"

"Actually, she doesn't know." Riley told them. "No one knows yet."

"They don't?" Cathy was clearly surprised. "Aren't you on shaky ground then, Riley?"

"It's complicated. Maggie's husband is away overseas on business at the moment and she wants to tell him first, before she tells the rest of the family." Riley shrugged. "I think that's fair enough. I'll admit I would have preferred having Maggie tell them all in the beginning, but with her husband away it hasn't worked out that way. When he comes home she'll tell him first and then Jayne and the boys."

"The boys?" Lisa echoed in astonishment. "What boys?"

Riley smiled crookedly. "I have two half brothers. One's eighteen and at university in Townsville and the other one is thirteen and lives at home."

"Fuck!" Lisa shook her head. "Complicated is an understatement. You can't say I didn't warn you, Riley. I told you to let sleeping dogs lie."

"Oh, come off it, Lisa! Not all families are as dysfunctional as you're always saying yours is," Cathy said, glaring at her.

Brenna rolled her eyes at Riley. "You'd think these two would get sick of arguing for argument's sake, wouldn't you? But I'm beginning to think they enjoy it. Or maybe not," she added when Cathy looked at her with pursed lips.

"Whatever," said Lisa. "But if I was Riley's mother and I was so glad to find her after all these years, I'd want to tell everyone. That's what I think, Riley."

"She will tell her family," Riley said firmly. "Maggie and I have been getting to know each other and that's going well. And I completely understand her reason for waiting to tell her husband. It's not something you'd blurt out on the telephone. Anyway, it's Maggie's decision and I don't intend to push it. What would be the point?"

"That's fair enough," Brenna crossed one booted foot over the other. "So your birth mother's okay?"

Riley grinned. "She's more than okay. She's just great."

"That's wonderful, Riley." Cathy smiled. "Do you look like her?"

Riley thought about that for a moment. "Sort of, I guess. Maggie says I'm more like my father, but I certainly have Maggie's coloring and the same hair."

"What about your father?" Cathy asked. "I take it she's not married to him now? Did she tell you anything about him?"

"A little. And no, Andrew Easton isn't my father." Riley sighed. "I think there's a bit of a mystery there. Not about who my father was or anything. But I get the impression it's still a little painful for Maggie to talk about it."

"I told you so. He probably did the deed and left her in the lurch," Lisa said snidely and Riley shook her head.

"No, I don't think it was like that. From what I can gather Maggie's family and his family lived next door to each other. They fell in love when Maggie was seventeen and he was twenty-six."

Lisa pulled a face. "Ugh! Cradle snatcher."

"Let Riley get on with the story, Lisa," Brenna admonished.

"Maggie's parents thought she was far too young to go out with him and they forbade her to see him. They sent her to Brisbane to stay with an elderly aunt. Maggie said she was so miserable. She missed my father and she had trouble finding a job. Then he started driving up to see her and, well, the inevitable happened."

"The guy was old enough to know better," said Lisa.

"Perhaps. Maggie said it may have seemed that way but she said she knew what she was doing, that it was her fault as much as it was his."

"Yeah, right. At seventeen."

"Lisa!" Cathy turned back to Riley. "So what happened? Why didn't they get married when your mother became pregnant? Surely she told your father."

"Yes, she did." Riley sighed. "Apparently, she rang him and told him and he said they'd get married straightaway. He was driving up to Brisbane, it was raining, a semitrailer jackknifed and there was a pileup. My father was killed instantly."

"Oh, no. How awful." Cathy reached out and gently squeezed Riley's arm.

"Maggie said she was devastated. She thought her life was over and she got terribly depressed."

"So that's why she didn't keep you and had you adopted out," Lisa said.

Riley shrugged. "Not entirely. Maggie's father was ill, she was away from home, pregnant, and then losing my father like that—I suppose the whole thing was too much for her. Anyway, Maggie's elderly aunt was worried about her and she rang Maggie's parents. With Maggie's father being so ill her elder sister—oh, Maggie only has one sister who's about twelve years older than she is. Well, Joan, the sister, came up and Maggie told her she was pregnant. They decided it would kill their father if he found out, so they swore the elderly aunt to secrecy, Maggie had me and—" Riley raised her hands and let them fall—"that was what happened."

"So no one knew about you except the sister and the aunt?" Cathy said.

"That's right. And the family wanted Maggie to go back home, but she got a job in a bank in Brisbane and that's where she met her husband a few years later."

"She never went back home?" Brenna shook her head. "That's sad."

"She said she couldn't go back because she thought—" Riley swallowed. "She didn't want to leave Brisbane because she thought a Brisbane couple would have adopted me and that one day she might see me. She said she looked in every baby pram she saw."

"Oh, Riley." Cathy stood up and gathered Riley into her arms. "The poor woman."

"She wouldn't have known what you looked like," Lisa said skeptically. "They would have taken you away from her as soon as you were born and one baby just looks like another."

Cathy shook her head at Lisa. "Of course they don't."

"And you're speaking from experience?" Lisa quipped.

"Yes, I am. I can tell you my nephews and nieces didn't. They all had their own little features."

"Cut it out, Lisa." Brenna said sternly as Lisa opened her mouth to speak. "Can't you see Riley's upset?"

"I'm fine, Bren. Really. But it is pretty sad, isn't it?"

Cathy nodded sympathetically. "I can see why your birth mother was so pleased when you contacted her."

"She said she can't remember much about the time when I was born. It was so awful she blanked a lot of it from her mind. But she did see me, Lisa. She said one of the nurses let her hold me before they took me away. She said she never forgot me."

Cathy tskcd. "It must have been so traumatic for her. That's why it's doubly wonderful you've found each other, Riley. Have you told Lenore all this?"

"Oh, yes." Riley grinned broadly. "We both wept buckets on the phone. My father suggested we hang up, cry ourselves out and then call again to save the phone bill."

Cathy laughed. "I can hear him saying that. I was just unsure how much you wanted me to tell Lenore because I'm playing bridge with her this week and she knows we're down here and that we're seeing you. You can bet she'll quiz me about how you're getting on."

"It's okay, Cath. Mum knows everything." Except how Riley felt about Maggie's stepdaughter. Riley hadn't confided that. To anyone.

Lisa straightened and stretched. "So, what time are we leaving for the game?"

Brenna looked at her watch just as a car door slammed and she raised inquiring eyebrows at Riley.

"It must be Jayne," Riley said, her mind a jumble of emotions.

CHAPTER SEVEN

"I'll just go and see if it is her. I told her this morning you were calling in."

"Bring her around," suggested Cathy. "We'd love to meet her."

Brenna and Cathy were close friends and Riley wanted them to meet Jayne. She knew she could depend on them to be discreet. Lisa, however, was a different matter. If Lisa guessed how Riley felt about Maggie's stepdaughter she didn't know how Lisa would react.

Jayne was just unlocking the front door when Riley walked around the corner. Jayne wore dark tailored slacks and a matching jacket, the pale blue of her shirt collar folded back over the lapels. Her fair hair was loose today and she pushed a strand back behind her ear as the breeze blew it across her face.

"Hi!" Riley greeted her and Jayne smiled back. "My friends from Rockhampton arrived about an hour ago. We're just sitting on the side veranda. If you have time would you like to come and meet them?"

"Of course. I'd love to. If you're on the side veranda we might as well go through the house." Jayne set her briefcase just inside the door and Riley opened the French doors.

The three women turned as Riley and Jayne joined them.

"Brenna, Cathy, Lisa, meet my boss, Jayne Easton."

Brenna stood up and shook Jayne's hand. "Nice to meet you. Riley's told us all about you. You have a great house."

"Thank you." Jayne smiled. "I hope she didn't tell you I was a dreadful boss."

"Not at all." Cathy said with a smile as she shook Jayne's hand. "Quite the contrary."

"Are you down in Brisbane on holiday?" Jayne asked politely. "I don't think Riley mentioned how long you were staying."

"Just for the day—well, actually, the night. We're going to the Friday night football game at the stadium down the road." Brenna laughed at Jayne's expression of surprise. "I know. It's a long way to drive just for a rugby league game."

"Rugby league? Oh, then I understand completely," Jayne said with mock seriousness. "Please don't tell me you don't follow the Broncos."

"What other team is there?" Brenna asked, and they laughed together. "Actually, some relatives of Cathy's have a private box at the new stadium and they can't use it for the game tonight. When they offered it to us, well, how could we refuse? So we're all going along tonight. Riley's coming with us."

"Oh, I see. It should be a great game. They take on the Bullbogs, don't they?" Jayne smiled at Riley. "Jake will be green with envy." She turned back to the others. "Jake's my young brother. He's a true-blue Broncos fan."

Brenna glanced at Cathy.

"We have extra seats, so he's welcome to come with us," Cathy offered. "Could he get here in half an hour?"

"Jake just lives around the corner," Riley said, knowing he'd love to go to the game. She should have thought of asking Cathy if Jake could join them.

Jayne looked uncomfortable. "Oh, I didn't mean to sound as though I was angling for an invitation for Jake."

Brenna shrugged. "We know that. And, as we said, we do have a couple of spare tickets, so what about yourself? Are you a footy fan too?"

"I watch as many of the Broncos' games as I can but I feel as though I've foisted Jake and myself upon you."

"No worries," Brenna assured her. "The tickets are there to be used. We'd be delighted if you'd join us, wouldn't we, Riley?"

Jayne glanced at Riley, who was having trouble keeping up with the change in plans.

She was pulled in two directions. While she wanted nothing more than to spend the evening with Jayne, she was also aware of the watchful eyes of Lisa. Riley knew she'd be on tenterhooks all night trying to make sure Lisa didn't pick up on her feelings for Jayne.

Jayne's smile faltered a little and Riley pulled herself together. She smiled back at Jayne. "Sure. And Jake would probably like you to come. Why don't you?"

"I'm not really dressed for a football game."

Riley gazed at her and wondered if the others were thinking what she was thinking. Jayne Easton would look good anywhere, dressed in anything.

"You can get changed while Riley rings your brother," Brenna said. "We're all ready to go and we're going to get something to eat at the game."

"Well, if you don't mind my tagging along I'd love to join you."

"That's great." Brenna smiled. "And Riley, you'd better go and ring young Jake to see if he wants to come."

Riley nodded and started along the veranda.

"Oh, Riley," Cathy said, and Riley turned back to her. "Ask your—Why not ask Jake's mother too."

It was Jayne's turn to laugh. "You can ask Maggie, Riley, but I don't think she'll accept. She's not a rugby league fan so I doubt she'll join us. She always complained when Dad and the boys and I watched the games."

88

"Riley can still ask." Brenna grinned. "And we'll see what sort of excuse your mother can come up with."

"I'll leave that to Riley then, while I get changed." Jayne went into the house.

"Wow!" breathed Brenna, keeping her voice low. "What a babe."

"Yeah," agreed Lisa. "What a waste she's straight."

"You two can stop drooling," said Cathy. "It's very unbecoming and it makes you both look very needy, doesn't it, Riley?"

Riley chuckled. "Now don't be too hard on them, Cath. She is very attractive."

Cathy laughed. "I had noticed."

"And you're sure she's straight?" Brenna asked.

Lisa snickered. "You can even ask that, Brenna? She has 'uptight and straight' written all over her. Still, you never can tell with the Ice Maiden types. Maybe you should push the envelope, Riley. Who knows, you could get lucky."

Before Cathy or Riley could reply Brenna stood up. "That's overstepping the bounds, Lisa. Now, let Riley make her phone call."

Thankful for the reprieve, Riley escaped to her flat. If only Lisa knew how much Riley wished Jayne was interested in her. But she wasn't, so there was no use crying for the unattainable. With a sigh she picked up the phone and dialed Maggie's number.

Riley explained the situation to Maggie, and when Maggie asked Jake if he'd like to go to the game Riley could hear his excited bellow in the background.

"Something tells me that's short for yes, he'd like to go." Riley laughed. "What about you? Would you like to come too?"

"Oh. Well. Thanks, Riley, but I have a few things to do," Maggie said hurriedly, and Riley laughed again.

"Like cleaning out your linen cupboard? Jayne said rugby league isn't your favorite game."

"I cannot tell a lie." Maggie chuckled. "Do you mind if I don't go, Riley?"

"Of course not. It's up to you. But could you tell Jake we'll pick him up in about ten minutes so he'll have to be quick with the hair gel."

She said good-bye to Maggie and set the receiver on the hook. She took a few deep breaths to regain her composure. She knew she'd have to be relaxed and together in front of her friends.

Brenna and Cathy would understand, she knew that. She wished again she could have talked to them about it all but with Lisa along she knew she probably wouldn't get an opportunity to be alone with the other couple. Riley genuinely didn't want to intentionally hurt Lisa's feelings, but she was concerned if Lisa realized Riley was attracted to Jayne, Lisa wouldn't be pleased. She suspected Lisa would find some way to embarrass Riley, and in doing so, embarrass Jayne as well.

With some misgivings Riley rejoined her friends.

The view from the private box was magnificent, the emblems and colors of the two teams etched into the field, in stark relief to the green of the grass. Riley only wished she could relax so she could enjoy the atmosphere, the excitement of the game, but with Jayne sitting behind her she found her awareness of the other woman totally distracting. And she could almost feel Lisa's disapproval.

Clearly Lisa wanted to sit beside her and she was thankful that Jake, in all his innocence, had taken the seat instead. Lisa had to sit next to him, with Cathy and Brenna beside her in the first row.

On the fourth level on the western side of the impressive stadium, the private box seated ten people in two rows of five comfortable seats, and an icebox was provided containing drinks. Separated from the other boxes by a low wall, the seats were in a perfect position to watch the game.

"Man, this is so cool, Riley." Jake was looking about him excitedly. "I can't believe it. It's wicked. My mates won't believe me when I tell them. You and Jayne will have to back me up, Riley, tell them I'm not having them on."

"We can do better than that," Brenna told him and held up her camera. "We can provide photographic evidence."

90

"Take my picture with Riley." Jake wrapped an arm around Riley and posed. "Oh, and with Jayne." He turned to his sister. "Come down here, Jayne, and have your photo taken with Riley and me. Mum would love that."

Brenna looked at Riley and she felt herself flush. "Great idea," Brenna said. "Riley and Jake, stand up. And Jayne, just lean forward between them."

Riley shivered slightly as she felt the feather touch of Jayne's breath on her neck. Then Jayne rested her hand on Riley's shoulder and Riley's knees almost gave way.

"Smile!" said Brenna and the camera flashed. "Lovely. One more just in case."

"Have you got a tele-lens?" Jake asked. "We get such a great view from here you can take photos of the players."

"She has it all." Cathy laughed as Brenna fiddled with her prized camera. "All the bells and whistles."

"Come and I'll show you," Brenna offered and Jake left his seat and scrambled over near Brenna.

Lisa grabbed the opportunity to slip into the seat Jake had vacated. She slid a sly smile at Riley.

"Nice one, Brenna," she said so that only Riley could hear. She touched Riley lightly on the thigh. "I've missed you."

Riley stiffened, fighting the urge to turn around to see if Jayne had noticed Lisa's overt familiarity. She felt her face grow hot and realized she'd leaned unconsciously away from the other woman, her shoulder coming up against the wall of the box.

"How did our team go in the quarter finals?" she asked Lisa as evenly as she could.

"They romped in. Four tries to one. Do you think you'll be home in time for the finals?"

"I'm not sure." Riley replied. "Probably not. The job I'm working on will take a while."

"You can always ask your boss for a few days off," Lisa said with a smirk.

Riley desperately wanted to turn around to see if Jayne was listening to their conversation.

"Hey, Jayne!" Jake called out at that moment. "I can see Matt's friend Craig over a couple of rows. Can I go down and see him?"

Jayne moved around past Lisa to look down into the stand below their box.

"See. On the left." Jake pointed out. "He's with his father and his sister. Can I go talk to him?"

"I'll come with you," Jayne said. "Your mother would never forgive me if I lost you."

Jake guffawed. "Like I'd get lost."

They went out the back door and Riley relaxed a little. She turned to Lisa. "I wish you wouldn't do that," she said with a frown.

"Do what?" Lisa feigned innocence. "I don't know what you mean."

"Yes, you do. Please stop it. It's embarrassing."

"Oh, lighten up, Riley." Lisa thrust her booted feet up onto the front of the box. "Who cares? We're on our own. Your boss and her brother aren't here and Cathy and Brenna already know about us."

"There is no us. You know that," Riley said through clenched teeth.

Lisa pursed her lips. "So you have found someone else!"

"No, I haven't. But if I had it wouldn't have anything to do with you, Lisa. I told you before I left."

Lisa stood up and stalked out into the hall. Riley sighed and Cathy looked across at her and shook her head.

"I'm sorry, Riley. Lisa was at our place when my aunt rang about the tickets. True to form Lisa asked herself along."

Brenna leaned forward. "Did Lisa tell you about Ruth?"

"Ruth? No. What about her?"

Cathy looked at Brenna and then back at Riley. "We didn't know whether or not to tell you."

"You mean Ruth Williams who works with you? I thought she'd drifted away from the scene."

"That's her. She went through a messy breakup last year. She's started coming along to the club's weekly dinner again and she's been paying Lisa a lot of attention. We thought, well, we hoped you wouldn't mind." She looked at Riley to ensure this was so.

"Of course I don't mind about Lisa and Ruth. I'm just happy Lisa's found someone else. And I'm relieved," Riley added truthfully.

"We thought you would be. Anyway," Cathy continued, "Ruth was at our place too and she was coming down with us as well as Lisa so we thought it would be okay. But, as with all good plans, it went awry. Ruth had to work at the last minute."

"It's all right, Cathy. I realize now it was a mistake to . . . Lisa and I agreed to be just friends from the start, but when I said I was coming down here for a while Lisa wanted to come with me." Riley shrugged. "I tried to tell her it was something I needed to do alone. It took some time for me to convince her."

"If you ask me, Lisa only wants things she can't have," Cathy stated.

"She'll come around once she gets used to the idea," Riley told them. "Especially if Ruth's waiting in the wings."

"So you aren't upset Lisa's seeing Ruth?" Brenna repeated. Riley shook her head and Brenna smiled.

"That's a relief, Riley. Cath and I were a bit worried, because she *is* seeing Ruth, regardless of what she says. We see them everywhere together. Cath and I can't say we thought you and Lisa were suited, but if she was your choice, well, we didn't want you to be hurt."

Riley stood up and gave her friends a hug. "I'm fine with it. In fact, I'm more than fine." She glanced at her wristwatch. "I guess I'd better go and talk to her before the game starts, give her a chance to tell me herself."

Riley went out of the box and looked down the hallway. Lisa was leaning against the wall and as Riley watched she drew on her cigarette. Riley walked down to join her.

"I don't think you can smoke in here," Riley said and Lisa looked up.

"I know," she said and blew out a cloud of smoke.

"Look, Lisa, I'm sorry if I upset you but please be fair. You know there's nothing between us."

"So you keep saying." Lisa took another drag on her cigarette and then looked at Riley through the curling smoke. "You know, while you've been away someone else has been giving me the come-on. She's pretty hot too. You remember Ruth Williams? If you don't come back soon, Riley, I may not keep refusing her offer."

"That's up to you, Lisa. I didn't know Ruth very well but she seemed to be a very nice person. I'm really happy for you."

Lisa crushed her cigarette beneath her heel and took hold of Riley's arm, pulled her closer. "For Christ's sake, Riley, I think I'm in love with you."

"You aren't in love with me, Lisa. And please, let me go."

Lisa dropped her arm but took a step closer to Riley. She went to say something but stopped, her gaze going past Riley, and her expression changed. "Here comes Miss Rich-and-Straight," she said and Riley stiffened, turning to see Jayne walking along the hall toward them. Lisa glanced sideways at Riley. "You know, if I wasn't so sure you hadn't already been burned by a straight woman I'd think you had the hots for her," she whispered in Riley's ear.

Riley forced herself to smile as Jayne approached them. Jayne's eyes went from Riley to Lisa.

"Did you catch up with your friends?" Riley asked, her voice almost steady.

"Yes." Jayne smiled. "I think Jake only wanted to tell Craig he was sitting in a private box. He won't be long. He's getting himself a meat pie." Jayne continued on into the box.

Riley went to follow her but Lisa stopped her. "Is there really no chance for us, Riley?" she asked and Riley shook her head.

"No, Lisa. There isn't," she said gently.

Lisa grimaced. "Well, it's your loss, Riley. Now I think I need some fresh air." She turned and walked away.

With a sigh Riley went into the box. Jayne was sitting in her seat talking to Brenna, who was standing with her back to the front of the box.

"Hi there, Riley." Brenna held out a bag of popcorn. "Want a snack? Salt and vinegar."

Riley nodded and went down to join Brenna. She ate some popcorn and glanced at Jayne. She'd crossed her denim-clad legs and folded back the sleeves of her tailored black shirt. Her fair hair gleamed beneath the lights and Riley thought she'd never looked more attractive. She forced herself to look away and her eyes locked with Brenna's.

Brenna raised her eyebrows slightly and silently passed Riley the popcorn. "Mmm. Don't you love this stuff?"

"You'll have indigestion for a week," warned Cathy.

"It's worth it. Want some?"

Cathy took a handful. "Only to save you from yourself." She put some in her mouth and dropped some down the front of her shirt. "Oh, damn!" she said, shaking out her shirt.

"Nobody move," ordered Brenna. "We have a disaster here. Some popcorn has ventured down Cathy's famous cleavage. Someone will have to make the sacrifice and go down there."

Riley laughed. "You're a clown, Brenna."

Cathy laughed too. "I'm quite capable of retrieving my own popcorn, thank you very much. And Jayne might just like some more," Cathy added, giving Brenna a warning look.

"Oh. Yes. Sure." Brenna passed the popcorn to Jayne.

Riley looked down over the football field. Maybe Jayne would drop some popcorn and Riley could offer assistance. She bit off a hysterical giggle that drew Brenna's attention, but before she could more than wonder if Jayne would pick up on the by-play between the three of them, Cathy's cousin and his wife arrived.

There were introductions and the shuffling of seats and by the time the teams ran onto the field Riley found herself sitting between Jake and Jayne. The first half of the game seemed to flash past. Riley was so unsettled by Jayne's nearness she was totally unaware of the scores of either team. She told herself she was being foolish. She had to let this thing with Jayne go, and she resolved to make herself concentrate on the second half of the game. Jake had helped somewhat in the first half by giving Riley a running commentary, until Jayne took him to task and told him to let Riley watch the game for herself.

At halftime they all got up to stretch their legs. Lisa went out for another cigarette with Cathy's cousin and his wife. Jake decided he was starving and Jayne went with him to get hot dogs, admonishing him as they left about how much he could eat. Relieved, Riley sat down again. She'd use this time to strengthen her determination to get her feelings for Jayne into perspective.

"And I'm off to find the restrooms," Cathy said, following everyone outside.

Brenna slipped into the seat beside Riley as Cathy left. "Sorry about the cleavage joke before. I forgot it was a mixed group," she said softly when they were alone.

"That's okay."

"It *was* a mixed group, wasn't it?" Brenna asked.

Puzzled, Riley raised her eyebrows in surprise. "Yes, of course. Why do you ask?"

"Because I saw the way you looked at her."

Riley laughed. "I didn't look at her any way."

"If you say so."

Riley sighed. "She's straight, Brenna. It can't go anywhere."

Brenna patted her knee. "I'm sorry, Riley. I like her. Sure you can't change her mind?"

"I wish." She shook her head. "She's engaged. And she's Maggie's stepdaughter."

"I really am sorry, Riley."

"I am too, Bren." Riley paused as Cathy rejoined them.

"Sorry about what? Lisa?" Cathy inquired.

"Not exactly." In a lowered voice Riley filled Cathy in on the subject of their conversation. She shook her head sadly. "Jayne's, well—I've never felt so attracted to anyone before. Not even Gem."

Brenna slipped her arm around Riley's shoulders and gave her a squeeze. "I take it you haven't told her how you feel?" Cathy asked.

Riley bit her lip. "No. And I won't. She's supposed to be getting married in the new year."

"Married?" Cathy moved up closer to Riley. "Oh, no. And have you met her fiancé?" she whispered conspiratorially.

"I have had that misfortune, yes." Riley grimaced. "He's awful."

Brenna raised her eyebrows, clearly doubting Riley's judgment.

"No, Brenna. He really is," Riley repeated. "He's quite good-looking but he's arrogant and condescending. Heaven only knows what Jayne ever saw in him. She said he'd changed since they started their business but—" Riley shrugged—"it's her life, I guess."

"What does her family think of him?" Cathy asked with a concerned frown.

"I suspect Maggie's not all that keen on him. When she first mentioned him she referred to him as Jayne's business partner rather than her fiancé."

"Well, there you go." Cathy nodded. "I'd say that was a surefire indication she doesn't like him."

"Not that it's any of my business," Riley added. "But Jayne deserves better."

"Perhaps Maggie thinks that, too."

They sat in silence for a moment.

"I'm glad we got to meet Maggie when we collected Jake," Cathy told Riley. "I really liked her. Didn't you, Brenna?"

Brenna agreed. "Which is good because you can be sure Lenore will be pumping Cathy for information at bridge next week."

"And it was kind of Maggie to offer us a place to stay when we told her we were driving back tonight," Cathy added.

Brenna nodded and relaxed back in the seat. "And you know there's quite a family resemblance between you and Maggie. And young Jake as well, for that matter."

"I noticed it, too. Has anyone else?" Cathy asked.

Riley shook her head. "Thankfully, no. Maybe they don't see it because they're not looking for it. But anyway, Maggie will tell everyone as soon as her husband comes home."

"How do you think they'll take it when she tells them?" Brenna asked.

"Okay, I hope. If only for Maggie's sake. I think Jake likes me." Riley gave a self-derisive smile. "And your idea to ask him to the game tonight has surely earned me brownie points. Jayne thinks I'm a good painter. My older half brother, Matt, won't be home till the end of his Uni semester, so he's an unknown quantity. And Maggie assures me she has the best husband in the world."

"It's hard to say how her husband will take it," Cathy reflected. "He might well see it as a betrayal, Maggie's not telling him something like that."

Riley nodded. "I know. In the beginning I said as much to Maggie. I also told her I didn't intend to put any pressure on her to tell the rest of her family about our relationship. But she's adamant she wants them to know."

"When's Maggie's husband due home?"

"In a few weeks, I think. So I have a couple of weeks' grace. Actually I haven't really thought about what I'll do if he does take all this badly."

"You can always come home, you know," Brenna said softly. "Cathy says your mother misses you. So do your friends."

"Thanks, Bren. And I will be home as soon as I finish painting Jayne's house."

"Good." She patted Riley's knee again and got up as Jake and Jayne returned to their seats for the second half.

"The game was awesome," Jake told his mother when the taxi dropped Jayne, Riley and Jake at Maggie's later that night. "We won in the last five minutes. Up till then it could have gone either way. You should have come with us, Mum. Talk about exciting."

98

Maggie rolled her eyes. "As you know I just can't get into rugby league, even if the rest of you are Broncos fans. But I'm glad you all enjoyed it."

"We did. Thanks for asking me, Riley."

"No worries, Jake."

"I can't believe your friends are driving back to Rockhampton tonight." Maggie frowned. "Why didn't they leave it until tomorrow. They could have stayed here. As I told them, we have spare beds."

"That's really generous of you, Maggie. They appreciated the offer very much. But Cathy's a nursing sister and she has to work tomorrow night. She didn't want to have to go straight to work when they got home. Anyway the three of them will be sharing the driving."

"It's still a long way to drive at night and it's already after ten."

"You worry too much, Maggie," Jayne said and gave her stepmother a hug. "Cathy said they come down to the games quite regularly, so I'm sure they're used to the trip." She smothered a yawn. "I should get off home, too. I have an early meeting tomorrow." Jayne turned to Riley. "Do you mind, Riley?"

"Of course not."

"You have a meeting on Saturday?" Maggie frowned.

"Unfortunately, yes. I have to catch a client between flights."

"Then I'll drive you both home," Maggie began and Jayne gave her another squeeze.

"No, you won't. Riley and I will walk. We'll be home in minutes and we'll protect each other."

With Maggie's protests ringing in her ears Riley set off with Jayne. They walked along in silence and Riley smiled to herself, enjoying this moment alone with her.

"It's a great evening, isn't it?" Jayne stopped, her hands in the back pockets of her jeans. "Look at those stars and that moon." She sighed. "It's a pity to call it a night."

Riley could second that. She wished they could walk into the house, hold hands as they climbed the stairs, fall into each other's

99

arms and watch the stars from Jayne's bed. Yes, jeered her inner voice, and bring on the string quartet playing something romantic.

Jayne walked on. "Jake so enjoyed himself tonight. So did I. It was nice of your friends to invite us."

"That's okay. Brenna and Cathy are two of the most generous people I know."

"And Lisa's a mutual friend, too?"

Riley tensed. "Yes. Lisa and I played touch football. We were on different teams," she added, asking herself why that would matter.

They continued on in silence, and when Jayne's mobile rang they both jumped. Jayne excused herself and answered it while Riley walked on a couple of steps in an effort to give her some privacy. It was no use because Riley could still hear the conversation.

"I'm sorry, Darren. It was a spur-of-the-moment thing and I didn't have the opportunity to call. I had the phone switched off during the game."

Riley kicked at a crack in the pavement. Darren Wardell, checking up on his fiancée.

"I've always liked rugby league," Jayne said defensively. "Eons ago, when I had some spare time, I used to go to the games with Dad and the boys. Now I'm lucky to occasionally catch a game on TV."

Riley reflected dryly that Darren Wardell didn't seem to know his fiancée very well.

Jayne's laugh seemed a little forced. "Yes, I really enjoyed it. And Jake had a great time."

Jayne caught up with Riley, and they walked on together as Jayne held the phone to her ear.

"It was a private box. Some friends of Riley's from Rockhampton asked us. No. They were relatives of Riley's friends." Jayne's step faltered. "I don't—I have no idea. Now, it's late, Darren. What did you want to talk to me about?"

Riley looked sideways at Jayne but her face was in shadow so she couldn't see the other woman's expression. And her tone was non-committal.

"I know that, Darren. And I'll address it at the meeting in the morning. In fact, I intended to. I thought you knew that." Jayne was silent for a few moments. "All right. Yes. I'll see you then. Good night."

She switched off the phone and slipped it back into her pocket.

"I don't know why I didn't leave the phone at home," she commented wearily.

"Habit, I guess," Riley said. "At least that's how I am with mine."

"Mmm."

"Is everything all right?" Riley asked and Jayne seemed to gather her thoughts.

"Oh, yes. Darren was just reminding me about the meeting in the morning."

"You sound like you'd like to play hooky again," Riley ventured and Jayne laughed lightly.

"That would be divine. Don't tempt me."

Riley laughed, too, but didn't pursue the subject. When it came to temptation Jayne herself was temptation personified. If there was any tempting being done, Riley decided, it would be Riley who was being tempted. By Jayne. She stifled a giggle and Jayne stopped.

"What's so funny?"

"Oh, nothing. Really." Riley was glad of the shadows to mask her blush. How she wished she could tell Jayne what she was thinking. "I was just seeing you stretched out on the sand sunbathing while your client sat at a conference table looking at his watch, fingers tapping the table, waiting for you."

Jayne chuckled. "And as I said before, don't tempt me."

"Doesn't your fiancé like rugby league?" Riley ventured, deciding she even had difficulty saying the man's name.

"No, not at all. Darren doesn't like any sport, period."

"My sister-in-law is always complaining about my brother's being an armchair sports fanatic," Riley said. "So I guess some women would consider a man who wasn't interested in sport to be a prime catch."

Jayne paused for a moment. "I suppose they might." She sighed. "Personally, I think there are worse traits than wanting to watch footy."

What Jayne meant by her cryptic comment Riley didn't get a chance to ask because they had reached the house. They walked through to the veranda and after a quick good-night they separated, Jayne going into the house and Riley to her flat.

The following Tuesday afternoon Riley was just about to leave the main house when she heard a key in the front door lock. She crossed the living room, expecting to see Jayne, but her smile died on her lips when Darren Wardell walked into the room, leaving the front door open behind him. There was a moment of heavy silence as they faced each other.

"Jayne isn't home yet," she said, acknowledging the fact that this man disliked her as much as she disliked him.

He frowned down at his wristwatch. "It's after four. She said she'd meet me here."

Did he get irritated every time Jayne wasn't where he expected her to be? Riley wondered. "As far as I know she's still at the office," she said, keeping her tone as pleasant as she could.

"She'll be here soon, I guess," he said, a little less belligerently. "Don't let me keep you from your work."

Riley folded her arms across her chest. "Actually, I've finished for the day." Riley could have told him she had been about to take the timber she'd purchased for Andrew Easton's bookshelves over to Maggie's but, as Riley saw it, it was no business of Darren Wardell's.

"You seem to be able to stop and start work as the mood takes you." His eyes narrowed. "Perhaps Jayne's too easy on you."

Riley shrugged. "She hasn't complained about my working arrangements."

"Yes, well, Jayne wouldn't. She's too softhearted. But I wouldn't be getting too comfortable around here if I were you."

"Meaning?" Riley let her hands fall to her hips.

He smiled nastily. "Jayne can just as easily change painters. I mean, anyone can paint a house."

"I suppose they can. But can they do the job properly?"

"How do we know you can?"

"I guess you'll just have to trust me," Riley replied lightly, telling herself to remain calm.

"Jobs aren't so easy to come by when you have bad references," he said, an edge to his voice.

"Which I don't. A fact Maggie will attest to."

He strolled past her to take a high stool from the breakfast bar. Turning the chair around he straddled it, resting his elbows on the chair's high back. "Strange sort of job for a woman, isn't it? Painting houses," he remarked, his expression snidely challenging.

"Why would it be a strange job for a woman?" she asked him. "You know what they say? Women can do anything these days."

He gave a skeptical laugh. "That's debatable. There are some things women will never be able to do."

Riley itched to ask him what he thought women would never be able to do but she refrained, knowing he'd surely reduce it to something sexual. "Perhaps." She went to turn away, continue on to her flat and leave him to it.

"I'm disappointed," he jibed. "I didn't expect a woman like you would give in so easily."

Riley stopped. "A woman like me? What exactly do you mean?"

He raised his hands and let them fall. "You tell me."

Riley held his gaze. "Now I'm disappointed in you, too," she said with a humorless smile. "I didn't expect a man like you would be able to back down from this illuminating conversation, seeing as you're such a tell-it-like-it-is sort of guy." She shrugged. "I expected worse of you."

"Just being honest. However, since you insist. A lezzo. A dyke," he said baldly. "A real man-hater."

"And you base this assumption on what?" Riley asked through gritted teeth, while the rational part of her told her to walk away.

"It's elementary." He counted off on his fingers. "No boyfriends. A man's job. You look like one."

"I have friends who are men. A job's a job. And appearances are just that."

"And you cozy up to Jayne at every opportunity."

Riley felt color flood her face.

"Isn't that what you lesbians do?" he continued. "Can't get a man for yourself so you try to turn normal straight women against men."

Riley laughed. "Do you realize just how ridiculous that sounds?"

"Well, they do."

"And you've had personal experience of this? I'd say you would turn women off you without any help from anyone, straight or gay. If you've lost or are losing any girlfriends I'd start by looking closer to home rather than blaming someone else."

Darren stilled and Riley thought she caught a flicker of uncertainty in his eyes. She hesitated. He must love Jayne but he certainly had a strange way of showing it. And if he did love her, didn't he have a right to be upset if he felt that, for whatever reason, he was losing her? Someone should tell him that putting on this ugly macho veneer would hardly help his cause. Maybe he had trouble expressing his more sensitive feelings. If that was the case, she admonished herself, perhaps she should be more sympathetic.

"I'm not losing Jayne," he said succinctly.

"Then you don't need to be concerned," Riley said a little more reasonably.

"Jayne is straight as a die and I'm not having some two-bit lesbian threatening me."

"No threats," Riley said evenly. "Just simple observations."

"Then keep your observations to yourself."

"Thanks for the advice. Right back at you."

He pushed himself to his feet and walked across toward Riley. She tensed, ready to react if he became physical. He stopped in front of her, loomed over her.

"You just stay away from Jayne."

"If Jayne's straight, I can't see what you've got to worry about."

"She is straight. And if I were you I'd start looking in the Positions Vacant column. I don't think you'll be working here much longer. Jayne won't want some ball-breaking lesbian living in her house."

"Don't you think that's up to Jayne?" Riley lifted her chin defiantly. "It's Jayne's house."

"You won't win this argument, you know," he said nastily. "Because nothing you can offer will be good enough. The bottom line is, you don't have one of these." He grabbed his crotch.

Riley's gaze raked him disdainfully, any sympathy she'd had for him disintegrating. "That's not what it's about."

"That's what it's all about with you dykes."

Riley bit off a laugh. "Oh, come on. Give me a break. That is so tired. Can't you come up with something more original?"

"A finger will never replace a penis."

Riley shook her head. "Your ignorance is showing and it's only surpassed by your distastefulness."

"Ooh! Big words. But guess what?" He folded his arms. "Big words will never cover the bitter truth. Most real women prefer men."

"Ah." Riley lowered her voice. "But we're not talking about most women here, are we? And you and I both know it."

CHAPTER EIGHT

He tensed, his lips twisting as he glared down at her. "I'm warning you again. Stay away from my fiancée."

"Can't you see that the fact you feel you have to warn me off Jayne is very telling in itself? If you were so secure in your relationship with her you wouldn't even be having this conversation with me."

"My relationship with Jayne is no business of yours," he said through clenched teeth. "And you might as well start packing now because your days here are numbered."

"And, as I said, that's up to Jayne. Now, I think you've said enough. I know I've heard more than enough. Perhaps you should leave now. I'll let Jayne know you called."

"It's not your house to issue any orders." He gave a harsh laugh. "And there's no need for you to let Jayne know anything. I'll be telling her myself, you can bet on it." He glanced at his watch again and swore. "Fucking dyke."

With that he strode past Riley, slamming the front door as he left. The crash was followed by the sound of breaking glass. Riley hurried into the entrance to see that a small lead-light panel had fallen from the door.

She opened the door carefully to examine the damage. Heaven preserve us from bigoted offensive oafs, she thought as she bent down and began collecting the small pieces of colored glass. It looked as though none had broken. They'd simply fallen out of one section of the glass panel.

As she stood up she caught a movement out of the corner of her eye and she took a step back, thinking Darren had returned. But it was Jake who stood uncertainly before her.

"Oh, Jake. I—" Riley struggled to regain some composure. "How are you?" How much had Jake overhead?

"Can you fix the door?"

Riley nodded. "Yes, I think so."

"If you hadn't told that jerk to piss off, I would have," he said with a frown. "He's such a drop shit."

Riley drew a breath and expelled it. "I'm sorry, Jake, that you had to overhear . . . How much did you hear?"

"Don't apologize, Riley. Actually, I heard pretty much all of it I think. I was going to leave and then I was worried. That he'd get rough or something. He was so mad he didn't even see me as he left."

"I really am sorry, Jake. I shouldn't have let him get to me."

"You should have laid him out." Jake paused. "You know, guys only call women lesbians if they feel threatened by them. I heard that on TV." He bent down and picked up the last couple of pieces of glass and handed them to Riley. "And if you were what that loser called you, well, he had no right to say anything to you. It's your business and none of his."

Riley swallowed, not knowing what to say to her half brother.

"Are you? What he said?" Jake asked.

Riley motioned him inside and closed the door behind him. She set the pieces of glass down on a side table and they sat down on the

107

lounge facing each other. She took a deep breath, knowing she couldn't lie to him. "Look, Jake—"

"It's okay. Honest. You don't have to tell me if you don't want to."

"I don't like keeping secrets but it's just not that simple, Jake." Riley looked at him and her throat tightened. "How would you really be with it? If it was true."

"That's what I wanted to tell you. If it was true, well, it doesn't matter to me. I'd be cool." He grinned, his expression reminding her of Maggie. "So I guess I must be secure in my own sexuality."

"Or you watch too much daytime TV."

Jake laughed. "Probably. Apart from that I like girls myself so—" He shrugged. "So you like girls. I can understand that. So do I."

"Well, I like just some of them," she said softly.

"Yeah. I know what you mean. I only like some of them, too." Jake looked away from her and then back again. "So why do you really think Darren was so upset? What's it to him?"

"That's a bit complicated," she said.

"You like Jayne, don't you?"

"Jake," Riley began, her face flushed with heat.

"I can tell you do. I mean, I knew you did. Well, not until just now. But it didn't—you know, my thoughts just sort of fell into place." He paused. "I guess it is kind of complicated, isn't it?"

"That it is," Riley agreed resignedly. "I'm sorry you've had all this heaped on you."

Jake shrugged. "I don't mind, Riley. Why wouldn't you like Jayne? I know she's my sister but I'd have to be blind not to see how awesome she is. And she's a great person, too. So why wouldn't you fancy her?"

"Why indeed?" Riley muttered, absently rubbing at a paint splatter on her arm.

"Does Jayne like you, too?"

Riley looked across at Jake in surprise.

"Is that what Darren was going off his head about?" he asked.

"I don't—I really don't know, Jake." For wild moments hope soared inside Riley. How she wished it was so.

"Mmm." He frowned seriously. "That would explain it. But then, I've never liked him. He was always kind of condescending and he only talked to me when Jayne was there. Other times he ignored me. The rest of the family feel the same as I do."

Riley could understand that. She'd disliked him from the moment she met him, thinking him rude and crass. But she didn't want to be responsible for causing any more dissension between Darren and Jake. "You know, adults sometimes behave . . ." She swallowed. "What I'm trying to say is, Darren loves Jayne and I think perhaps he might have difficulty showing his feelings."

Jake exclaimed in disbelief. "You're right about that. He sure does have a weird way of showing it." He shifted uneasily in his seat. "Do you really think Jayne loves him?"

"They've been together for a long time," Riley replied carefully. "And they are engaged to be married."

"Well, I know Matt thinks he's a dickhead too," Jake stated. "Mum's never said anything to me but I heard her tell Dad he wasn't right for Jayne. Dad said Jayne would work that out for herself. I kept wishing she wouldn't take so long. Do you think she has worked it out now, Riley? She doesn't talk about him much these days." Riley thought about the way Jayne's expression clouded when she mentioned Darren, and Darren's anger toward Riley. "I'm not sure."

"Well, I sure hope she has. Apart from that, you'd be much better to have in our family, Riley."

"Oh, Jake." She wasn't quite sure what to make of this revelation.

"Mum really likes you. So do I. Dad will be ecstatic when you fix his shelves. And, as I told you, I'm cool about you and Jayne."

Riley swallowed.

"Plus, you barrack for the Broncos and you have friends with a private box at the stadium. Face it, Riley. You're in."

Riley laughed despite her misgivings. "Jayne and I—there's nothing between us. But she's lucky to have a brother like you."

Jake went a little pink about the ears. "She hasn't always thought brothers were so cool." He gave a chortle. "Matt loves to tell the

109

story about when Jayne went out on this date. He sneaked outside and waited behind a bush. And when the guy kissed Jayne goodnight he made really loud slurping noises. She chased him up the stairs and around the house. Mum and Dad weren't pleased."

Riley joined in his laughter. "Not nice, Jake."

"No, I know. But I wish I'd had the chance to play such a good joke. It was really wicked. And it turned out the guy Jayne went out with was the older brother of one of Matt's mates. Matt said he was really packing it the first time he saw the guy afterwards. He thought he'd get flattened but he didn't. Wow! He was lucky."

"Very lucky," Riley agreed dryly. "Jake, can I ask you a favor?"

"Sure. What?"

"Can you not tell anyone about this? I mean, I should be the one to tell Jayne myself."

"That's cool, Riley. I can keep a secret, you know. But on one condition," he added with mock seriousness.

"Oh. What's that?"

"I won't tell anyone you're a lesbian if you don't tell I watch daytime TV. Is it a deal?"

Riley laughed despite herself. She stood up and held out her hand. "It's a deal."

Jake pushed himself to his feet and they shook hands, but before Riley could say anything else a car door slammed.

"If it's that idiot come back just don't let him in, Riley," suggested Jake, frowning belligerently.

"He has a key," Riley replied, drawing herself up to her full height.

They headed toward the door, only to see it swing open as Jayne came inside.

"Hello. What are you two up to?" she asked with a smile as she put her briefcase down on the lounge chair.

"Ah, nothing," Riley began, feeling guilty that she had been discussing Jayne and her fiancé with Jake. And how could she explain to Jayne that she'd had an altercation with Darren Wardell? Should she tell Jayne what had happened? Because if Darren ran true to form he'd delight in complaining about the hired help. But would he tell Jayne that Riley was a lesbian?

"You just missed your lover boy," Jake stated without preamble.

Jayne stilled, her eyes going from Riley back to her brother. "Darren was here?" she asked, a small frown furrowing her brow. "I've been trying to get in touch with him but he wasn't answering his mobile. And please don't call him that, Jake. I don't like it." She turned back to Riley. "What did—? Did he leave a message?"

Riley shook her head, hoping Jake would keep his knowledge of the incident to himself. "No, he didn't leave a message but he might have gone back to the office. You could try him there."

"And he smashed your door," Jake said with relish, indicating the front door Jayne had closed behind her. "Now Riley has to fix it."

Jayne turned around. "The door? I didn't notice." She touched the section where the glass was missing.

"It's nothing. I can repair it quite easily," Riley put in, wishing Jake had left it alone.

"Darren did this?"

"Well, the door slammed and I guess the panel wasn't set in very securely." Riley felt herself color. Why was she defending Jayne's fiancé when he was such a creep?

Jake went to add his observations but he stopped when Riley frowned at him with a slight shake of her head.

He pulled a face and muttered something under his breath. "He's a loser, Jaynie. You deserve better." Folding his arms he glared at his sister. "And Riley agrees with me."

Riley swung around to face Jake, heat washing her cheeks. "Jake!" She turned back to Jayne. "Look, I'm sorry. I really didn't—"

"But you were thinking it," Jake stated. "And he was really rude to Riley," he told his sister.

"He was?" Jayne's gaze met Riley's. "What did he say?"

"It was nothing. Really." Riley wanted to strangle Jake for putting her in this position. "He was just annoyed you weren't here, I think."

111

"He knew I'd gone to Ipswich to see a client." Jayne's lips thinned. "Apart from that there's no need for him to be rude to you. I'll speak to him. I'm sorry about this."

"It's all right. Honestly, I'd appreciate it if you didn't say anything to him." Riley was horrified at the idea of Darren repeating his accusations to Jayne. As long as Jayne made no comments about it there was a slim chance he might have been all talk and wouldn't carry out his threat. Not that Riley believed that for a moment.

"Actually, Riley did sort him out," Jake said with glee.

Riley wanted to slap him. "We did sort *it* out," she said weakly.

Jayne looked from one to the other and seemed about to say more when the phone rang. She went to answer it.

"Jake, I'm going to kill you," Riley said in an undertone.

He grinned and whispered back, "Jayne wouldn't like that."

"Only because I think she wants to kill you first," Riley mouthed in reply.

"Of course not. I'll get her for you." Jayne held out the receiver. "It's for you, Riley," she said expressionlessly.

Grateful for the intervention Riley took the phone. "Hello," she said, wondering who could be ringing her at the main house rather than the flat.

"How's the love of my life? Not still working, are you? I should have told your boss to give you time off for good behavior."

"Mac?" Riley smiled despite herself and then she sobered. "What's up? Nothing's wrong, is it?"

"Don't be such a worrywart. Everything's fine. Can't I just ring to see how you are?"

Riley relaxed. "I'm fine. How did you get this number?"

"From your mother. Knowing you, I thought you'd still be hard at work. So, aren't you going to ask how I am?"

She laughed. "How are you then?"

"Missing you. But I'm about to remedy that. I'm actually in Brisbane."

"You are? How long will you be here for?"

"Want the good news or the bad news?"

"Mac! What are you talking about?"

He laughed. "I came back down by car with my uncle and aunt and I'm flying back to Rocky early in the morning. Any chance you can take me out to the airport?"

"Sure. When's your flight?"

"Six a.m."

Riley groaned. "That means you'll have to be out there at least an hour earlier."

"I know. It was the only flight I could get. As you know my uncle and aunt are on the opposite side of town to the airport so I thought I could stay the night with you. At least your flat's on the right side of town."

"Stay with me?" Riley repeated as she watched Jayne give Jake a hug. He waved at Riley from the doorway, obviously on his way home.

"Yes," Mac said again. "Stay with you. Would that be a problem?"

Riley paused. Jayne had to be hearing Riley's side of the conversation. "Oh, I don't know, Mac. You see, my flat's pretty small. It's sort of part of the house I'm working on. What about a motel?"

"You'd put me in a motel when your own mother suggested I stay with you so I could surreptitiously check to see you're all right?"

Jayne touched Riley lightly on the arm. "Your brother's welcome to stay here," she said.

"He's not—it's a friend," Riley stuttered, feeling decidedly foolish and not knowing why.

"He can still stay," Jayne said and turned to climb the stairs to her room.

Riley looked after her. Had Jayne meant the offer or had she simply had it foisted upon her? Riley hadn't been able to glean any emotion from her expression.

"Mac?" she said into the phone.

"I heard. So all's well. My aunt wants to go out for a meal so my uncle suggested the Caxton. That's not far from you, is it?"

"No. Not far. Around the corner and down the hill."

"Thought so. We'll pick you up at six-thirty and you can eat with us. I'll shout. And then my uncle will drop us back after dinner. For dessert you can have your wicked way with me."

Riley bit off a laugh. "You're hopeless. And I take it your aunt and uncle aren't listening to you?"

"Are you kidding? My aunt would ring my mother, who'd then ring your mother and whatever happened next you can be sure would involve shotguns and getting a preacher out of bed to perform the ceremony."

Riley laughed out loud, clutching her side. "Mac, you fool."

"I am. And I've just had a thought. I could wait till my aunt comes back upstairs and repeat what I've just said. Then you'd have to make an honest man of me."

"Don't you dare or that black eye I gave you when you were twelve will be chicken feed."

"You're a hard, hard woman, Riley James. So. See you at six-thirty. Okay?" He checked the address and Riley gave him directions before he rang off.

She turned around with a smile still on her face just as Jayne came back down the steps.

"Jake said Maggie sent him over to ask you how much the timber cost for Dad's bookshelves but I'll pay for it. It's his birthday in a couple of weeks so it'll be my birthday gift." She opened the briefcase she'd left on the lounge chair and took out her checkbook.

Riley took her wallet out of the back pocket of her shorts and found the receipt. "I did plan on taking the timber over this afternoon. It's on the back of my ute." Jayne looked at the receipt. "I got a trade discount," Riley added quickly.

"But what about your labor?" Jayne frowned. "Have you worked out an overall cost?"

"Oh, I wasn't—I mean, it shouldn't take that long. I was going to do it at the weekend."

"We asked you to do the job so we'll pay you for it." Jayne gave Riley a level look.

Riley felt decidedly uncomfortable. "Actually, I offered to do it."

Jayne shook her head. "I'll discuss it with Maggie." She wrote out a check and handed it to Riley.

Riley gaped at the amount. "You can't—that's too much."

"I can and I have. And I think it's a fair price." Jayne gave a faint smile. "Take it, Riley. It's Dad's birthday present."

"What if he doesn't like it? I mean—"

"He'll be over the moon. Now put it away before you lose it."

"Thank you." Slowly Riley folded the check and slipped it into her wallet.

"Good. Oh, and speaking about my father, Jake was also supposed to tell you Dad's coming home early. Maggie expects him the weekend after next."

"Oh." Riley took in this information. That meant Maggie would tell her husband the truth about Riley, and Andrew Easton's reaction to his wife's revelation could mean Riley might have to leave. Return home.

A wave of sadness engulfed her. She knew she'd regret having to leave this house. It already had the feel of home to it. And leaving Jayne would be—it would be a wrench, she thought inadequately.

"Why don't you get the job underway when you take the timber over, rather than wait till the weekend. With Dad coming home early it doesn't leave you long to get the shelves done."

"Oh, but, what about—?" She waved her arm to encompass the house and Jayne smiled crookedly.

"The painting has been waiting this long, a little longer won't make much difference."

Riley stood undecided.

"Go on, Riley. And I told Jake to give you a hand to unload the timber." Jayne grimaced. "It's the least he can do after embarrassing you."

"Oh, it wasn't as bad as Jake made out," Riley said, wondering why she wasn't struck down for such a deliberate untruth. "It was a, sort of a misunderstanding."

Jayne nodded and started to turn away.

"And Jayne. Thanks for letting Mac stay. He wants me to get him out to the airport before five so I'll be able to get back and then get started on the painting on time."

"That's fine. I'll see you later then." With that Jayne crossed to her study, went in and closed the door behind her.

Riley headed out to the garage and her truck.

Riley spent an enjoyable evening getting reacquainted with Mac's aunt and uncle. She hadn't seen them for a couple of years and they'd been out when she'd dropped Mac at their house when she'd first arrived in Brisbane.

The Caxton Hotel was famous for its steaks and they had a delicious meal together in the casual surroundings, Mac entertaining them with his lively sense of humor. Riley was still chuckling when she waved good-bye to Mac's relations and led him toward the house.

They were headed toward the side veranda and Riley's flat, but the security light came on and the front door opened.

"Oh. Riley. I'm sorry. I thought I heard someone outside," Jayne said as she opened the ornate door wider. "You may as well come through this way."

"I'm sorry we disturbed you," Riley said.

"That's okay. I was working in the study."

Riley stepped into the lighted entrance and Mac joined her. Jayne's eyebrows rose just slightly as she took in Riley's companion and as Riley turned to make the introductions she reassessed Mac Bradford.

Tall. Lean. Dark-haired. Blue-eyed. A slight shadow along his jawline where he needed to shave. He was dressed in faded blue jeans and a deep blue shirt with the sleeves rolled halfway up his tanned arms. Riley wasn't blind to his attraction so she was sure Jayne wouldn't be. "Jayne, this is a friend of mine, Mac Bradford. Mac, meet my boss, Jayne Easton."

Mac smiled, the corners of his eyes crinkling, a deep cleft, too long and masculine to be a dimple, furrowing one cheek. Riley knew Mac was devastating. Her straight friends had been telling her for years how hot he was and how lucky she was to have such an attractive boyfriend. So she watched Jayne's expression to see if she recognized Mac's good looks.

"Nice to meet you, Mac," Jayne said easily and reached out to shake his hand.

"Likewise," Mac said with equal aplomb.

Riley could pick up nothing from either of their expressions.

"Great house," Mac was saying, looking around appreciatively. "Riley told me it's been in your family since it was built."

"That's right. Come through and have a look inside. Riley's doing wonders with the painting."

"Riley's an artist," Mac said. He put his arm around Riley's shoulder and gave her a squeeze. "She painted our place at home last year and Dad's always singing her praises. He'd have jobs lined up so she could do painting full-time if she didn't prefer carpentry."

"Well, I'm very pleased with her work." Jayne took Mac on a tour with Riley following along behind. Back in the living room Jayne opened the French doors onto the back veranda.

Mac whistled. "Wow! Talk about a top view."

Riley pointed out a couple of landmarks. "And that's the MLC Building. The light changes and flashes when the weather changes."

"Now *that's* handy. We can look at it to see if it's raining," Jayne said with a straight face and then she and Mac burst out laughing.

Riley smiled at them. "Aren't you two funny?"

"Sorry, Riley. I've always wanted to say that." Jayne was still grinning. "I've just brewed myself some coffee. Would either of you care for a cup? Or maybe a nightcap?"

"Oh, no—" Riley began to refuse.

"I'd love some coffee," Mac said. "Thanks."

"What about you, Riley?" Jayne asked.

"If Riley has coffee this late it keeps her awake all night," Mac put in.

Riley felt her cheeks go warm. Mac was being far too familiar, giving Jayne a totally wrong impression of their relationship.

"And we can't have her losing her beauty sleep, now can we?" he added, taking Riley's hand and giving it a squeeze.

Riley removed her hand, making a mental note to give Mac a piece of her mind at the earliest opportunity. "I think I will have a cup. Can I help you get it?"

"No. No. You sit down with your friend and enjoy the view." Jayne went inside to get the coffee.

"Why did you agree to have coffee?" Riley whispered. "We just had some."

"Just being sociable." He sat down at the patio table.

"And as for that comment you made," Riley said through clenched teeth.

"Comment? Which one?" Mac sat back, obviously enjoying Riley's annoyance.

"You know very well which comment. The one about coffee keeping me awake. Heaven only knows what Jayne thought."

"It does keep you awake. You know that," Mac said so rationally that Riley wanted to hit him.

"That's not the point. It sounded suggestive."

Mac laughed softly. "Did you think so? I was hoping it would. But enough of that. You didn't tell me your boss was so easy to look at."

"That's what I'm getting at, Mac. She *is* my boss."

"I wish my boss looked like that," Mac said ruefully.

Riley bit off her comment as Jayne approached.

They sat chatting, Jayne easily drawing Mac out about his job. Riley could barely swallow her coffee as she worried about what Mac would say. That was the trouble with childhood friends, she thought. They knew too many of your secrets.

Not that Mac would be likely to out Riley. In fact, not long into the conversation he'd moved his own chair so he could rest his arm affectionately along the back of Riley's chair. Riley leaned forward, ostensibly to blow on her hot coffee, wondering what Mac was up to.

Eventually Mac sat back and stretched. "I guess we should be calling it a night. Thanks for the coffee." He turned to Jayne with one of his winning smiles. "And thanks for letting me stay with Riley. It will mean we won't have to get up so early in the morning." He rested one hand affectionately on Riley's shoulder and gave it a squeeze.

Riley almost laughed. This was the third male she'd wanted to throttle today. First, Darren Wardell, then Jake and now Mac. As Lisa would say, *Thank God I'm a lesbian.*

"There's no problem with you staying," Jayne said lightly enough and Riley asked herself what she had expected Jayne to say. That she would be devastated at the thought of Riley's spending the night with a man? Tell Riley she was jealous because she wanted Riley for herself? Dream on, Riley, she told herself derisively.

"And I'm sorry I kept you when you have to be up so early." Jayne stood up and gathered their empty mugs. "It was nice to meet you, Mac. Good night, Riley." She disappeared inside.

Mac stood up, too. "Come on, Riley. I'll toss you for first shower, or I'm not averse to sharing a shower and conserving water."

Riley bit off a retort. She could only hope Mac's voice didn't carry through the open doors into the kitchen where Jayne was stowing the used coffee mugs in the dishwasher.

"Now, no snoring and I want your word you'll stay on your side of the bed," Riley said firmly.

Mac sighed loudly. "I'm just a little concerned I might roll uphill over those pillows you've cruelly stuffed between us."

"It's that or the upright lounge chair," Riley warned and patted the pillows. "And these are to keep you honest."

"Honest? Now that hurt." Mac pushed himself up on his elbow and looked across at Riley. "I mean, it's not as though we're strangers who haven't fooled around before."

"Mac, we were twelve years old, and a quick kiss behind the garage isn't exactly fooling around."

"I told you before, that's not how I remember it. I've been having fantasies ever since about your tongue in my mouth and the way we swapped our chewing gum."

"Chewing gum? Yuck! That's gross, Mac. That isn't fantasy, it's a nightmare. And besides, it never happened," Riley stated with conviction.

"There's nothing sadder than a lesbian in denial."

"Denial? And what exactly am I denying?"

Mac leaned on the pillows and grinned at her. "For starters, you're denying yourself a night of pure ecstasy with the hottest stud in the village."

"The hottest stud in the village? I take it you mean you?" Riley tried not to laugh. "Somehow I'll just have to cope. Let's call it the cross I'll have to bear."

"Why be so hard on yourself, Riles? I can provide the hard on for both of us."

Riley groaned. "Mac Bradford, please stop embarrassing yourself."

"You're a woman of stone, Riley James. And let me tell you, hardness is very unattractive in a woman. That's why I can't understand why women constantly fall at your feet."

Riley gave an exclamation of disbelief. "Constantly, my foot."

"No. Constantly at your feet."

"Ha! Ha!" She settled the sheet up to her chin. "You seem to have more fantasies than a fairy story."

"No pun intended I take it."

Riley laughed and shoved him off the pillow. "Very funny, Mr. Comedian. And I'd like to know where all these women are who, you say, are supposedly falling at my feet."

Mac frowned seriously. "Well, there's Lisa. But I think you know how I feel about her."

"You never said anything." Riley turned to look at him and he shrugged.

"Truthfully, Riley. I don't like her much. Besides, you two have nothing in common."

"I know, Mac." Riley sighed. "And I think I've finally convinced her that I just want us to be friends." She looked at Mac. "So are you going to say I told you so? When I introduced you two you did make a cryptic comment about it being difficult to get out of a sticky relationship."

Mac gave a soft derisive laugh. "I'm not that much of a hypocrite."

"Hypocrite? What are you talking about?"

"Sandy Schofield."

Riley sat up. "You went out with Sandy Schofield. When?"

"A couple of weeks ago." Mac grimaced. "Heaven only knows why I did it."

"I didn't even know you fancied her. And isn't she going out with Tom Jervis?"

"They'd broken up. And I don't fancy her." He ran a hand through his hair. "But I—hell, she was down at the club, crying over Tom breaking up with her, and I somehow heard myself asking her out to dinner. I don't know why. I barely knew her. But you know I can't stand to see a woman cry."

"Right!" Riley said sarcastically. She held up her hand when he gave her a wounded look. "But in your defense—and I don't know why I'm defending you because you don't deserve it—in your defense Sandy Schofield is pretty attractive."

"She has great boobs."

Riley shook her head. "That's not what I meant."

"But you can't say you haven't noticed."

"There's more to being attractive than being well endowed," Riley said, her tone reproving.

"If you say so. But that wasn't quite what I meant either. I knew you would have noticed she was attractive because she's your type."

"My type? What on earth are you going on about, Mac?"

"Tall. Blonde. Good figure."

A picture of Jayne Easton popped immediately into Riley's mind and she frowned. "I really don't know what you're talking about." Riley stopped. Gem had been tall and fair, too.

"Of course, Lisa was the exception so maybe I'm generalizing."

"Only maybe?" Riley asked dryly. "And I know why you're saying all this, Mac. You're trying to change the thread of the conversation. We were talking about you. And the fact that I couldn't see you with Sandy Schofield."

Mac sighed. "I know. I guess it was just like you and Lisa. Sandy and I had nothing in common. I still feel guilty as hell and I hated having to tell her I didn't want to see her again. I felt like an absolute shit." He paused. "I probably was an absolute shit."

"No kidding! I don't know, Mac Braford. I leave home for a few weeks and my very best friend—"

"Makes a complete fool of himself," he finished. "Well, not a complete fool. I did dig myself out of the mess I'd made, but only just, on a couple of counts."

"I'm afraid to ask what you mean," Riley said with a grimace.

"Well, you know how big Tom Jervis is? He'd have made mince-meat of me."

"I thought you said they'd broken up?"

"Jervis is the jealous type. Anyway, he came groveling and Sandy made up with him, as she apparently does. And before you ask, no, Sandy and I didn't *do* anything."

Riley held up her hand. "I would never have asked you that. I'm too much of a lady."

"I would have asked if I was you. But anyway, as I said, we didn't do it. Tom Jervis came back to town before Sandy and I had a chance to consummate our mismatch. Which, as I said, was lucky. I have a feeling our big footballer wouldn't have cared much for it if he'd found out, and you know what it's like at home. Someone would have told him. My beautiful face could have been ruined."

"Heaven forbid," Riley said sarcastically.

"Pity, though. I mean, I'm feeling guilty anyway. I might as well have had something to be guilty about."

"Mac," Riley begged, "can we change the subject. I'm not comfortable lying here in bed with you discussing your sex life."

"My lack of sex life, you mean. But my fault and I apologize. I got distracted when we were talking about you and your sex life."

"Oh, no, we weren't."

"Stop splitting hairs. If you want to be absolutely specific I was talking about women falling all over you."

"Yes, well, I'm not sure I want to talk about that subject either," Riley said.

"Don't be boring, Riley. Your love life—and I apologize for being vulgar enough to say sex life—your love life is fascinating. So, I was talking about women falling all over you. One particular woman, actually."

"I have no earthly idea what you're talking about, Mac."

"Sure you don't! Your gorgeous boss."

Riley stilled and Mac propped himself up again so he could look at her.

"No comment, Riley? Well, that was a bit of a fizzer."

"Jayne Easton is straight," Riley said as evenly as she could.

"She is? Mmm. She's pretty hot."

"Yes. She is very attractive." Riley swallowed. Did Mac fancy Jayne? Why wouldn't he? And Jayne couldn't help but notice how handsome Mac was. Her heart constricted. "But she's a few years older than you are," she couldn't prevent herself from adding, knowing she didn't want to picture Jayne and Mac together.

Mac laughed delightedly. "Maybe I secretly like older women."

Riley couldn't think of a thing to say. What if Jayne and Mac—? No. Jayne was engaged to be married. But she'd been very friendly, chatting to Mac. A sinking feeling began in the pit of Riley's stomach.

"I know they like me."

Riley blinked uncomprehendingly at him. "They?"

"Older women," he explained. "They like me. It started with Mrs. Gardner, our first-grade teacher. And I know my mother and yours think I'm wonderful." He chuckled at Riley's expression. "But we were talking about your boss, the divine Jayne, and you completely misconstrued. I wasn't talking about me. I somehow don't think I have the right equipment for her either."

"The right equip—good grief, Mac! She's engaged. She's getting married."

"Yeah. Right."

"No, Mac. She is." Riley clutched his arm to get her point across. "To her business partner. She's known him since they were at university together. I've met him."

"What's he like?"

Riley hesitated. "The pits."

"That bad? Or is the little demon jealousy coloring your opinion?"

"He called me a dyke and warned me off Jayne."

Mac frowned. "He did. What a bastard. Interesting, though." He glanced thoughtfully at Riley. "I didn't imagine it then. If he said that, then she is sending very mixed messages."

"What—? What do you mean?"

"She has the hots for you, sugar. And her boyfriend knows it."

CHAPTER NINE

Riley felt her face flame. "Mac, that's not funny."

"It wasn't meant to be, Riley. I wasn't joking. I wish I was. You get all the best women."

Riley's fingers curled into his arm and he protested. "Hey, that hurt."

"Sorry." Riley took a steadying breath and he rubbed at his arm where she'd clutched him.

"You know, it's not my fault she fancies you. And I can tell you she didn't like the fact that I was staying the night one tiny bit."

"That's ridiculous. You don't know that."

"Ha!" Mac lay back and put his hands behind his head. "I do know that. She was all set to offer me the spare bedroom in the house to keep us apart."

"The spare bedrooms are being painted," Riley put in and Mac laughed.

"Don't be so literal. Look, all I'm saying is I know the look she was giving you, and I'm speaking from experience. She looked like I felt when you went out with your first girlfriend, Gem what's-her-name."

"Mac, please. I don't feel much like joking about this."

"I'm not joking. I'm serious, Riley."

Riley considered what he'd said. "You must be mistaken." Even as she said the words a tiny ember of hope burst into flame inside Riley. What if it was true? "She's straight," she said, more for her own benefit than Mac's.

"Have you told her you're a lesbian? Is that why her boyfriend came out beating his chest?"

"Of course not. No one knows. Except maybe Jake."

"You told—? Isn't he just a kid? Heck, Riley, was that wise?"

"He's thirteen and he overheard Darren. He doesn't like Jayne's fiancé either and he says he's cool, his words, with my being a lesbian. I swore him to secrecy."

"Do you think you can trust him?"

"I hope so. I haven't even told Maggie yet."

"Are you worried about telling her? Maggie, I mean."

Riley shook her head. "Not worried exactly. I just have no idea how she'll take it. I'm hopeful, but who knows how people will react when push comes to shove. I may not even tell her at all."

"Don't you want to tell Jayne, give her the opportunity to take advantage of you?"

"You have a wonderful way with words, Mac," Riley remarked dryly. "And even if I did want to tell Jayne I wouldn't know how."

"Maybe you could paint a big rainbow feature on the wall. That should give her the clue she's looking for."

"Very droll. Jayne Easton's not looking for anything. She has it all. Looks. Nice car. Nice clothes. Travels all over. She's a self-confessed workaholic. She's in a long-term relationship with her business partner. And there you have it." Riley's burst of hope flickered and died.

"All that might be so but how do you know she isn't looking to change the direction of her life. How old is she?"

"About thirty, I think."

"Well, there you are. She's hit the big three-oh and she's reevaluating her life."

"I hate to shoot your misguided theory down in flames but it's the big four-oh when people do that."

"You're just so negative, Riley. I'm telling you, and take it from one who knows, your boss lady fancies you." Mac ran his finger down Riley's bare arm. "We all do."

Riley slapped at his hand and turned to make a show of plumping her pillow. "Go to sleep, you clown. It's almost eleven and we have to be out at the airport at sunrise. Remember?"

"So what about you?"

"*What* about me?"

"Do you fancy her?"

Riley sighed loudly. "Jayne's my birth mother's stepdaughter, Mac. It borders on incestuous."

"Your birth mother's stepdaughter. Yikes! When you put it like that it makes me feel like I've stepped into a daytime soapy. But seriously, Riley, she's no blood relative to you."

Riley made a noncommittal sound and Mac chuckled.

"I knew you'd thought about it. And I could see the way you look at her, too."

Riley stiffened. "I don't look at her any way." She swallowed. "Do I?"

Mac laughed softly. "Sweet dreams, Riles."

Riley slept fitfully and she was in the bathroom pulling on her cargo shorts the next morning when there was a knock on the door. She heard Mac open it and then the murmur of voices. Hurriedly she slipped her T-shirt over her head and emerged from the bathroom just as Mac was gathering his things.

"Get a move on, Riley," he said as he picked up his backpack. "Change of plans."

Only then did Riley see Jayne Easton standing just outside the door, illuminated by the light from the flat. She was dressed in a dark gray business suit, the straight skirt showing off her long shapely legs. Heaven only knew how her business associates kept their minds on business, Riley reflected, as she fought to keep her expression bland in case Mac was watching her.

"I hope you don't mind, Riley," Jayne began. "I had a call after you left last night and I have to fly down to Sydney for a couple of days. My flight leaves just after Mac's so I thought I could save you a trip out to the airport by giving him a lift myself."

Mac had his back to Jayne and he waggled his eyebrows suggestively at Riley. She struggled to ignore him.

"Unless you want to drive out there, that is," Jayne added and Mac turned around with a grin.

"I don't think being driven out to the airport in Riley's old truck quite measures up to having a gorgeous blonde in an open sports car drop me off. No contest. Sorry, Riles."

"My ute isn't that old," she said defensively as she followed Mac out onto the side veranda, hoping Jayne hadn't seen the unmade bed. *And that matters?* jeered a voice inside her. Jayne knew exactly how many beds were in the flat.

"You don't mind, Riley?" Jayne reiterated and Riley shook her head.

"No, of course not." She shrugged. "I can get to work sooner."

"Yes," Mac put in. "I hear your boss is something of a wicked despot."

They both laughed at the horrified look on Riley's face.

"She's got the reputation for being a real tyrant," Jayne said, her smile lifting the corners of her perfect mouth.

Riley fought the urge to throw her arms around the other woman, feel those wonderful lips on hers. Then strong arms folded her in a bear hug and Mac was nuzzling her ear.

"Thanks for putting me up." He stood back, keeping her in the circle of his arms. "I had a great evening." He winked outrageously

128

and Riley felt her face flame. He laughed softly and kissed her warm cheek before turning back to Jayne. "I'm ready when you are. See you, Riley. And I'll be sure to report to both our mothers that you're doing fine."

Riley glanced at Jayne. The other woman's smile had gone and she was looking at the lightening skies over the city. "Thanks again. For taking Mac to the airport."

Jayne seemed to gather herself. "It's fine. Could you—? This meeting was a sudden thing and it was too late to ring Maggie last night. I didn't want to disturb her this early, so would you mind telling her I'll be back on Friday, probably late afternoon."

"Of course. I'll tell her," Riley said quickly.

"Thanks. Well, I'll see you then."

Mac started along the veranda and Jayne went to follow him. She paused and turned back to Riley. "If you need, Maggie has my mobile number." Her gaze met Riley's briefly before she continued after Mac.

He waited for her to catch up to him and grinned. "You know, if you ask me nicely I'll tell you about the time Riley climbed up to the top of our mango tree and couldn't get down. We had to call the fire brigade."

Jane laughed delightedly as they disappeared around the corner of the house.

Riley watched them both go into the garage, heard the doors bang, the engine purr to life. Then they were gone, leaving Riley feeling unexpectedly alone.

Standing up, Riley flexed her tired muscles. She'd cleaned her brushes and she glanced at her wristwatch. 7:45 p.m. All of a sudden she realized how hungry she was. But at least she'd finished painting the door and window frames, the worst part of painting as far as Riley was concerned.

And this morning, with Maggie and Jake's help she'd replaced Andrew Easton's book collection on the shelves she'd renovated. Maggie had been so pleased with the results.

So Riley supposed she'd had a few good days. Even if she knew why she'd been driving herself so hard. She was distracting herself so she wouldn't have to think about what Jayne's fiancé might be telling her. She knew Jayne was back from her trip to Sydney because Maggie had spoken to her just after lunch. Jayne told her she was going straight to the office from the airport. And Darren would be waiting for her. At least having Mac stay the night might negate any of Darren's accusations.

With a sigh she shed her overalls and flicked off the lights before heading tiredly upstairs. It was all too complicated. She hadn't slept terribly well since her run-in with Darren and it annoyed her that she had allowed the man to get under her skin the way he had.

The house was quiet and Riley knew Jayne hadn't returned home from the office. She was certainly late tonight.

Riley went out to her flat, locking the door to the main house behind her. She crossed to the bathroom and peeled off her shorts and shirt. Under the shower she started to relax.

Maybe Jayne had gone out for dinner. Riley stiffened. Had she gone out with her fiancé? And was Darren Wardell warning her to keep away from Riley and why she should? What if Jayne—? Angry with herself, Riley told herself it was all out of her control and worrying about what might or might not happen was pointless.

She switched off the water and toweled herself dry before pulling on a pair of cool cotton shorts and a tank top. Even this late it was still fairly humid. It was surprising they hadn't had a storm to clear the air.

She put together a salad and poured some iced tea. She'd eat outside where it was a little cooler. As Jayne wasn't home Riley took her meal around to the back veranda and settled at the small table to eat.

There was a slight breeze but it barely rustled the leaves on the trees. Riley sighed and watched the flickering lights as she ate. She'd miss this view when she left here. And she'd have to leave when she finished painting Jayne's house. She couldn't impose on Jayne or Maggie.

She supposed she'd have to go home. She'd done what she'd come down to Brisbane to do. She'd met Maggie, got to know her, and in a week or so Maggie's husband would be home. Then the Eastons would know Riley's connection to their family.

Of course, she may not have the opportunity to finish painting Jayne's house or to see the family's reaction to Maggie's revelation. If Darren Wardell had his way Riley would be gone as of yesterday.

She told herself she should simply tell Jayne the truth. It would ensure Darren's threats to do just that wouldn't apply. Riley knew it was the best course of action. Just tell Jayne. But—

What was she so afraid of? she asked herself. That she would lose Jayne's friendship? That Jayne would in turn tell Maggie? That her birth mother would be disappointed in her? Riley shook her head, wishing she was back home with her family and friends where she was accepted unconditionally.

She finished her dinner and picked up her plate and glass, walked around the veranda toward her flat. The motion light over the front door flicked on and Riley paused. Jayne must be home. Would she be alone?

Just then living room light came on and before Riley could move Jayne had opened the French doors on the side veranda. She stopped when she saw Riley standing there. "Oh, Riley. I was coming out to the flat to see you."

"I've just finished my dinner," Riley said inanely, indicating the plate and glass in her hand. You could tell Jayne now, prompted her inner voice. It would be better coming from you. Riley nearly dropped her plate. She drew a shallow breath, her resolve flickering and dying. "It's still pretty hot, isn't it?"

"Yes. I can't wait for the air-conditioning to be up and running again. If they haven't got that part by Monday I'm going to get really terse." Jayne still had hold of the door and Riley could see she looked tired and strained.

131

"You'd probably find the part would miraculously appear and a tribe of guys would fix the problem immediately. A case of the squeaky wheel gets the most oil." Riley smiled weakly, butterflies fluttering in her stomach. "I guess you'd notice the heat more after being in air conditioning all day at work."

"Mmm. You're right." Jayne played with a strand of her hair.

Was she nervous about something? Riley suspected she was. That made two of them. Riley's heartbeats were tripping over themselves in her chest. "Well, I'll say good night then." She took a step toward the flat but stopped when Jayne spoke.

"Oh, Riley, before you go."

Riley turned back to face her.

"Can I talk to you for a moment?"

"Sure." Riley's heart sank. There was only one reason why Jayne might want to talk to her. Darren must have carried out his threat to warn Jayne against her and now she was going to ask Riley to leave.

"Come on inside." Jayne stepped back into the living room.

Riley set her plate and glass down on the lounger and reluctantly followed Jayne into the lighted room. She'd never felt so dispirited in her life.

Jayne nervously rubbed her hands together. "Perhaps we could sit down?"

Sinking into a lounge chair Riley waited for the words she knew were coming. Jayne was about to say, *"Sorry. I've decided to get someone else to finish painting my house. And I'll be needing the flat."*

She watched as Jayne shrugged out of her light jacket, laying it over the back of a chair before she in turn sat down. She wore a thin short-sleeved top under her jacket, the low scooped neckline hinting at the shadow of the valley between her breasts. She crossed her long legs and her short skirt rode up a little.

Riley's heart constricted. Now that the moment she'd been dreading had come she realized her feelings for Jayne ran far deeper than she knew was sensible. Far deeper.

Flashes from the past few weeks came back to tease her. When she'd turned around that first day to see Jayne standing behind her.

132

Jayne across the candlelit table out on the veranda. Jayne laughing in the surf, the salt water running over her skin. An ache of regret rose inside Riley as she sat waiting for Jayne to speak.

"I don't quite know where to start," Jayne said, not meeting Riley's eyes. "Perhaps I should begin with an apology. And I should have made it sooner, because Darren had no right to speak to you the way he did the other day. But—" She paused.

"It's okay," Riley said flatly. "And you don't need to explain. I can wait until you get a replacement painter or I can leave tomorrow if you'd rather."

"Leave?" Jayne looked across at Riley in surprise. "You want to leave? Riley, I'm sorry Darren was so rude. He has no say in who I hire to work on my house."

"It isn't Darren. Really. And I don't want to leave. But I thought—" Riley shrugged.

"You thought that was what I wanted to talk about? That I wanted to tell you to leave?"

Riley nodded. Had she been wrong? Hope flickered inside her.

"And you thought I was going to fire you? Because of what happened with Darren?" Jayne asked. "Oh, Riley. I'm sorry. But you know I've never been dissatisfied with your work."

"Thank you. But I thought you would have spoken to your fiancé and, well, I said a few things to him that perhaps I shouldn't have."

"Reading between the lines I don't think he was totally blameless. But yes, I have spoken to him." Jayne sighed. "That's where I've been tonight. We—I needed to talk to him. I've been meaning to for some time, long before you started painting the house. But I kept putting it off." Jayne leaned back in the chair and closed her eyes.

Riley watched her, not daring to breathe.

"I've been so snowed under at work these past few months I just let the rest of my life slide." She sat forward again. "What happened the other day between you and Darren simply brought it to a head." She absently rubbed the ring finger on her left hand. Only then did Riley notice she wasn't wearing her engagement ring. "This afternoon I told Darren I didn't want to marry him."

Riley was surprised and then concerned. As much as she thought Jayne was too good for Darren she knew it wouldn't have been easy for Jayne to come to this decision. And if her altercation with Darren had had anything to do with it, well . . . "Look, Jayne, I'm really sorry. I didn't mean to cause any problems between you and Darren."

"It wasn't you, Riley. Don't think that," Jayne assured her. "This has been coming for a long time." She rubbed her hand tiredly over her eyes. "Darren and I haven't been happy for ages. Not for years, I don't think. We were simply drifting along out of habit."

"I'm sorry," Riley repeated softly and Jayne nodded.

"As I said before Darren's changed over the years." She made a dismissive gesture with her hand. "I don't know. I spoke to Maggie tonight, told her I'd called the wedding off, and she suggested Darren and I might have grown in different directions. Whatever it is, I've known for a very long time I didn't want to marry him."

Riley didn't know what to say.

"And, looking back," Jayne continued, "I'm not completely certain I ever did want to marry him. Perhaps we drifted into it. We dated at uni, had our interest in computers in common. Then we worked long hours together to get the company up and running. It seemed marriage was the natural progression. But now I know we weren't—Well, I can't marry him because I don't love him. Not the way, well, the way I should." She glanced at Riley and flushed a little. "But enough of that. I should leave it that Darren and I are no longer engaged to be married."

"It must have been a difficult decision to make," Riley said cautiously and Jayne shrugged.

"Not once I'd admitted it to myself. I know Maggie's worried I'll fall apart." Jayne gave a soft humorless laugh. "But, quite honestly, I'm just relieved it's over at last. I know I wasn't happy, neither of us was. And as soon as he's had time to think about it rationally Darren will realize I'm right."

"Didn't he—? How did he take it?" Riley couldn't stop herself from asking.

134

"He was upset. But I expected that." Jayne shook her head and her fair hair swung around her face. She absently reached up to tuck a loose strand behind her ear. "The problem was, once I'd started talking, voicing my concerns so to speak, I couldn't stop. I also told him I wanted to resign from my position in the company."

Riley raised her eyebrows. "You do?"

"Yes. And that's also not something I decided on the spur of the moment or decided lightly. I'll keep my share of the company but I don't want to work at the pace I have been these past few years."

Riley knew Maggie would be overjoyed that Jayne would be slowing down.

"Darren wasn't pleased about that either," Jayne continued, "but I see no problem. We can find new staff, restructure the staff we have. And we have some fantastic people working for us who deserve promotions. I'm convinced it won't cause too much drama."

Riley hoped Darren would feel that way.

"I know I've turned Darren's world upside down but I knew I couldn't keep working the way I was. I'm tired and I'm unmotivated. Between work and how I felt about our relationship I knew I was heading for a breakdown."

"What will you do then?" Riley asked and Jayne raised her hands and let them fall.

"Rest for a while. I might take a holiday. I'll still be involved in the company but more on a consulting level. It will give me more time to do what I did in the beginning, what I really enjoy doing. Working on the software programs. I told Darren I was worth more to the company doing that. He'll see I'm right."

Riley suspected the last was said more for Jayne's own benefit. Somehow she couldn't see Darren Wardell agreeing easily with something that wasn't his idea. But Riley had to admit she was secretly ecstatic that Jayne wouldn't be seeing him anymore. Then she chastised herself. She was letting her own antipathy for the man overshadow the gravity of the situation. It must have taken a lot for Jayne to come to these decisions and, as much as it irked Riley to

135

admit it, she could understand that Darren would be upset at losing Jayne, personally and professionally.

"It will take a few months to sort everything out," Jayne said, "but I've given Darren my assurance I won't be taking a back seat until the restructure is in place. I'll be working all out to see the transition runs smoothly. Tomorrow we'll schedule meetings with all those concerned—the staff, lawyers." She pulled a face. "I'm not looking forward to it but it has to be done."

"I suppose so."

Jayne sighed again. "But I didn't mean to go into all that. It had nothing to do with you, Riley. What I wanted to say was I really am sorry about the other afternoon. Darren had no right to be rude to you because he was angry I was late."

"It's okay." Riley gave a quick smile. Now that she knew Jayne didn't want her to leave Riley felt she could be generous. "I'm sure I was just as rude back to him."

Jayne paused, her tongue tip moistening her lips. "Darren accused me of being involved with someone else." She glanced at Riley and away again, a slight flush coloring her face.

"I suppose it was only natural for him to think that was why you were breaking off your engagement," Riley acknowledged carefully, feeling the conversational ground shift just slightly. Her nerve endings snapped to attention.

"Perhaps, but I don't know why he should have thought that. Maybe it was guilty conscience on his part. I suspect there's a certain personal assistant who will be more than happy to console him. And she has my blessing. But anyway, I asked him when he thought I had the time to develop another relationship when I didn't have time for the one I had. He was still convinced there was someone else."

Riley swallowed. Was Jayne trying to let her know that Darren had voiced his accusations?

"I asked him what he'd argued with you about." Jayne looked at her. "He said he accused you of not being a qualified painter. Which was why you thought I wanted you to leave?"

136

Riley nodded. "I guess you could say he intimated that painters were a dime a dozen."

"But that wasn't all he said, was it?" Jayne persisted. Her fingers nervously smoothed the seam of her skirt. "This evening things got pretty heated between us and he suggested I might be having an affair." She paused and Riley felt the air between them grow heavy with tension. "With you," Jayne added softly.

CHAPTER TEN

Heat rose inside Riley and she knew her face had suffused with color. "You know that's not true," she said, her voice sounding thin in her ears.

"He made those accusations against you, too, the other afternoon, didn't he? I can't believe he—" Jayne shook her head. "I asked him what he based his assumptions on and all he could say was that it was plainly obvious that you were a lesbian. That you did a man's job and that you had short hair and looked like one. I disagreed. I told him women worked in all sorts of jobs these days, regardless of the length of their hair."

Riley's stomach churned.

"Reading between the lines I take it some of the things Darren said to you were quite crude."

"It was pretty standard stuff," Riley said carefully and there were a few moments of electric silence.

"Do people usually accuse you of being a lesbian?" Jayne asked gently.

"No, they don't," Riley said. The people around her knew she was a lesbian. No one had to accuse her. She drew herself together, knowing she'd have to tell Jayne the truth. All this subterfuge went against Riley's nature. It meant she'd have to tell Maggie sooner rather than later but she did have to tell Jayne. "Jayne, I need to say something."

"You don't have to say anything you don't want to say," Jayne put in quickly.

"I know. But there is something I've wanted to tell you for some time. And not because of anything Darren said. Not because of him. But because of, well, just me. The person I am. And I'm not ashamed of who I am. I just don't—" Riley took a steadying breath. "What Darren said was true. I am a lesbian." Riley's heartbeats rose to thunder inside her. There. She'd said it.

She searched Jayne's face for her reaction and she watched as Jayne swallowed, saw the flutter of her pulse at the base of her throat. Her fingers moved nervously on the arm of her chair and she glanced down before she finally met Riley's gaze.

"I thought you might be," she said softly.

They looked at each other for long, heavy moments.

Riley was the first to look away. "Perhaps I should have told you when I took the job."

"No, Riley." Jayne shook her head. "There was no reason why you should have told me. As I see it, it was your business, and it had nothing to do with your ability to do the job."

Riley felt herself relax a little. At least Jayne wasn't totally repulsed.

"It certainly wasn't in the job description," Jayne added with an attempt at lightness and Riley gave her a quick smile.

"Now, there's a thought," she said, her throat tight, and that same charged silence grew between them.

"Riley," Jayne began. "I'd like to—there's something—"

Riley watched the other woman's face, could see she was struggling to say more. Her heart felt like lead in her chest again. Now Jayne was going to tell her it didn't matter because she herself was straight, totally heterosexual.

"May I ask you something?" Jayne got out and Riley nodded. "When did you—I mean, how long have you known you were a lesbian?"

Riley's eyebrows rose in surprise at the unexpected question. Why did Jayne want to know? Was it just polite interest or—? Riley stopped her wayward thoughts as that persevering spark of hope flickered inside her again.

"You don't have to talk about it if you'd rather not," Jayne added quickly.

"It's okay. I suppose I've known since my teens. I guess I always knew I was different but I didn't have a name for it."

"But how did you know?"

Riley sat forward, rested her elbows on her knees. "I realized I'd fallen in love with a friend of mine. A girlfriend."

"You're not still together?"

"No. We broke up. She married a guy, has a family."

"You've never wanted to get married?"

Riley gave her a crooked grin. "Not to a man."

"What about your friends? Do they know?"

Riley raised her eyebrows.

"Cathy and Brenna. Lisa and—" Jayne paused just slightly. "Mac."

"Cathy and Brenna are a couple. They've been together for years. Lisa's a lesbian, too." It was Riley's turn to pause.

"Is she your girlfriend?" Jayne asked.

"No. We're friends."

"And Mac?" she asked casually.

Riley looked at the other woman. Was this where the conversation had been leading all along? After all, Jayne was now a free woman, free to form other relationships. And there was no denying Mac was extremely good-looking. It would be no surprise if she was interested in him. But Riley suspected it would break her heart if that were the case. "Mac's just what I said he was. My best friend. He was the first person I confided in."

"Oh." Jayne had gone a little pink again. "I thought you said when you first mentioned Mac that he was your best friend. So you and Mac, you're not a couple? I mean, you're not bisexual? You don't—"

Riley shook her head. "No, we're not. And no, I'm not. Mac and I *are* just good friends."

Jayne smiled faintly. "I see. I'm sorry. It was just that the other night I thought you and Mac were, well, involved."

"Not physically. I do prefer women. Exclusively."

"I didn't mean to pry. It's just—"

"You've never met a lesbian before?" Riley finished with a teasing smile.

"Not that I was aware of. And certainly not one I felt I could—" She paused again—"talk to." She looked across at Riley. "What about your parents? Do they know?"

"Oh, yes. They've known pretty much from the start."

"How did they take it?"

"They were concerned at first but I suppose they're used to the idea now."

"So you—" Jayne's gaze fell again, concentrating on the hem of her skirt where her fingers now nervously pulled at a stray thread. "You live as an out lesbian?"

Riley laughed. "Since I've been in Brisbane, not so you'd notice. But at home, yes."

"That must be difficult for you."

"Not usually. It's not really so different from being heterosexual. The difficulties only arise because being heterosexual is the default setting."

Jayne smiled at that. "Which can cause problems."

"Well, it's why people ask you if you have a boyfriend. They don't even consider you might have a girlfriend."

Jayne frowned. "But what about the people at the other end of the scale, the ones who hate anyone who's different from themselves?"

"They're the dangerous ones," Riley conceded. "And being different comes with the territory. But I can't live my life thinking about

141

them all the time. Otherwise I'd have no life at all. As I see it, people are the same, no matter what. There's good and bad in both communities."

"I suppose there is."

"To answer your original question," Riley continued, "I don't consciously hide the fact that I'm a lesbian but, well, I guess the subject didn't come up when Maggie asked me to take over from your painters." She grinned crookedly. "And speaking about that, can I keep the job?"

"Of course," Jayne assured her. "There was never any reason why you couldn't. Regardless of what Darren said."

"Thanks. I appreciate that." Riley smiled. "You have a magnificent house and I'm really enjoying painting it."

"And as I said before I have no complaints about your work. Oh, and Maggie said you've done a great job on Dad's shelves. She's ecstatic. So thank you for that, too."

"Just doing my job, ma'am," Riley said with a pseudo-TV detective tone and they both laughed. "I really enjoy restoration work."

Jayne nodded and stifled a yawn.

Riley pushed herself to her feet. "You're tired. I should let you get to bed."

Jayne stood up too, color warming her cheeks. "I'm okay. But I am just a little tired, I guess. Probably because I'm relieved I've had the courage to address all the things I've been sweeping under the carpet for so long. It was a long time coming and now it's finally over. But I did promise Maggie I'd ring her and let her know I'm all right." Jayne glanced at her wristwatch. "I should do that before it gets too late."

"Then I'll leave you to it." Riley crossed to the door. "And Jayne, thank you."

She nodded and smiled tiredly.

Riley said a soft good-night and returned to her flat. Only when she was inside did it occur to her that Jayne might tell Maggie that Riley was a lesbian.

A loud clap of thunder woke Riley with a start. She sat up and blinked, hearing the deafening deluge of torrential rain on the corrugated iron roof of the flat. Although it was a little unseasonable she was hardly surprised by the tropical storm. It seemed to Riley it had been building all week and today had been almost unbearably humid, the air still and heavy. She flicked on her bedside lamp and rushed over to close the window as rain splattered on the carpet.

She'd just thrown a towel on the floor to sop up the water when she realized she'd left the window in the downstairs bedroom open slightly to dissipate the smell of fresh paint. Riley grabbed her keys to the main house and left her flat, careful to close the door behind her.

Unlocking the door to the main house she padded softly inside, her bare feet not making a sound on the polished wooden floor. It wouldn't do to wake Jayne and scare her into thinking she was being burgled.

Riley suppressed a giggle as a flash of lightning lit her way down the stairs. With the din of the rain on the roof above her bedroom Jayne would be hard pressed to hear herself think, let alone Riley's creeping about downstairs.

Turning on the light Riley raced across the room to close the window. Luckily she'd left the drop sheets down and they'd contained the small amount of rain that had blown in the window. She checked the other rooms and then began climbing the stairs, feeling her way up as she clutched the banister.

She'd just reached the top step when the light over the stairs to Jayne's room was flicked on. Riley looked up to see Jayne standing at the top of the staircase. She was wearing a mauve silk robe and when she saw Riley her hand moved to her chest in fright.

"It's me. Riley," she said quickly. "I didn't mean to scare you. I've just been closing the window I left open in the bedroom downstairs."

"It's okay. Actually, I was coming down to get a hammer. I can't— one of the windows up here is stuck and the rain's pouring in. Maybe you could help me with it? I mean, I'd appreciate it if you could give me a hand to close it."

"Of course." Riley started up the stairs, trying not to look at the thin silk covering Jayne's body, trying to stop herself imagining what was underneath.

"I hate bothering you in the middle of the night," Jayne said as Riley followed her into the bedroom.

Riley tried to find something to say to put the other woman at ease. Since she'd told Jayne she was a lesbian she was certain Jayne was tense in her presence. "It's all right. It's not as though I wasn't out of bed. The storm's pretty loud and wild but I think it's passing over."

"I hope you're right," Jayne said. "I don't mind the rain but I hate the wind."

Riley crossed to the half-open window and examined it, realizing it had somehow worked itself off kilter. She banged the dropped side with the heel of her hand a couple of times until it righted itself and she could slide it downwards. "There you go," she said as lightly as she could, hoping her voice wouldn't betray the fact that Jayne's proximity made her whole body taut, her nerve endings tingling as her heartbeats skipped over themselves.

"Thanks." Jayne crossed her arms and then raised one hand, her fingers playing nervously with the neckline of her robe. "I hope you didn't get too wet." Her blue eyes moved over Riley's faded old T-shirt and mismatched boxer shorts.

Riley went decidedly hot all over and she was amazed her weakened knees continued to hold her upright. And Jayne's bed was so invitingly close.

Desire swelled inside Riley, and she felt her nipples tingle and harden, thrusting sharply against the soft material of her T-shirt. She brushed at her shorts. "Oh, no. Just a bit damp," she said quickly. Taking hold of the front of her T-shirt, she held it away from her body, feigning giving it a deep scrutiny for errant rain spots. A wayward draft of wind teased her bare midriff and she dropped the edge of the short T-shirt, turning desperately toward the glass doors, aware now of the splinters of jagged lightning spearing across the thundery night sky. "Mother Nature can be scary," she said breathily.

Jayne walked over to the doors, drew the curtains across the large expanse of glass, shutting out the storm, before turning back toward Riley. "I was so busy trying to battle with the window I didn't get to the doors." She stopped, looked at Riley and then away.

The tension in the room was as electric as the storm-torn air outside. Or so it seemed to Riley. She told her shaky legs to move her away, toward the door and the safety of her flat. But there was a breakdown in communications somewhere and she simply stood there, her eyes on Jayne, her entire body poised, tuned to the other woman. Spirals of arousal clutched at the pit of her stomach and the ache between her legs was almost unbearable.

Jayne had moved a few steps closer to Riley. Now there was only an arm's length between them.

"Are you sure you're not wet?" she repeated.

Riley shook her head. "Not much. But you—you'd better get a towel and I'll wipe up the water on the floor."

Jayne took another step closer. "You don't have to do that."

"I know." Riley was sure Jayne must be able to hear the thudding of her heart. And just when Riley thought she would be unable to bear the intensity a moment longer, Jayne turned away.

"I'll get a towel."

She walked into the en suite and Riley let out the breath she'd been holding. In no time Jayne came back. She spread a fluffy white towel on the floor and, as she bent forward to move the edge of the towel the lapels of her robe parted slightly.

Riley's eyes were drawn to the tantalizing glimpse of Jayne's cleavage. And she couldn't look away. Her mouth went dry and she swallowed a soft moan that started deep in her chest.

Jayne straightened slowly and Riley's eyes rose to lock with the other woman's. The expression on Jayne's face told Riley she was aware of Riley's scrutiny and Riley was sure she didn't care for it.

"I'm sorry." Riley felt her face flame. "I wasn't—I didn't mean to—" Her voice failed her.

What would Jayne be thinking of her, openly ogling her? Riley was mortified with herself. She knew she had to leave, go back to her flat before she did anything else to upset Jayne. Like telling her just how attractive, how desirable she was. And how much she wanted to make love to her.

"I'll leave you to it." Riley told herself to head toward the door. She took one step and paused. "I'll look at the window tomorrow. It probably just needs adjusting. It shouldn't take me long to fix it." She knew she was babbling but she couldn't stop herself. She gave the window her attention because she was unable to look at Jayne. Anything was better than seeing the revulsion on Jayne's face. "I'm pretty sure the storm has passed over now. Sounds like it anyway." Riley chattered on, her voice thin in her ears. She made herself take another step toward the door only to find Jayne standing in her path. Startled, she looked up and what she saw stopped her in mid step.

Jayne's eyes were inky deep blue pools, and their focus seemed to settle on Riley's trembling lips.

"Riley." Jayne breathed her name in a tone Riley had never heard her use. It was soft and sensuous, pouring over Riley like warm honey.

Riley's blood raced through her veins, her nerve endings on alert, gathering in such a surge of hot desire she moaned deep in her throat.

At the low sound Jayne's lashes fell to shield the expression in her eyes, and her tongue tip nervously dampened her lips.

"I've read in books," she said softly, brokenly, "about people saying they'd die from wanting someone. Now I—" She swallowed, the pulse at the base of her throat beating a wild, erotic tattoo. "Now I know what they mean."

146

CHAPTER ELEVEN

Jayne looked up, her eyes glowing brightly. "If I don't kiss you now, Riley, I think I might die." She raised one shaking hand, ran it lightly along Riley's jaw until one finger settled oh-so-gently on Riley's lips. "So soft. So very soft," she murmured thickly, so that Riley barely caught the words.

And then she leaned forward and her lips met Riley's, settled, drew back, touched again. Riley felt light-headed, as though she might faint. She reached out, her arms sliding around Jayne's waist, luxuriating in the sensuous, silk-clad feel of her. With a broken sigh Riley moved into Jayne's body, felt the exquisite thrust of her breasts, the jut of her hips. She ran her hands over the curve of Jayne's back, settled on her firm buttocks.

She moaned again, or was it Jayne, as her mouth claimed the other woman's, her tongue-tip seeking to taste as the fire of desire raged inside her. Her body tuned to every nuance as she lost herself in the wonder of the sensation that was Jayne Easton. Her taste. Her softness. Her fire.

Even the steady splatter of rain on the roof above them couldn't drown out the sound of Jayne's inciting responses, the ragged headiness of their mingled breathing. Riley tenderly nibbled on Jayne's lips, along the line of her firm jaw, her sensitive earlobe, and she felt Jayne's shuddering response. She moved her lips then, slowly sliding down over her throat, lingering in the hollow where her pulse raced, then downward toward the velvet valley between Jayne's breasts.

Jayne gasped and clutched at Riley's shoulders. "I can't stand. My knees have gone to water." She sank back against the metal frame of the high bedstead, drawing Riley with her.

"Lean on me," Riley whispered, one of her legs slipping between Jayne's, their bare skin sliding silkily. Jayne's short robe parted, displaying a smooth thigh and a tantalizing glimpse of a light triangle of curls.

And Riley burned for her. Molten fire seemed to race through her veins, the heat inside her clamoring for a release she knew only Jayne could give her. For one emotion-charged moment her breath caught somewhere in her chest, only to escape erratically as a surging ache of desire rose to wrap her in its tentacles.

"God, Jayne! I need to touch you." Riley said thickly, her fingers finding the loosened ties of Jayne's robe. She made herself pause then, her eyes meeting Jayne's, silently asking for permission.

Jayne's reply was to shakily take hold of the bottom of Riley's T-shirt and lift it over her head. She gazed at Riley's breasts in wonder, then slowly ran her hands over Riley's midriff to cup their throbbing fullness. When her thumbs rasped lightly over Riley's erect nipples Riley's head fell forward and she murmured against Jayne's hot skin, the fire of wanting arrowing down between her legs, leaving her weak. She pulled shakily at the ties of Jayne's robe again, sliding the silky fabric from her shoulders.

She stared at Jayne's full breasts and she whispered her name as she leaned forward to capture one upturned rosy peak in her mouth.

She grazed the tip with her tongue, sucked gently, and Jayne fell forward, her knees giving way beneath her as she orgasmed. Riley caught and held her close, managing to guide them onto the bed as she held Jayne while her body quivered its release.

"I'm sorry. I—" Jayne murmured into Riley's shoulder and Riley smoothed back her damp fair hair. "I wanted you so much."

Riley reached down, lifted Jayne's chin so she could look into her eyes. "Don't be sorry. You're wonderful."

"But I—" Her lashes fell to rest on her flushed cheeks. "I couldn't stop myself. I was so—I've never wanted anyone so much in my life."

Riley kissed her tenderly, then more insistently, slid her hand over the curve of her hip, moaned as a surge of her own renewed desire took hold of her again. She felt Jayne's hips thrust toward her and knew the other woman was aroused again.

Jayne's fingers teased Riley's tingling nipples, and then she buried her face between Riley's breasts, her fair hair teasing Riley's skin, her tongue tasting. She nibbled with painful slowness over the taut rise of Riley's breast until she at last caught Riley's nipple in her mouth.

Riley shuddered, arching against her.

"Tell me what to do," Jayne said unevenly. "Tell me what you like."

Riley struggled for breath. "Touch me," she said in a voice she scarcely recognized as her own. "Please." She guided Jayne's hand downward over her midriff and when Jayne's fingers encountered the waistband of Riley's boxer shorts she barely paused before her hand slipped inside to settle on the tangle of now damp curls.

Riley thrust her hips against Jayne's fingers and covered the other woman's hand with her own, gently guiding.

"Like this?" Jayne asked, finding Riley's center with unerring ease.

"Just like that," Riley got out. She clutched at Jayne's shoulder, felt the heady imprint of Jayne's breasts, the heat of skin meeting skin, the heightened awareness of nerve endings raw with desire. And then she was cascading downward, falling into her own orgasm, until she lay spent, her face pressed against the softness of Jayne's breasts, her body still pulsing around Jayne's fingers.

"Jayne." She murmured. "God, Jayne."

"No one has ever said my name quite like that," Jayne said softly, and she pulled Riley impossibly closer.

They remained like that, wrapped in each other's arms, until Riley's breathing slowed. She could hear the steady thud of Jayne's heart beneath her cheek and she moved her head slightly, took one of Jayne's nipples into her mouth, nibbling, teasing, sucking. Her hand slid over Jayne's flat stomach, her fingertips circling her navel, then moved lower, paused, slid upward, taunting, and she felt Jayne's muscles flex. She let her hand trail lower again this time, sliding through her curls to cup her mound.

Jayne stiffened slightly and Riley looked up into her eyes. She murmured reassuringly and nuzzled Jayne's breast again before gently sliding her fingers into the wetness.

She took her guidance from the subtle movements of Jayne's body as it lay half beneath her. Riley stroked and circled as she watched Jayne's hands tense where she clasped the twisted sheets. Her hips rose and fell against Riley's hand until she dissolved in orgasm again.

Riley moved up a little in the bed, pulled Jayne to her and kissed her slowly, reverently.

"Oh, Riley. That was—in my wildest dreams I couldn't—" She drew a steadying breath. "It was so much more than I could have imagined."

Her gaze met Riley's and a tear welled, then overflowed to trickle down her cheek. Riley reached out with her tongue tip, caught the tear and kissed the spot where it had been.

"Shh," she said softly. "I understand."

Jayne sighed and they settled into each other's arms again, legs entwined, and they were soon fast asleep, the steady rain beating on the roof above them.

❧

The sound of the telephone ringing dragged Riley from her deep sleep the next morning. She opened her eyes and started to stretch out her hand, only to find Jayne's firm breast only inches from her lips. Last night came back in all its glorious detail. She opened her eyes properly and looked up to find Jayne watching her.

Riley sighed. It hadn't been just a delightful dream. It was a wonderful reality. Her heart soared even as something inside her called for caution. Until last night Jayne had given every indication that she was straight, reminded her inner voice. And until recently she'd been engaged to be married to Darren Wardell. She may simply have been carried away by the heat of the moment. She could have been experimenting, curious about—

Riley reined in her torturing thoughts. She owed Jayne time to make up her own mind, to come to terms with this huge change in her life. Riley knew she needed to trust her. But all her old insecurities came back to taunt her.

The phone trilled again and Riley went to move but Jayne's arm around her stilled her. She glanced at the clock. It was already after nine and a sliver of bright sunlight broke through a gap in the curtains.

Jayne had lifted the receiver. "Hello," she said with remarkable equanimity. Then her body stiffened slightly. "Darren." She turned slightly away from Riley. "What do you want?"

Riley watched Jayne's profile as she listened. She looked sideways at Riley but Riley could read nothing in her expression.

One night of passion with a woman does not a lesbian make, jeered Riley's inner voice, but she refused to listen.

"The meeting." Jayne glanced at the clock in surprise. "Damn. I completely forgot. Well, I didn't forget exactly. I overslept. We—" Jayne slid another glance at Riley and warm color washed her face. "I had a pretty bad storm here last night. I was up closing windows and, well, it was pretty wild."

She frowned as she listened and Riley could hear the imperious tone, if not the words Darren Wardell was saying.

151

"I know very well it's an important meeting. And I'm well aware it was my idea." Jayne bit her lip. "Look, stall them for a while."

Darren made some comment and Jayne's lips thinned.

"I don't know. Show them the view from the office. Take them on a tour. Give them coffee. You'll think of something. I'll be there as soon as I can."

Whatever Darren said made Jayne's fingers go white as she clutched the phone.

"All right. I said I'd be there." She flung the receiver back onto its cradle and turned to Riley. "I'm sorry about that. I have an important meeting I'm supposed to be attending in twenty minutes. I should shower and—"

"You could go like that," Riley suggested. "It would be guaranteed to distract them. You could ask for anything."

"No doubt," Jayne replied dryly. Her gaze fell to the rise of Riley's breast and she reached out, tentatively filled her hand, watching as Riley's nipple puckered in response. "Tell me last night wasn't a dream, Riley," she said softly.

Riley covered Jayne's hand with her own and she kissed her slowly. "If it was, we seem to have had parallel dreams."

"Riley, I don't know—I don't know what to say. I have no point of reference, no experience of this. I've never—"

"Woken up beside a woman?" Riley finished gently.

Jayne shook her head. "Never." Her gaze roved hungrily over Riley. "God, why haven't I?" she asked thickly, and she was leaning toward Riley when the phone rang shrilly again.

They both started and Jayne reached for the receiver again. "Yes, Darren. I said I'd be there," she began curtly. "Oh, Maggie. Sorry." She sat up. "I thought it was Darren again, reminding me about a meeting."

Riley could hear the murmur of Maggie's voice and she felt a pang of disquiet.

"Yes. The storm woke us both up and we were running around checking and closing windows. No. No damage, I don't think.

Actually, I haven't looked outside. I sort of overslept. That's why Darren rang." She paused. "Yes, a meeting with the lawyers." She looked at the bedside clock and grimaced. "In fifteen minutes."

Fifteen minutes? Riley's heart sank in disappointment.

Jayne listened for a few moments. "Okay. Glad you're all right, too." She replaced the receiver and looked back at Riley. "That was Maggie checking we were all right after the storm." Jayne's gaze roved over Riley again, setting Riley's skin aflame. Jayne took a deep breath. "I should shower," she said without a lot of conviction.

Riley nodded, wanting to let her fingers glide over the contours of Jayne's body, the swell of rounded hip and breast. She sat up, rested her lips on the smooth roundness of Jayne's bare shoulder. "I'd like to shower with you but fifteen minutes isn't nearly long enough." She smiled at Jayne. "I'll go down and make some coffee." Sliding off the bed, she grabbed her T-shirt and went to pull it over her head but paused when Jayne stood up too, exquisite in her nakedness.

"Riley. I wish I could stay."

"I know. And I wish you could, too." She took Jayne's hands and kissed her slowly on the lips, leaning into her, feeling her warm, smooth skin against her own.

Jayne moaned softly, pulled Riley's hands around her as their kiss deepened, and their bodies strained against each other. Riley's breasts tingled, her nipples hardening as desire once again clutched at the pit of her stomach. They drew reluctantly apart, each breathing raggedly, and the expression in Jayne's eyes mirrored the wanting in Riley's aroused body.

Riley closed her eyes for a moment and drew a steadying breath. "You'd better have your shower. And if I stay here a second longer you won't have a chance in hell of making your meeting." She gave Jayne a crooked smile, shrugged into her T-shirt and hurried downstairs.

She filled the coffeepot and put some slices of bread into the toaster, all the while imagining Jayne in the shower, her body sleek, her skin glistening with soap bubbles and water droplets. She made herself attend to the toast and as she spread a slice with honey she realized she was ravenous.

Must be her night of earth-shattering sex. But it wasn't just sex, Riley admonished herself. Not with Jayne. It had been—wonderful. Indescribably wonderful. And Jayne was wonderful, too.

Then Jayne was coming down the stairs and into the kitchen. As Riley watched her approach, she knew without a doubt she was desperately, unequivocally in love with her.

Jayne was shrugging into a lightweight navy blazer. She wore a crisp white shirt and a straight gray skirt that finished just above her knees, displaying her long shapely legs. She'd coiled her hair into a French knot and she looked so beautiful Riley could only stare at her for long moments before she made herself move.

She handed Jayne a covered mug of coffee and reached up to kiss her lips before proffering a slice of toast. Jayne held the toast between her teeth as she picked up her briefcase and stuck it under her arm.

"Thanks." She swallowed a mouthful and balanced the remainder of the slice on top of her coffee mug. "I'm so hungry."

"Me, too."

Then eyes met, held, and Jayne shook her head faintly. "I have to go. I—I'll be caught up all day but I'll be home as soon as I can. We'll have the whole weekend. We need to talk."

Riley nodded.

"Oh, Riley. You know if I kiss you again I won't go," she said, her voice thick.

Riley put her finger to her own lips and then touched her finger lightly to Jayne's mouth. Jayne's lips settled around Riley's finger, nibbled, sucked. She groaned and turned away.

"I'll be counting the moments," she added softly as she turned and hurried through the door.

After Jayne left, Riley hummed to herself as she showered and changed. She cleared away the damp towels from the storm the night before and put them through a washing cycle. Then she carried her toolbox upstairs to repair the window in Jayne's bedroom. The job took her ages because she kept pausing to look at the bed, the rumpled sheets, reliving those tantalizing hours she'd spent with Jayne.

About eleven she went downstairs and continued with her painting, putting a final coat on the third bedroom before she stopped for lunch. When the doorbell rang a couple of hours later she grinned and bounded up the steps. For one moment she imagined it was Jayne and she was halfway up the steps before reason told her Jayne had her own key and it was unlikely she'd ring the doorbell.

"Are you there, Riley?" Maggie's voice caused Riley's step to falter as she crossed toward the door.

She'd just slept with Maggie's stepdaughter. If Maggie knew . . . She took a deep breath and opened the door.

"I thought you may have been out," Maggie said as she kissed Riley's cheek.

"No. I was downstairs. Would you like a cuppa? I was just going to take a break." Riley stepped out of her overalls and hung them over the banister. "I just have to clean myself up."

"I'd love a cup of tea. But I'll make it while you do that." Maggie disappeared into the kitchen and Riley hurried into her flat to wash off the paint splatters.

The wind had picked up, making it far too breezy on the veranda, so they sat in the easy chairs in the living room.

"The storm was fierce, wasn't it?" Maggie remarked after they'd settled in with their cups of tea. "And I read in the paper that houses were unroofed on the north side. Luckily no one was hurt though."

Riley murmured agreement.

"And, do you know, Jake managed to sleep through the whole thing. 'What storm?' he asked me, when I mentioned it this morning."

Riley laughed. "I can't believe the thunder didn't wake him up. He must be a heavy sleeper."

"He always has been." Maggie took a sip of her tea. "There's nothing quite like a tropical storm." She paused and frowned slightly.

155

"Is something wrong?" Riley asked, a hundred questions racing through her mind. How would Maggie react when Riley told her she was a lesbian? And when she found out that Jayne—

Guilt rose inside Riley. Her life was careering along like a runaway train. She knew she'd have to speak to Maggie about it, and the sooner the better, but—

Maggie sighed. "Actually, I did want to talk to you about something else. I wondered how Jayne was?" Maggie's expression was full of concern. "I'm worried about her. She's been so tense lately. And now, well, did she tell you she's broken up with Darren?"

Riley nodded. "She told me last night."

"She assured me she wasn't upset but I don't know." Maggie shook her head. "I worry about her."

"I'm sure you don't need to. She seems all right. Tired." Riley swallowed. If Maggie could have seen Jayne this morning she couldn't have helped but notice the change in her stepdaughter.

"Did she say anything to you? I mean, it seemed so sudden."

Riley hesitated. "Not a great deal. But I don't think it was a spur-of-the-moment thing. She seems to have given it quite a bit of thought."

Maggie nodded. "She told me that, too. I knew she wasn't totally happy but I just didn't consider she'd break her engagement. Do you think she'll reconsider?"

"Well." Riley shifted uncomfortably. "She seemed pretty adamant that she didn't want to get married."

"It's just that Darren rang me last night." Maggie took another sip of her tea. "He wanted me to talk to her. See if she'll change her mind."

Riley was taken aback. She couldn't see Darren Wardell pleading his case with Maggie.

"I have to admit I was surprised that he'd ask me to intervene," Maggie continued. "Darren's never been one to want to be involved with family. His own parents live in South Australia and, as far as I know, he rarely sees them. I know we've never met them in all the years Jayne's known him. From the little Jayne has said I take it he had a rather awful homelife, poles apart from ours." She sighed and looked worriedly at Riley. "My first instinct was not to get involved. It's Jayne's business and ultimately, her decision. But I felt a little guilty. You see, I've never cared for Darren. I didn't think he and Jayne were suited. He was so, well, self-centered."

Riley could agree with her on that point.

"Then, last night, after the storm woke me," Maggie continued, "I started thinking about how much time they had invested in each other, let alone in the business. They've known each other for over ten years and they've been engaged for four. I just—" She shook her head. "It seems such a pity."

"If they're unsure of their feelings perhaps it's not a bad thing if they do postpone getting married until, well, until they are sure," Riley said, feeling decidedly uncomfortable about commenting on this particular subject.

"Perhaps you're right." Maggie grimaced. "I know you're right. But according to Darren it's Jayne who's unsure. He said he still wants to get married but Jayne doesn't. He even hinted there was someone else in the picture."

Riley swallowed guiltily.

"I know I shouldn't pry. I mean, Jayne's a grown woman. But I love her, Riley, and I'm so worried about her. Has Jayne—" Maggie bit her lip. "Has she mentioned anyone else to you, Riley?" she asked in a rush, and Riley shook her head.

"No, not to me."

"She hasn't to me either. And I'm sure she would have." Maggie continued to frown. "Jayne also said she was looking at stepping down from her position with her company. I don't know what that means. She's worked so hard I don't want to see her throw any of that away."

"I'm sure she won't do that," Riley put in. "But she did say she was exhausted and unmotivated."

Maggie nodded. "There's no doubt she is tired. I've been so concerned for her. And as much as I want her to slow down I wish she'd wait till her father gets back so she can discuss it with him."

"Try not to worry, Maggie. I'm sure Jayne's given this all a lot of thought."

"I suppose she has. But I shouldn't be involving you in this." Maggie smiled at Riley. "I did come over to see how you were, too. Jayne tells me a friend from home called in to see you."

"Yes. Mac. I've known him since I was a child." Riley smiled, relieved that Maggie had changed the subject. Discussing Mac was far safer than talking about Jayne. "Mac and I grew up together."

"Is he your boyfriend?" Maggie laughed softly as Riley stilled. "You know, we've never talked about that part of your life, have we? We've discussed so much about you, but not that."

"No, Mac's not my boyfriend. He's just a friend. A good friend. I think Mum sent him down to check to see I was all right."

"I can understand she'd be worried. Do you think perhaps one day we could meet? Your mother and father and I? I know we've spoken on the phone but I'd like to get to know them, too."

"Mum would like that." Riley knew this was so.

"So, do you have a special man in your life?" Maggie persisted.

Riley shrugged. "Just my Dad. And my big brother."

Maggie laughed. "I can't believe the young men in Rockhampton are so blind they've let you slip through their fingers."

Riley knew she'd passed up any number of opportunities. Now one was presenting itself again. She took a deep breath.

"Are you sure you and Mac aren't—" Maggie raised her eyebrows teasingly.

"Maggie, I—there was something I wanted to talk to you about," Riley began. "I just, well, didn't know how to tell you."

Maggie's smile had faded and she looked across at Riley. "You know you can tell me or ask me anything."

"I just don't know how you'll feel about it."

"What is it?"

"Well, I—I haven't talked to you about, well, boyfriends because I don't have any."

"Heavens, Riley, that doesn't matter. I didn't mean to make you uncomfortable. It was only thinking about Jayne and Darren that made me realize I'd never asked you if you had a special friend."

"I do have lots of friends, like Mac and Cathy and Brenna, but until I came down here to Brisbane there wasn't, I mean, I wasn't involved with anyone."

Maggie set her cup down and sat forward. "Well, there's plenty of time for that. You know, after your father was killed and after you were born it took me years to even begin to notice the world around me. And then I met Andrew and I realized how—" She shook her head and laughed softly. "People joke about finding Mr. Right but it's true." Her eyes held a faraway look for a moment. "I loved your father very much, Riley, and if he hadn't been killed I like to think we would have had a good life together. But when I met Andrew I knew what 'finding Mr. Right' meant. I'm sure when the right man comes along you'll know too. It's worth waiting for."

"That's not quite what I meant." Riley stood up and paced nervously across the floor. "I don't have any boyfriends because I prefer women." She swallowed again and turned to face her birth mother.

Maggie stared back at her. Then she stood up too. "You prefer—? You're a lesbian?"

Riley nodded. "I've wanted to tell you for, well, since we met but I didn't know how you would react."

"Your parents, they know?" Maggie asked and Riley nodded again.

"I told them pretty well as soon as I was sure." Riley held Maggie's gaze for long moments and then her birth mother looked away. Riley stiffened. "I hope I haven't upset you."

"No. No, of course not." Maggie looked at her wristwatch. "Oh, dear. Is that the time? I have to be—I promised Cora Bertoni I'd stop by for afternoon tea. I have to go, Riley." She started toward the door.

"Maggie?"

Maggie paused but didn't turn around. "Riley, I just need some time. To take all this in. Please."

Riley's heart sank. "Sure. I'm sorry, Maggie."

Maggie stood with her back to Riley for long moments before she continued to the door and was gone.

Riley sank down on the chair and rubbed a shaky hand over her eyes. So much for Jake's assertion that his parents were tolerant and accepting. Pain clutched at her. She'd expected more of Maggie, could have sworn Maggie's reaction would have been totally different.

For some reason Riley thought about Lisa. She gave a bitter laugh. If Riley confided in Lisa, Lisa would delight in telling her she'd told her so. Unfortunately Lisa was right this time. She shouldn't have told Maggie.

Then there were her feelings for Jayne. Riley's heart sank. God, what a mess!

After a while Riley stood up, made herself go back downstairs and tidy up her paint and rollers. She didn't have the heart to do any more work today. She wandered out on the veranda gazing miserably at, but not seeing, the magnificent view, and the sun was low in the sky when she made a decision. She'd have to go and talk to Maggie. It was that or ring her mother. She longed to just hear the sound of Lenore's voice but if she did ring her Riley knew she would know by the tone of Riley's voice that she was unhappy. All Riley could do was go over and see Maggie, try to explain.

She went inside and her resolve wavered. It was almost four-thirty so Jayne would be home soon and Riley wanted to be here when she arrived. She wanted to feel Jayne's arms around her, feel her strength. Undecided, she walked up and down the living room before scribbling a note for Jayne letting her know she was at Maggie's.

Before she could change her mind she propped the note on the breakfast bar and went into her flat to replace her work shorts and T-shirt with a fresh outfit. She pulled on her cross-trainers and

160

walked out onto the street. Heading along the footpath she broke into a jog. If she walked it would give her more time to talk herself out of it.

Riley rounded the corner and jogged through the gate, coming to a stop as Maggie turned from locking her front door. She paused, too, when she saw Riley.

"Riley. I was just coming over," she said uncertainly.

"So was I," Riley said with a crooked smile.

"Will you come in?" Maggie relaxed a little and Riley went up the steps, waiting while Maggie unlocked the door, following her into the living room. "Riley, I—"

"Maggie—" Riley said at the same time and they both laughed a little. "You first." Riley shifted from one foot to the other.

Maggie put her bag on the sofa. "Well then, firstly, I should admit I didn't have to go to Cora's place."

"I know," Riley said softly.

"I don't know why I ran away from you." Maggie shook her head. "And I don't know why I was so shocked by what you told me. I suppose it was because it just didn't occur to me."

"I shouldn't have just sprung it on you like that."

"How else could you have told me, love?" Maggie sighed. "No, this wasn't your fault. It was mine."

Riley didn't know what to say. "I'm just sorry I had to upset you."

Maggie gave a derisive laugh. "You know I've always considered myself to be a fairly tolerant person. I mean, my own life wouldn't bear a lot of scrutiny so I don't see that I have a right to judge anyone. I did just that. And I've always taught Jayne and the boys to be accepting, to respect others. That people were not more, or less, but different. And that our differences made up a wonderful whole. This afternoon you put all my theories, my beliefs, to the test. And I failed miserably."

Riley swallowed.

Maggie took a couple of steps toward her and stopped. "In the short time I've known you, Riley, I've come to love you, the person

161

you've grown into, and I—" She put her hand on Riley's arm. "I wouldn't want to change you," she finished, her voice breaking.

Then they were in each other's arms, hugging each other close.

"You're the little piece of my heart I thought I'd lost forever. Finding you, getting to know you, has made my life complete," Maggie said as she held Riley in the circle of her arms. "After I lost you, I thought my life was over. It wasn't, and I've made a good life. I love Andrew. He's my rock. And I love Jayne and the boys. But you're a part of my life too, Riley. I lost you twenty-five years ago and I couldn't bear it if I lost you again. Can you forgive me?"

"There's nothing to forgive. It was just a shock. I can understand that."

Maggie gave a sigh of relief. "Perhaps we can start again, hmm?"

Riley smiled. "Sure."

"Thank you." Maggie stepped back. She looked down at the floor and then her gaze met Riley's. She smiled crookedly. "So, Riley, do you have any girlfriends?"

Riley chuckled. "No, not really. I went out with Lisa for a while. You might remember her. You met her when we went to the football game."

"Oh, yes. But you're not going out with her now?"

"No. She—" Riley shrugged. "Lisa's okay. But anyway, we're just friends."

"Does your mother like her?"

Riley laughed and shook her head. "Not much. I think Mum still has a small hope I'll end up with Mac."

"And there's no hope of that?"

"I'd be doing Mac a great disservice. I like him too much for that. So no."

Maggie frowned. "It must be difficult for you."

"It's just the way it is. I have lots of good friends."

"Cathy and Brenna, are they a couple?" Maggie asked.

"Yes. They've been together for seventeen years. They're great. Cathy plays bridge with Mum at their bridge club every fortnight."

"It's a shame you don't have anyone special," Maggie said sympathetically and then grinned. "I'm sorry. I'm a hopeless romantic. Jayne used to get quite annoyed with me when I tried to matchmake before she met Darren."

Riley's mouth went dry and her mind threw up a picture of Jayne leaning over her, her head thrown back, totally aroused. How could she tell Maggie there was no need to matchmake. For either of them. That she'd fallen in love with Jayne. Having just restored her relationship with Maggie, Riley didn't want it to dissolve into tatters again.

"I did—Once there was someone," Riley said quickly, pushing all those disquieting thoughts to the back of her mind.

"What happened?"

"I was in love with her." Riley was hard-pressed to recall Gem's face. Another face, a beautiful, incredible wonderful face, seemed to push all else from her mind. "And I thought she loved me. But she married someone else."

Maggie raised her eyebrows. "A man?"

"Yes. They have a couple of kids now. I thought she broke my heart."

"Oh, Riley. I'm so sorry." Maggie put her arms around Riley again. "How awful."

"It was a long time ago. I guess I'm over it," Riley said, feeling more than a little guilty.

"We all seem to suffer from love, don't we?" Maggie smoothed a strand of hair back from Riley's face. "I love you, Riley. So much." She rested her lips on Riley's forehead for a moment. "I'm so glad I found you."

"And I feel the same way," Riley said, her throat thick with tears.

Maggie stepped back as the phone rang. She was still holding Riley's hands and she gave them a squeeze before she released her. "I'd better see who that is. I'm expecting a call from Andrew tonight." She left Riley and then stopped momentarily in the hallway. "Jayne. I didn't hear you come in, love. How are you? Riley's in the living room. I'll be with you after I answer the phone."

At the sound of Jayne's name Riley's entire body seemed to come totally alive and she found herself smiling. A whole gambit of emotions raged inside her. Her nerve endings tingled with awareness as though they'd been silently on alert, simply waiting for Jayne's return. Riley wanted nothing more than to touch her, feel Jayne's arms around her, melt into the softness, smell the heady scent of her, taste her so soft lips, hear her sensuous murmurs of surrender.

Riley had started toward the hallway when Jayne stepped into the room. She hadn't stopped to change for she was still wearing her gray skirt, but she'd discarded her navy blazer and she'd folded the sleeves of her white shirt back to her elbows.

Jayne was here. Riley's gaze drank in the beauty of her, her soft hair, her pliant body, her long shapely legs that had entwined with Riley's, the gentle curve of her breasts Riley's hands had cupped. And those wonderful lips Riley had kissed.

"Hi!" Riley said, suddenly tongue-tied, a smile lighting her face. Then she paused, her smile of welcome dying at the closed expression on Jayne's face. "What is it? What's wrong?"

She would have gone to her but Jayne held up her hand, as if to fend her off. Jayne glanced into the hallway as though to check Maggie had left them before she turned back to Riley. "How could you?" she whispered harshly.

Riley was completely nonplussed.

"How could you do that, Riley?" Jayne repeated.

"Do what?" Riley found her voice, although her brain seemed to be functioning at half pace.

"With my own stepmother." Jayne's voice broke.

"Maggie?" Riley heard herself say. Did this have something to do with her relationship to Maggie? Had Jayne found out? Riley flushed slightly and Jayne swung angrily away from Riley as though she couldn't bear to look at her.

"I can't believe you could do that." She looked angrily back at Riley. "Last night I thought—" An expression of pain crossed her face. "Didn't last night mean anything to you?" she asked, her voice low and thick.

"Of course it did. It was wonderful." Riley went to close the space between them but stopped when Jayne held up her hand again.

"God! I don't know why I thought this would be any different." Jayne gave a bitter laugh and shook her head. "I'm such a fool. As far as I know you could, and obviously do, make a habit of seducing—"

"Seducing?" Riley frowned. Jayne's tone had put the very worst connotations on the word. "Jayne, please. It wasn't like that."

"And wasn't it like that with Maggie either?" Jayne bit out.

"With Maggie? What do you mean?" Suddenly realization hit Riley like a blow to the solar plexus. A wave of heat suffused her face.

"I saw you just now. In Maggie's arms."

"You think Maggie and I—? Jayne, you're mistaken. It *wasn't* like that."

"It looked just like that. And I heard what Maggie said. *'I'm so glad I found you.'*" Jayne bit her lip, fighting for control. "Funny. That's just what I thought, too." She glared at Riley. "You must be good, Riley. I suppose I should be impressed. But right this minute, I'm not."

"Jayne, I can explain." Riley stopped. She'd almost told Jayne the truth about Maggie. Yet she knew she couldn't do that, not without her birth mother's permission. "I'm not involved with Maggie."

"Maybe I should ask Maggie when she returns."

"Don't do that, Jayne. Please. It really isn't what you think."

"Then what is it?" Jayne hissed.

"Not that." Riley raised her hands and let them fall. "You'll just have to take my word for it."

"Your word?" Jayne shook her head. "At the moment your word doesn't mean much to me. Why should I believe you?"

"Jayne! Riley!" They both looked toward the doorway at the sound of Maggie's approach.

"Because I love you," Riley said softly. She slid a glance at Jayne but she gave no indication she'd heard Riley's whispered words.

165

CHAPTER TWELVE

And then Maggie had joined them. "Thank heavens you're here, Jayne. That was your father. He's flying into Sydney in the morning and he wants me to go down there to meet him. Oh, dear. I can't believe it." She looked at her watch. "I scarcely have time. I'll have to throw some clothes into a bag and I'll need you to drive me to the airport. Can you?" She appealed to Jayne.

"Of course, but—"

Maggie laughed excitedly. "Your father wants us to have a romantic weekend in Sydney before flying home on Monday night. The only flight down he could get me leaves in—" She looked at her wristwatch again—"just over an hour. I'll have to pack."

"We'll make it." Jayne said, starting toward the hallway.

Maggie turned to Riley. "And, Riley, can you pick up Jake from his mate's place? Number twenty-three. Just down the road, by the craft shop."

Riley nodded. Jake had told her about his best friend, Brett, the day he'd helped her with his father's bookshelves.

"Oh, and the car. It's booked in for a service on Monday. Do you think you could cancel it, Jayne?"

"No need to, Maggie." Jayne offered, "I can take it down and collect it for you."

"Would you, love? Thanks so much. I was getting it done early so I wouldn't need to do it when Andrew got home. Maybe it would be easier if Riley took my car to collect Jake and then she could take the car home with her tonight? Oh, this has thrown me into such a muddle I don't know where I am. And Jayne, can Jake stay with you over the weekend? I know he's old enough to stay on his own but I'd feel better if he was with you."

"Of course. And there's no need for Riley to pick up Jake. I'll go and collect him while you're packing your bag."

Maggie squeezed her arm. "Thanks, love. Now, what am I going to take with me? Riley, can you come and help me pack?"

Jayne looked as though she would say something but, with a quick glance that skimmed from her stepmother to Riley, she headed out the door.

Riley followed Maggie into her bedroom, her mind reeling. How could Jayne think she and Maggie were involved? It was ludicrous. Why would she think that? Riley replayed the scene in her mind and she frowned. Maggie had given Riley a hug. She'd kissed her and told her she loved her. Riley bit her lip. Jayne must have overheard them, totally misconstrued.

"Oh, Riley, I'm so excited and so nervous. I don't know if I'm coming or going." Maggie opened a drawer in her beautiful silky oak dressing table and took out a pile of undies.

Riley pulled herself together. "Where's your suitcase?"

"On the top shelf in the closet," Maggie replied, indicating the walk-in wardrobe. "Just the small one will do. It's only for a couple of days."

Riley's gaze went from the row of neatly hung dresses, skirts and blouses hanging on one side to the masculine suits and shirts on the other, and Andrew Easton suddenly became very real to her. She swallowed and lifted down the overnight bag Maggie wanted.

Opening the case on the bed, Riley ticked off a list on her fingers. "Undies. Nightgown." She turned and grinned at Maggie. "Make that a sexy one. Or maybe none at all. No, better take one in case of fire."

Maggie giggled and blushed. "I feel like a schoolgirl."

"Well, you haven't seen him for weeks."

"And I've missed him so much." Maggie wiped away a tear. "Wait till you meet him, Riley. He's a wonderful man."

"I'm looking forward to it," Riley said, not totally truthfully. She still wasn't sure that Andrew Easton would take the knowledge of his wife's secret as well as Maggie said he would. "Now, let's get you packed or you'll miss your flight."

"I hope I haven't forgotten anything." Maggie was clearly worried but Riley zipped up her case and slid it off the bed.

"You can buy anything you need. I'll take this outside while you change."

"And, Riley." Maggie stopped her as she went to leave the room. "I'm going to talk to Andrew while I'm down there. In fact, I'll ring Matt and see if he can come home for a few days. Then Andrew and I can tell the three of them when we get home. It should be a family thing."

Riley nodded, her mind a turmoil of jumbled thoughts. Now that Maggie was about to tell her family the truth, Riley was nervous that they might not like the idea of a long-lost sister. But she desperately wanted to tell Jayne, to explain how wrong she was about Riley's relationship with Maggie.

"It'll be fine, Riley. I know it will," Maggie said softly. "In my own way I've been preparing Andrew for this for a long time. He'll be all right about it."

"I hope so, Maggie. I really do. But I'm okay with your not telling the others as well."

168

Maggie patted her cheek. "Don't worry about it, love. Jayne and Jake already like you so I see no problem there. And Matt will be fine with it too. You'll see."

Riley could think of a hundred problems but only one burned inside her. How was Jayne going to react to the truth? And Riley had the whole weekend to keep the secret.

"I'll tell them when they're all together. And I'll have a chance to talk to Jayne about Darren on the way to the airport. She still looks so tired."

Riley made no comment and left Maggie alone to change. She set the suitcase down on the veranda and leaned on the railing, wishing she could turn back time. Or wind it on. It was completely dark now and Riley flicked on the outside light.

The blue sports car purred to a stop at the gate and Jake bounded up the steps, Jayne following more slowly behind him.

"Hey, Riley! Isn't it great Dad's home?" Jake grinned at her. "I'm coming over to stay for the weekend. Maybe we could go fishing. What do you say?"

Riley gave a half smile as she looked at Jake's excited face. And suddenly she remembered a photograph of herself taken when she was about Jake's age. It was at a school sports meet and she'd just won her race. Lenore had taken the photo as Riley ran toward her mother and father. Jake looked just like her as he ran up the steps. Tears stung her eyes and for the first time she really realized what having found her natural family meant.

She reached out and gave Jake a hug, momentarily taking him by surprise, before he hugged her back.

"That hug means yes, doesn't it?" he asked with a grin and Riley laughed with him.

"I guess it does."

"Wicked. I'll go pack my stuff." He turned back to Jayne. "Can I bring my Xbox? And Riley said she'd take me fishing. Can we go tomorrow, Riley?"

"Jake!" Jayne admonished. "Just hurry up and get your things."

"Right." He disappeared inside and Jayne and Riley were left alone on the veranda.

Tears welled in Riley's eyes again as Jayne turned away from her. The harsh outside light threw her profile into dark curves and angles and Riley was sure she could almost physically feel her beauty. It was as though Jayne had crawled inside Riley, indelibly leaving every nuance of herself inside, making Riley ache with the need to hold her.

"Jayne—"

"Don't say anything, Riley. I couldn't bear it." Jayne's voice sounded choked with her own tears and Riley could only stand there impotently as the heavy silence grew between them like an insurmountable mountain range.

The next evening Riley sat looking at the flickering television. It was her own fault she was sitting here alone. She could have stayed in the house, shared a meal with Jayne and Jake. Jake had asked her to. And Jayne had reluctantly added her invitation.

But Jayne hadn't wanted Riley to stay. Riley was sure of that. Jayne was only being polite. Since yesterday when Maggie left she'd barely registered Riley's presence. She'd declined Riley's suggestion that they go to the movies, so Riley and Jake had gone alone.

How could she not be as aware of Riley as Riley was of her? Just looking at Jayne caused a pain somewhere in the region of Riley's heart.

The telephone rang and Riley started, taking a few seconds to recover before she could pick up the receiver.

"And g'day to you, Riley James," Mac said cheerily. "How's my favorite girlfriend? Any repercussions from our night of unbridled passion? No, wait a minute. That's right. It was my night of unbridled passion. You slept like a baby."

Riley laughed despite herself. "Mac. It's so good to hear your voice."

170

"It is?" He questioned suspiciously.

"Yes, it is."

"I'm not sure I like the sound of that. I half expected you not to answer your phone."

"Why did you think that?" Riley asked.

"I thought you might have had better things to do. And talking of better things to do, have you got that beautiful woman into bed yet?"

"Oh, Mac." Riley's voice broke.

"Uh-oh. Now *I* don't like the sound of *that*. What's up?"

"She thinks I'm having an affair with Maggie," Riley said flatly.

There was a moment of dead silence. "She thinks what? How come?"

"She saw Maggie put her arms around me and kiss me. On the forehead. Oh, Mac, it's such a mess. I love her so much and I thought, well, I thought she loved me." Riley drew a steadying breath. "I wish you were here, Mac. I think I need a friend."

"I think you need to tell Jayne about you and Maggie, that's what I think," Mac said firmly.

"Maggie's in Sydney at the moment. She's spending the weekend with her husband and she's going to tell the family when she comes home on Monday night. I'm hoping then Jayne will understand."

Mac sighed. "So you're just going to wait it out?"

"I guess that's all I can do."

"I still say you should tell Jayne," Mac said. "Surely Maggie would understand if you explained the situation."

"We can't really talk at the moment anyway. Jake's staying with Jayne while his parents are away, which is a good and a bad thing. The bad thing is Jayne and I aren't getting any time alone together so we can't talk anyway. The good thing is I don't have to decide whether or not to break Maggie's confidence."

"Phew! You really get yourself into some situations, Riley, don't you? Can't you send Jake off to the movies or something?"

"That's where we've been today. Without Jayne."

"You know, the longer you let Jayne think about this the guiltier you'll look."

171

"I hope you're wrong, Mac. I just don't know what else to do."

"It sounds like it's going to be a long weekend," Mac said ominously.

"Well, Jake and I are going fishing tomorrow. And if today's any indication Jayne will probably be locked up in her study working."

"Work? On a Sunday!" Mac exclaimed. "Doesn't she know she needs a day of rest?"

"She's resigned from her position and will be taking some time off once things are sorted out." Riley paused. "And she's broken off her engagement."

"Ah-ha! Didn't I tell you so? The minute she set eyes on you that engagement was doomed."

Riley laughed despite herself. "You're totally mad, do you know that?"

"But I'm right," he stated. "You said yourself just a moment ago that you thought she loved you. What made you think that then?"

"Well, she kissed me."

"Just a kiss?" Mac teased her. "Must have been some kiss."

"Mac, please. Don't joke about this."

"I'm sorry, Riles. Hang in there. I'm sure it will turn out okay."

"I hope you're right. But until Maggie comes back I can't do a thing. Maybe even after that. I have no way of knowing how Jayne will feel when she finds out I'm Maggie's daughter."

"Will you be okay? I can come down if you do want some support."

"Thanks, Mac, but I'll be all right. It should be sorted out one way or another after the weekend. I should be finished painting the house in a week or so. Then I'll come home."

"We'll be happy to see you."

"I seem to be forever thanking you these days. You're my best friend, do you know that? Just—would you mind not telling Mum and Dad about this? I don't want them to worry. I'll talk to them when I get home."

"Sure. But don't sell your mother short, Riley. She knows something's going on. Wow! Did she cross-examine me when I got back last time."

"You didn't tell Mum about Jayne, did you?"

"Not about Jayne with respect to how you feel about her, but your mother played bridge with Cathy and it seems Cathy and Brenna were quite impressed by your boss."

"Do you think Mum knows how I feel about Jayne?" Riley persisted.

"I don't know, Riley. I sure didn't tell her. But she gave me that look she could always give me that made me feel she was downloading all the files in my mind. It was very off-putting."

Riley laughed softly. "I know that look." She sighed. "I'll ring her after Maggie's talked to her family. Until then there's not much I can tell Mum."

"Mmm," Mac murmured. "Well, I'll be thinking of you, Riles. Just call if you need me."

"Thanks, Mac. For ringing. And for everything."

Jake was alone when he pounded on Riley's door at daybreak the next morning. They decided to head up to the Sunshine Coast because Riley remembered her brother had said the fishing was good up there. Despite her concern about the situation Riley found she enjoyed the day in Jake's entertaining company. After lunch they went for a surf at King's Beach and then went back to fishing. It was after dark when they arrived home.

Jayne came out of her study as Jake clattered into the living room.

"We had the best day, Jaynie," he said. "You should have come with us. We caught some beauties, bream and flathead. And Riley said she'll cook them for us for dinner tomorrow night."

"I was about to send out a search party." Jayne avoided looking at Riley.

"I'm sorry we were late," Riley apologized. "The fish started biting just when we were about to leave."

"As they do." Jake smirked.

"Have you eaten?" Jayne asked.

173

"We stopped for a hamburger and chips on the way home," Jake told her. "We were starving."

"Well, it's getting late and you have to go to school tomorrow."

Jake pulled a face. "Thanks for reminding me. Don't suppose I could have the day off, could I? I could help Riley with the painting."

"Oh, I think Riley can manage on her own," Jayne said dryly. "Nice try though, Jake."

Riley smiled at his long face. "Well, I guess I'll see you both tomorrow."

"Thanks for taking me, Riley. I had a wicked time."

"I did too." Riley glanced at Jayne. "What about your mother's car? Do you want me to take it down to the garage tomorrow?"

"No, thanks. I'll drop it down myself after I've taken Jake to school and I'll get a taxi to work. And I'll get the mechanic to deliver the car here when they've finished the service."

"You mean you're not making me walk to school?" Jake gave a mock bow. "Thank you, warden."

Jayne smiled at him. "I aim to please. But you'll have to catch the bus home."

Jake rolled his eyes. "I still say I could be heaps of help if I stayed home. Don't you reckon, Riley?"

Riley held up her hands. "I think I'll leave you two to that discussion," she said diplomatically. "Good night."

And Riley made sure Jayne and Jake had left for work and school the next morning before she went back to her painting. Not that she got all that much work done. All she could think about was the imminent arrival of Maggie and Andrew and what the evening would hold. And the day dragged.

So she was more than pleased to see Jake when he came in from school, welcoming his company as he helped her clean up her rollers. She could tell how excited he was about his father's return.

The mechanic had duly delivered Maggie's car and when Jayne arrived home from the office the three of them sat down to the meal

Riley had prepared. Jake was impressed with the grilled fish they had caught yesterday. He chatted on, seemingly unaware that Riley and his sister rarely addressed each other.

Finally Maggie and Andrew arrived. They'd taken a taxi from the airport and Jayne met them at the door. She threw herself into her father's arms. "Dad. It's so good to have you safely home. We've missed you."

"Yeah, Dad. Great to see you." Jake hugged his father, too. "Did you and Mum have fun in Sydney?"

"We sure did."

Riley watched them, her body tense and anxious.

Now that Andrew Easton had finally arrived home, she hung back, trying to gauge Maggie's feelings from her expression. She looked calm and happy. Surely Maggie wouldn't be smiling if the weekend had turned out badly?

Riley shifted her gaze to the tall, broad-shouldered man beside her birth mother. Dressed casually in a pair of dark slacks, his blue shirt open at the neck, Andrew Easton was a handsome man, and it was obvious where Jayne got her height and classic good looks. Her father had a firm chin, square jaw, eyes that crinkled at the corners when he smiled, and his thick hair was flecked with gray. More importantly, Riley didn't think he looked like a man who had been dealt a blow and hadn't recovered.

Maggie hugged Jayne and then Jake. Over her son's shoulder she smiled at Riley and gave her a slight nod. Riley felt some of her tension leave her, although part of her still dwelled on Jayne and what she would think when she learned the truth. The one thing she clung to was the fact that when Jayne did find out the truth she would understand. If she didn't Riley wasn't sure what she'd do.

"Andrew, this is Riley." Maggie drew Riley forward. "As I told you, she's painting Jayne's house."

Maggie's husband reached out to shake Riley's hand. His gaze swept her face and then he smiled. "Nice to meet you, Riley. Maggie's told me a lot about you."

"Yes." Riley swallowed, tears choking her. "She's told me a lot about you, too," she said thickly.

"What about some tea or coffee?" Jayne suggested brightly.

"No. Don't worry, love. We're fine." Maggie said as they all sat down in the living room. "And we have a little surprise." Maggie beamed at her husband. "You tell them, Andrew."

Riley's tension returned. Had Maggie decided she was going to tell Jayne and Jake so soon? Riley hadn't expected this.

"We rang Matt and he's taking a few days off so we can all be together."

"Matt's coming home?" Jake was obviously delighted. "That's wicked."

"I thought he was in the middle of exams," Jayne put in and Maggie shook her head.

"He sat for his last one this afternoon and he's flying down tonight." She looked at her wristwatch. "His flight arrives in about an hour."

"How about you and Jake collect him from the airport, Jayne?" suggested Andrew. "You can take your mother's car. Didn't you say it had just had a service, darling?"

"Oh, yes. The service." Maggie turned back to her stepdaughter. "Thanks for handling that, Jayne. Were there any problems?"

Jayne shook her head. "No, I don't think there were any problems. I meant to ask. Riley spoke to the mechanic."

"He said it was fine," Riley assured them.

"Then thank you, too, Riley."

"That's okay. I'll get the keys." Riley went over to the breakfast bar and came back with Maggie's car keys. She held them out to Jayne.

Jayne paused before taking the keys and Riley knew Jayne made sure their fingers barely touched. Jayne's gaze went from Maggie to Riley. "Perhaps Riley might like to come out to the airport, too, Dad. It would give you and Maggie some time to rest and get over your flight."

Maggie glanced at her husband. "Oh. Well, I thought Riley could show your father the work she's done on the house."

"From what I can see it looks fantastic," Andrew Easton said as he looked around him.

"If you wait till Matt gets here Riley can show the both of them together," Jayne suggested. "Then she won't have to do the tour twice."

Maggie looked slightly flustered.

"It's okay, Jayne," Riley said. "You and Jake go. I'll stay here and make some coffee."

"That would be lovely," Maggie said quickly, clearly forgetting she'd only just refused Jayne's offer of coffee.

Riley went into the kitchen and filled the kettle as Jake headed for the door.

"Come on, Jayne. We don't want to be late and miss Matt's arrival."

Jayne made no comment but followed Jake out to the garage. Riley came back into the living room when they heard the car pull away and Maggie let out the breath she'd been holding.

Andrew laughed softly. "Jayne can be very astute."

"Like her father." Maggie took hold of his hand.

"And *your* daughter is very like you," Andrew replied and then smiled across at Riley. "Beautiful, just like her mother."

Riley flushed. "Thank you. You—you're okay. About this?" she asked gently.

"I can't say I wasn't surprised when Maggie told me, because I was. I still am. I couldn't quite believe it but, looking at you . . ." He shook his head, raised Maggie's hand to his lips and kissed it. "You know, Riley, it's incredible. You look so much like Maggie when I first met her."

Maggie wiped away a tear.

"As you know I have a daughter myself," Andrew continued. "I know how I would have felt if someone had taken Jayne away from me."

"Didn't I tell you he was the best husband in the world, Riley?" Maggie beamed.

Andrew grimaced. "Oh, I have my moments. But seriously, Riley, welcome to our family."

Riley smiled. "I'm honored. You have a wonderful family."

Andrew shook his head again. "I can't believe you look so much like Maggie." He slid his arm around his wife's shoulder.

"Do you think so?" Maggie asked him. "I thought it was just our similar coloring."

"She has your wonderful smile. But, our apologies, Riley, we didn't mean to discuss you like this. It's rude of us."

Riley made a negating gesture with her hand. "That's okay. My mother, my adoptive mother, saw a photo of Jayne, Jake and me that my friend Brenna took at the football game we all went to, and she thought Jake and I were very much alike."

Andrew nodded. "Jake is like his mother. So, tell me about your family, Riley. I believe your father's a builder."

Riley finished making the coffee with Maggie's help and they sat in Jayne's living room and talked. Riley told Andrew about her adoptive family and it seemed that in no time they heard a car pull into the garage and doors slam.

Maggie took a deep breath. "I'm so nervous."

Andrew gave her a quick reassuring hug and kissed her cheek. "Don't be. They'll be fine, love. Do you want me to tell them?"

Maggie shook her head. "No. I should do it." She looked at Riley. "Are you all right with this, Riley?"

"Yes, I am." Riley nodded and they all stood up. A million thoughts churned inside her. It was the moment she'd been living for over the long, stressful weekend. How would Jayne react to the truth?

"Oh, dear." Maggie blew her nose and wiped away a tear. "I just know I'm going to get emotional."

"You'll be fine, and I'm here if you need me," her husband said as Jayne led the boys into the room.

Riley had barely a moment to reflect that her half brother Matt was as tall as his father and very much like him, before she sought out Jayne.

Jayne's gaze met Riley's and a frown furrowed her brow, her expression tense. She was clearly concerned about what was to follow. Her eyes narrowed as she shifted her gaze to her parents, her father with his arm protectively around Maggie's shoulders.

Matt Easton strode across the room and hugged his parents. "I'm not saying I didn't welcome the chance to get away from my books, but I'm worried about why you wanted a family conference. Jake and I cross-examined Jayne on the way back from the airport but she vows she knows nothing."

"There's no need to worry, Matt," Maggie reassured him. "But we should introduce you to Riley. Riley James, meet my son Matthew."

Matt turned and smiled at Riley. "Hi. Nice to meet you. Jake's been raving about you on the way home. In fact I told him I suspected he had a crush on you. Now I can see why. Way to go, Jake." He gave his brother a shove and Jake burst out laughing.

"Oh, yeah. Riley's a chicky babe. She's going to marry me when I grow up, aren't you, Riley?" He winked at Riley and she laughed with him at what he considered to be their private joke.

"If I was going to get married, Jake," Riley said dryly, "it would only be to you."

Jake draped himself over a lounge chair and grinned at his brother. "Eat your heart out, Matt."

Andrew and Maggie sat down and Riley moved slightly away, remaining standing.

"Perhaps we should all sit down," Andrew said easily. "Your mother and I have something to tell you."

Jayne stepped forward then. "Anyone want anything to drink. Coffee? Coke?"

"I'll have coffee, Jayne. Please." Matt sat down.

"We've just made some fresh coffee." Riley started forward but Jayne motioned her to stay seated.

179

"I'll get it, Riley," she said and went into the kitchen.

"Could you bring me back a Coke?" Jake asked as he threw himself into a chair beside Matt's.

"What's wrong with your legs, mate?" Matt said. "Get it yourself, you lazy sod."

"You're not getting yours. Too old and decrepit to crawl into the kitchen, are you?" Jake retaliated good-naturedly as he followed Jayne.

Matt grinned. "It's good to be home. I miss getting a rise out of Jake."

"And I've missed hearing you two bickering," Maggie said as Jake came back and sat down, giving his brother a scowl as he did so.

"Want your coffee topped up?" Jayne asked and when her parents and Riley declined she returned and reluctantly sank onto the arm of the chair Matt was sitting in.

"If all this is about Jayne's breaking off her engagement to Darren, then we already know," put in Matt. "Jayne told us in the car she gave Darren the Di . . . um, Darren the Drongo the big A. We told her we'd have sent him on his way ages ago."

"It's not about that." Maggie spoke at last. She looked across at Riley and Riley wanted to go to her, put her arms around her.

"Maggie, don't." Jayne's words caused both Riley and Maggie to turn to Jayne in surprise. "I know what you're going to say and I—" She shook her head, swallowing to control her voice.

"You—you know?" Maggie's face was pale. "How could you know, Jayne?" She turned back to Riley. "Did you tell her?"

Riley shook her head.

"Riley didn't have to tell me. I saw you. The other day, before you left for Sydney."

"You saw us?" Maggie looked confused. "I don't understand, love?"

Riley stood up. She had to stop Jayne, let Maggie tell her the truth. "Jayne, please. You've got it all wrong. Let Maggie explain."

"Explain what?" Matt sat forward, his face tense. "Mum, you're not sick, are you?"

180

"No, love. No. I'm fine," Maggie hastened to reassure him as Jayne stood up, obviously distressed.

"Jayne, wait." Riley crossed to stand beside her, and she reached out to clasp Jayne's arm. "Don't say any more until you're heard what Maggie has to say."

"Yes, Jayne. Give Maggie a chance to tell you," said her father firmly.

"But, Dad," Jayne appealed to her father. "Surely you don't want Maggie to admit it."

Andrew Easton frowned. "Why would you even begin to think I wouldn't understand. I love Maggie and I'm disappointed in you, Jayne."

Maggie got to her feet. "Andrew. Jayne. Please." She looked about to burst into tears.

Riley went to her, slipped an arm around her shoulders. "Maggie, don't. It's not worth it. You don't have to tell them."

Maggie drew herself together. She smiled at Riley. "Yes, I do, love." She turned back to her children. "Please. Just let me say this. I've kept a secret from your father for twenty-five years because I was too much of a coward to trust him. And as the years went by it got even more difficult to confess. But now I want no more secrets."

Riley glanced at Jayne and her face was as pale as her step-mother's. She looked from Maggie to Riley and then she flushed. She put her hands to her lips. "Oh, my God! Riley," she all but whispered and Riley knew that realization had dawned on the other woman.

"Before I met your father," Maggie began shakily, "I was in love with a young man, the son of our neighbors in Murwillumbah. I found out I was pregnant and then before we could get married he was killed in a motor accident."

Maggie turned to her husband as he stood up beside her. He put his arms around her as she swallowed a sob.

"You had a baby? But what happened to it?" Jake asked solemnly. "Did it die, too?"

181

Maggie shook her head. "No, Jake. But I was just seventeen and it was decided it would be better for the baby and for me if I put my baby up for adoption."

"But you could have kept it," Jake persisted. "Lots of girls keep their babies."

"It wasn't what you did in those days. I wasn't well and . . ." Maggie paused. "Everyone thought it was best that I adopt my baby out. I love you all very much, you know that, but I've never forgotten about—" She raised a shaking hand to wipe her eyes. "A couple of months ago I registered my name with a group that reunites adopted children with their natural parents. And I found my daughter."

"You found her?" Jake started to smile. "So, can we meet—" He stopped, his eyes widening in shock as he looked at Riley.

Maggie drew Riley forward. "Riley's my daughter and your sister."

Matt and Jake stared at Riley in surprise and then Riley shifted her gaze to Jayne.

"I'm sorry, Jayne," she said softly, her voice thick with tears. "I couldn't explain. It wasn't just my secret to tell."

"Oh, Riley." Jayne breathed, the look in her eyes giving Riley the first ray of hope she'd had in days. "I had it all wrong. I thought—" She shook her head and turned to her stepmother. "Maggie, I'm so sorry." Jayne crossed the room and put her arms around Maggie. "Please, forgive me."

"For what, love?" Maggie drew back and gazed at Jayne. "I don't know what you thought but are you all right with this?"

Jayne wiped her eyes and gave a shaky smile. "I'm fine. Honest. I just thought you were—I thought you wanted to break up with Dad."

Maggie looked horrified. "Break up with your father? How could you—? Why would you think that?"

Jayne simply shook her head.

"You thought—" Maggie looked at Riley and then her face flamed. "Jayne, I don't know what to say."

"Don't say anything, Maggie," Jayne implored. "Just that you'll accept my apology." She looked at her father. "You too, Dad."

"Of course. Although I have no earthly idea—" He stopped and his eyes narrowed. "I see." He looked across at his sons.

"I'm sorry," Jayne repeated. "I—we can talk later."

Just at that moment Jake bounded across the room and grabbed Riley in a bear hug. "Well, I guess our wedding's off, Riley, but the next best thing is to have you for a sister." He swung her around and gave her a noisy kiss on the cheek. "Or sister-in-law," he whispered in Riley's ear. "And I've just thought of something. Lucky we didn't get married before we found out we were related, or we could have ended up on daytime TV."

Riley looked at him and they both burst out laughing.

"Somehow I don't think we should ask for an explanation for that," Andrew remarked.

When Riley sobered Matt joined them, his hands shoved into his pockets. He leaned forward and gave Riley a quick kiss. "Welcome to the family, Riley," he said, just a little embarrassed.

Riley smiled her thanks and looked back at Jayne.

"Yes, Riley. Welcome to the family," Jayne said, although Riley could glean nothing from her expression.

They all sat down again, talking, asking Riley questions.

"And you work as a carpenter?" Matt asked.

"She paints, too," Jake informed him as Riley nodded. "Have you seen what Riley's done yet, Dad?"

"No, not yet." He got to his feet. "We didn't get around to it while you were collecting Matt, but if Riley would like to we could have a look now."

"Of course." Riley stood up, too. "Shall we start downstairs?"

"I'll just wash up these few cups," Maggie said, beginning to collect their empty mugs.

"I'll help you." Jayne's gaze met Maggie's. "It will give us a moment to talk."

Riley paused. What did Jayne intend to talk to Maggie about? Maybe she was simply going to apologize again for her misconception about their relationship.

"Come on, Riley." Jake was waiting at the top of the stairs and Riley reluctantly followed him. "I helped Riley with some of it, didn't I, Riley?"

Jake led them on a complete tour of the house, including Jayne's freshly painted bedroom. Riley's gaze slid to the bed and quickly away as she tried to concentrate on Jayne's father's praise for the color scheme.

When they returned to the living room, Maggie and Jayne were sitting side by side on the couch. Jayne looked as though she had been crying and Maggie's face was pale. Maggie looked at Riley, went to say something, glanced at her sons and appeared to change her mind.

"The house looks magnificent, Jayne," Andrew was saying. "I really like the renovations upstairs. The last time I saw it the carpenters had just torn out the attic. It's amazing. And Riley's done a great job with the painting."

"Yes, she has." Jayne glanced at Riley and flushed. "Joe Camilleri couldn't have done better."

"And wait till you see what Riley's done at home," Jake started to say and them clamped his hand over his mouth. "Oops! That was supposed to be a surprise."

Maggie shook her head and laughed lightly. "It's still a surprise, Jake." She turned to her husband. "It's Jayne's birthday present to you."

Andrew grinned at his daughter. "Thanks in anticipation. I love surprises."

"You've had your share this weekend then, Dad," Matt said dryly and his father laughed.

"You're not wrong there," he said. "Apart from wanting to get home to see my surprise, I think we should call it a night. What with one thing and another, your mother's tired."

"I think we all are," Maggie said, "but I want you all to know how wonderful I think you all are for how you've taken this, for accepting that I . . ." She paused, controlling her voice.

"We love you, Mum," Matt said sincerely and Maggie burst into tears.

Riley dashed at her own tears and when she met Jake's gaze he rolled his eyes expressively.

"I think we'd better go, Dad," he said, "or these women will dehydrate themselves."

His father laughed and put his son in a mock headlock before giving him a hug. "Jake's right. We all need a rest. We'll head home," he said and smiled at Riley and Jayne. "No doubt we'll see you both tomorrow."

Maggie gave Jayne a final hug. "Maybe you and Riley and I could talk tomorrow, hmm?"

Jayne nodded and Maggie followed her husband and sons out to the car, leaving Riley and Jayne alone together.

"I don't—" Jayne shook her head. "I don't know what to say, Riley. I never even imagined—I was so far off the mark."

"I couldn't tell you. It was always Maggie's call. I wanted to the other night but I didn't know how your father was going to react."

Jayne nodded. "It must have been difficult for you," she added stiffly.

"If Jake hadn't been with us, well . . ." Riley shrugged. "But he was and I couldn't take the chance he'd overhear. I knew as soon as your parents returned, well, all would be revealed."

"I never suspected and yet, now that I know, your resemblance to Maggie is quite apparent. How could I not see it?"

"You weren't looking for it," Riley said and a heavy silence grew between them.

Tension twisted inside Riley and she swallowed as Jayne walked across to the French doors and gazed out at the view, her back to Riley.

What was she thinking? Riley wondered. All she wanted was to draw Jayne into her arms, hold her close.

185

Jayne turned, her face pale, and Riley's heart sank. "Riley, I can't seem to take all this in. I'm emotionally drained. I need some time." She shook her head again.

"Jayne—" Riley's heart ached.

Jayne held up her hand. "Would you mind if we—I just need some time, Riley," she finished softly.

"Of course." Riley had to force the words out. "I'll let you—I'll see you. Maybe tomorrow." Her throat closed on unshed tears.

"Yes," Jayne said, her eyes not meeting Riley's.

Riley turned and headed out the door. Surely Jayne would call her back. When she reached the door to her flat she knew Jayne wasn't going to follow her.

CHAPTER FOURTEEN

An hour later Riley was still sitting in her chair waiting for Jayne. She's not coming, jeered her inner voice, and Riley knew deep down it was so.

With a sigh Riley undressed and stepped into the shower. As the water streamed over her tears fell. She was falling apart.

She'd found her birth mother and gained a wonderful extended family but she'd lost her heart to Jayne. And Jayne didn't want her.

Riley switched off the shower and went through the motions of preparing for bed. She slid between the sheets and stretched out. She was exhausted yet hyped up, and she knew she'd never sleep.

She threw back the covers and went outside. The lights were still burning in the living room but Jayne wasn't there.

Riley tiptoed quietly around to the back of the house. She looked up to the balcony above her, the balcony off Jayne's bedroom. Slivers of light beamed through the decking, so if Jayne was in bed she wasn't sleeping either.

Should Riley throw discretion to the wind and go up there? Try to talk to her? Tell her she loved her? But if Jayne had changed her mind, what would be the point? Still, Jayne had asked for a little time and Riley acknowledged she had to respect that.

The twinkling lights of the city couldn't hold Riley's attention as they usually did and she slowly retraced her steps to the flat. She climbed back into bed. She should simply pack her bags and go home. She'd found her birth mother, and her adoptive parents and her friends were waiting for her at home.

Closing her eyes Riley willed herself toward the oblivion of sleep. In the morning she'd ring her mother. Then she'd talk to Maggie, make some excuse and go home. With her mind made up Riley eventually drifted into a troubled sleep and it was barely dawn when she stirred.

She groaned and climbed out of bed, then made herself some tea and toast. Half an hour later she reached for the phone. Her parents were early risers and Riley knew her father would have already left for work.

When she heard her mother's voice Riley fought back tears. "It's good to hear your voice, Mum," she said and she realized how true that was.

"And it's good to hear yours too. But you sound a little upset. What's up, love?" Lenore asked.

Riley told her mother about the evening before and Maggie's emotional get-together. "They all seemed to accept it quite well."

"I knew they'd think you were wonderful," Lenore said matter-of-factly. "Not that I'm biased."

"Of course you're not." Riley smiled and then sighed. "I love you, Mum."

"And I love you. Have you decided when you're coming home?"

"Well, I guess I've done what I came down here to do, found Maggie, got to know her, and I thought, well, maybe I'd head home in a day or two."

"That's wonderful. I just wasn't expecting you'd be coming home so soon?"

Riley laughed. "I thought you said you missed me."

"We do, Riley. You know that. I'm just surprised. I didn't realize you'd finished your painting job."

"I haven't. I just thought I'd come home."

There was a moment of silence.

"It's not like you to leave a job unfinished," Lenore said at last. "How much do you have left to do?"

"Not too much. Final coats on a couple of the bedrooms downstairs. Some finishing touches here and there." But if Jayne had changed her mind . . . Riley didn't think she could continue to work here feeling as she did about Jayne.

"Is there a problem, love?"

"No. Not exactly."

"You know your father can come and help you finish the painting. We were talking last night about coming down there for a few days. We'd love to see you. And we could visit the Kingstons. They're always asking us. You remember they moved to Brisbane a few months ago? Apart from that, we'd like to meet Maggie and her family."

"They want to meet you and Dad, too. But it's not the painting, Mum. It's just . . . there's something I haven't told you." Riley took a deep breath. "I've met someone."

"You've met someone! Oh, Riley. Is that all? You had me so worried. I thought you weren't well or something. So, what's she like?"

"She's attractive and—" Tears rose to choke Riley and she swallowed. "I love her so much, Mum, but I don't think she feels the same way."

"Has she told you that?"

"Not in so many words. It's a little complicated."

Lenore was silent for a moment. "Isn't she a lesbian?"

"Oh, Mum. It's Jayne. Maggie's stepdaughter. I thought—" Riley's voice broke on a sob.

"Oh, love. What happened?"

And then it was all spilling out. And once she started talking Riley couldn't seem to stop. She told her mother how she'd felt when she

189

met Jayne, how their friendship had grown. Riley's dislike of Jayne's fiancé. And how Jayne had misconstrued Riley's relationship with Maggie.

"She thought you were having an affair with Maggie?" Lenore repeated. "Oh, Riley."

"And I couldn't explain, not until Maggie got back from Sydney."

"But she knows the truth now?"

"Yes. But she said she needs time."

"Well, Riley, that's understandable," Lenore said reasonably. "It must have been quite a shock for her. Did you tell her how you feel?"

"No. Yes. I don't know. Not exactly."

"Then perhaps you should. Just tell her. You know, I've never been one to try to guess what someone else is thinking. You need to talk about it, Riley. Worrying yourself sick about endless possibilities doesn't achieve anything."

"But what if she says she doesn't love me?"

"What if she says she does love you? Wouldn't you rather know one way or the other?"

"I just—" Riley sighed.

"Talk to her, Riley," her mother said gently. "Tell her how you feel about her."

"I know you're right, Mum. I was just being, well, cowardly, I guess."

"You've been through an emotional few weeks, love. Don't be so hard on yourself."

"Oh, Mum. I love you. Thanks so much for listening."

"I love you, too, Riley. Now, off you go and talk to Jayne. And ring me later."

They rang off and Riley stood for a moment gathering her courage. She glanced at the time. It was already seven-thirty. Would Jayne be awake? Should she wait until she heard her moving about downstairs?

Riley looked down at her nightshirt. She'd have to change. But what to wear? Would it matter? she asked herself contemptuously.

She pulled out her favorite emerald green T-shirt and slipped on a near-new pair of denim shorts. She brushed her hair and looked in the mirror. Would Jayne think she looked all right?

Riley turned away in exasperation and started toward the door, only to realize she was still barefoot. She was searching for her slip-on shoes when there was a knock at her door.

Riley stilled. She pulled her tattered composure into some semblance of order and opened the door.

Jayne was just turning away. In those first few seconds Riley registered she was wearing her apricot cotton pants and a black cotton shirt with a drawstring neckline. Her fair hair was loose to her bare shoulders, the early morning sunlight catching it and burnishing it to a shimmer of rosy silver as she turned back to face Riley.

"Oh. I thought you might not have been awake yet," she said a little unevenly.

"I woke early," Riley said inanely. "I was just about to come over to the house."

They looked at each other for long moments and Riley was sure she saw a flicker of desire in Jayne's eyes before she glanced away. She ached to put her arms around her but she made herself stand her ground, take her cue from Jayne.

"I've made coffee," Jayne said at last. "Would you like a cup?"

"Please." Riley smiled nervously. At least Jayne had wanted to see her. Maybe they could talk, sort out this mess. She followed Jayne into the house and stood by the breakfast bar as Jayne poured the coffee.

"Shall we sit outside?"

Riley nodded and picked up the mug of coffee Jayne set in front of her.

They sat down opposite each other, the unlit candle on the small table between them reminding Riley of the evening they'd shared pizza. And suddenly she wanted to cry.

Riley took a deep breath. "Jayne, I wish I could have told you about Maggie and me. But Maggie wanted to tell your father first."

"I understand all that now, now that I've had time to think it all through. She wouldn't have wanted it any other way." She sighed. "And I know Maggie wouldn't be Maggie if she didn't act honorably. I allowed myself to forget that. I mean, deep down, I knew she was but..." Jayne gave a self-derisive laugh. "I wasn't thinking straight." She took a sip of her coffee. "I also don't know how I missed the resemblance between you and Maggie."

"No one was looking for it." Riley shrugged. "Why would you?"

Jayne nodded. "I can't imagine how dreadful it must have been for her when she had to give you up. And then to have to carry such a secret for so long. I wish she could have told us sooner." She looked at Riley. "Have you always known you were adopted?"

"Always. I have wonderful adoptive parents who've been very understanding. And I guess I always knew I'd want to find my birth mother, too, when the time was right." Riley shrugged. "About eighteen months ago I decided to register with the adoption group and eventually they gave me Maggie's name. It took me a while to get up the courage to make contact with her."

"It must have been a very emotional time for you."

"Initially it was," Riley agreed. "Then I got to know her."

Their eyes met and it seemed to Riley time paused, stood still. She knew the sun still warmed the morning, that the light breeze rustled the leaves on the trees and somewhere not far away a kookaburra laughed raucously, marking his territory. Yet all Riley could focus on was the deep blue of Jayne's eyes, the line of her cheek, the soft enticing curve of her lips.

"And you," Riley added, her throat suddenly tight.

"And I met you," Jayne said softly. "You came into my life when I needed the strength to take charge of it, to make the changes I'd wanted to make for so long. My work. And Darren."

Riley shifted uneasily on her seat. "Jayne, I didn't set out to create any problems between you and Darren. Please believe that. As much as I didn't like him, I didn't want to be the cause of you breaking off your engagement."

"You weren't the cause, Riley," Jayne hastened to assure her. "You may have been the catalyst I needed to change my life, but my relationship with Darren was undone long before you came on the scene. And at first I couldn't—" She gave a crooked smile—"or wouldn't, understand why Darren behaved so badly toward you. I know I'd barely mentioned you to him. I tried to tell myself he didn't usually treat people that way but then I realized that sometimes he did. I've used up a lot of energy over the years distracting him in social situations to sidestep his rudeness, or apologizing for him afterwards. Or both."

Riley told herself silently that she could believe that.

"Meeting you made me face up to a lot of things that deep down I'd known for some time. One of them was that I wasn't in love with Darren. Maybe after I returned from Melbourne he sensed that and he mistakenly blamed that on you." She looked at Riley. "And for that I apologize."

Riley shrugged. "You don't have to, Jayne."

"Yes, I do." She gave a derisive laugh. "I also didn't give him credit for being so perceptive. After he met you he made some derogatory remarks about dykes, and I lost my cool, got defensive out of all proportion. He said I'd better be careful because if I continued to champion the lesbian cause everyone would think I was one, too." She stood up, walked over to lean on her hands on the veranda railings. "That gave me some more food for thought."

Riley swallowed. What was Jayne trying to say?

Jayne turned back to face Riley. "When I was in Melbourne all those weeks I seemed to be working twenty hours a day, seven days a week. But one night, after all the guys had left, a couple of my female associates stayed behind for a nightcap. One woman was complaining about the lack of support she got from her husband. Every one of them told the same story and I realized it was the same for me with Darren. There was no reason why he couldn't come down to Melbourne to take some of the pressure off me. But he didn't."

Riley took a sip of her coffee, shakily replacing the mug on the table when she realized she was clutching it painfully.

"Of course, eventually the conversation turned to why women bothered with men. Sex, someone suggested." Jayne crossed her arms, as though she was cold. "I couldn't remember the last time Darren and I made love. I suspect we never did. We had sex and we discussed work. That was it. Not much to base a relationship on, is it? I'm not saying he didn't love me. I know he did in his own way, but we were never in love. We both acknowledged that the other night." Jayne sat down again. She nervously pushed a strand of hair back behind her ear. "Riley, when I, well, asked you when you knew you were a lesbian I wanted to . . . It wasn't just idle curiosity."

Riley's stomach muscles contracted. She could barely breathe, as she worried about what Jayne would or wouldn't say.

"Looking back, I suppose I settled on Darren as a partner because I felt the urge to conform and he was there." She picked up her mug and looked down at the dregs of her coffee. "I'm not proud of that. And yet it didn't consciously occur to me that I might be a lesbian, not until that night in Melbourne when I realized I was more at home in the company of women than men, that I always had been. Oh, I was too much of a coward to give it a name but—"

She glanced at Riley and away again, her face flushed. Riley wanted to take her in her arms, tell her she was anything but a coward.

"I also remembered Dayna. We'd been such good friends. But when I met Darren and started going out with him I forfeited that friendship. I knew somewhere inside me that when I was with Darren I would have rather been with Dayna, that I was sacrificing the pleasure I got from her company, all because I didn't have the courage to choose the so-called unconventional path. I was a coward back then too, and that night in Melbourne, I felt like a coward again. It so unnerved me. I wanted to come home to get it all into perspective. I thought it might have been because Darren and I hadn't had any time together for months." Her gaze met Riley's, and warm color touched her cheeks. "So I came home and, well, you stepped out of Joe Camilleri's overalls and into my life." A pulse beat a tattoo at the base of Jayne's throat. "And I knew my work, my fiancé, had nothing to do with what was wrong with me."

A lump rose in Riley's throat and she blinked back her tears.

Jayne's fingers clutched her coffee mug as though her life depended on it. "I didn't get much sleep last night. I spent the time thinking. About you and Maggie. Mostly about you. Riley, I—"

The peal of the telephone cut callously between them and they both started at the sound. Jayne seemed to need a moment to gather herself before she stood up.

"It might be Maggie," Riley said.

Jayne glanced at her wristwatch. "Perhaps. But it will probably be Darren. I said I'd be in to work early this morning. I'm rather late. If I let it go to message bank he'll only keep trying," she said flatly. She looked as though she was about to say more but she sighed and went into the house.

Riley slowly stood up. Some of her tension had left her, yet she didn't dare think Jayne had meant she cared for Riley. Deciding she preferred women was one thing, but making such a mammoth lifestyle change was another. Riley took herself to task. It wasn't like her to be so negative. She walked around the table and glanced into the living room.

Jayne was using the phone on the wall by the breakfast bar. After a moment she hung up the receiver. Her shoulders seemed to sag and she took hold of the breakfast bar for support, as if she was exhausted.

Riley took a tentative step into the room, wanting to go to her. "Jayne?" she said softly. When Jayne turned Riley saw the dampness of tears on her cheeks. Concerned, Riley walked quickly across the room to her. "What is it?" she asked gently.

"Just Darren's usual. I should be used to it by now. I guess I'm a bit—" She drew a steadying breath. "Did you mean it, Riley?"

Riley's eyebrows rose in surprise. "Mean what?"

"What you said. At Maggie's on Friday."

Riley swallowed.

"You said you loved me. Did you mean it?" Jayne looked at her then and Riley smiled crookedly.

"Oh, yes. More than I've ever meant anything in my life."

A tear trickled down Jayne's cheek. Slowly Riley reached out, her hand gently cupping Jayne's face and she brushed at the tear with her thumb.

"Oh, Riley. I'm so glad. I thought I'd—" Jayne turned her head, her lips caressing Riley's palm. "I love you, too. So much. I think I have from the first moment I saw you."

Riley grinned broadly, scarcely daring to believe the words Jayne was saying. "I did too. I thought you were the most beautiful woman I'd ever seen in my life."

Jayne reached out, drew Riley into her arms. She seemed to dissolve into Riley and they stood together just holding each other, until eventually Jayne took Riley's hand and led her over to the couch.

They sat down together, arms around each other, and their lips met again.

Riley moaned softly. "Last night. I thought I'd lost you."

"I'm so sorry." Jayne lifted Riley's hand to her lips, gently, sensuously kissing each fingertip. "Part of me simply wanted to take you in my arms. But I think I was in shock. I couldn't believe I didn't see the resemblance between you and Maggie and I was ashamed I'd made such a fool of myself. I was so jealous. Of you and Maggie. When I saw you in her arms I . . . Rational thought completely deserted me. The way I felt about you, that night together, it was all so new. Can you forgive me for that?"

"Of course." Riley chuckled. "Although when Maggie's had time to think about it I'm not sure how she'll feel about your mistaking her for a lesbian."

"She's already forgiven me."

Riley looked at Jayne in surprise. "She has? When?"

"Last night. When you were showing Dad and the boys the house. I told her the truth, that I was in love with you, but that I didn't know how you felt about me."

"You told her? What did she say?"

"Not much. She asked me if that was the reason I'd broken up with Darren. I told her you weren't the reason, that I was the reason. We may have some work to do there but I know she'll come round. She loves us both."

"Oh, Jayne." Riley frowned. "I don't want to cause any ill feeling between you and your family."

"You won't." Jayne grinned. "Dad will be won over by the bookshelves, Jake adores you, and so will Matt once he gets to know you."

"You sound just like Maggie, and Jake as well. In fact, he said much the same thing."

"Jake knows? About us?"

"He overheard Darren that afternoon. We talked about it and he asked me if I fancied you. I had to swear him to secrecy, hence his joke last night about my marrying him. He's a great kid."

"I guess I'd better talk to Jake about it." She grimaced. "Darren has a lot to answer for." Jayne shook her head and her hair swung against the curve of her cheek.

Riley took hold of a fair strand, twined it lightly around her finger, and her gaze met Jayne's. Jayne's lips parted, her tongue tip moistening their dryness and Riley felt the heat, the wild surge of arousal swell inside her, spiraling down to settle in a throbbing ache between her legs. Shakily she let her fingers slide out of Jayne's hair, her fingertip resting on the curve of Jayne's throat, feeling the pounding of her pulse, languidly tracing down over her smooth skin, pausing at the neckline of her shirt. She slowly and deliberately untied the drawstring.

Jayne's breath caught in her throat and she murmured softly, "Talking about marriage, I know Jake asked you first, but I was wondering if you might be able to see your way clear to sharing the rest of your life with me, Riley James?"

"The rest of my life?" Riley began to nibble the path traced by her fingertips.

"Mmm. Because I think I know now exactly what Maggie was talking about all those years ago when I asked her how I'd know when I was in love."

Riley looked up.

"You're the other part of me, Riley. The part that makes me whole. And I love you. So very much."

"I love you, too."

Jayne smiled tremulously. "I'm so glad you do. I've been totally out of my depth these past weeks. I couldn't seem to allow myself to think you might be as attracted to me as I was to you."

Riley rolled her eyes. "It's a wonder you didn't see it written all over my face. Mac knew right away. And he told me you weren't indifferent to me."

"Did he now? Was this before or after he left me in no doubt about what he had planned for you the night he stayed with you?" she asked dryly.

Riley chuckled. "He's incorrigible, isn't he? Can I take it you were jealous then?"

"Absolutely green."

"You were? Mac said as much. You hid it very well."

"I didn't sleep a wink that night either. I kept reminding myself you'd told me on two occasions that he was just a friend. Then I'd think about the one bed in the flat." Jayne shook her head.

"I was worried about that bed," Riley admitted with a grin. "There I was trying to give you the message that I preferred women and Mac was, well, being Mac."

Jayne slid a glance at Riley. "You must care a lot for him."

"I do." Riley reached up and gently lifted Jayne's chin, held her gaze. "But he doesn't kiss like you do."

Jayne gave a quick smile. "So you have kissed him, hmm?"

"When I was twelve. You'll have to ask him about it one day. But even then I knew he wouldn't kiss like you do."

Jayne slid her hands over Riley's hips and around her waist. "How did you know that?"

"I just knew. I'll show you," she said softly, leaning forward, kissing Jayne gently, slowly, on the lips.

Their kiss deepened and when they drew apart they were both breathless.

"The other night," Jayne said, her voice catching in her throat, "I couldn't believe how wonderful it could be. Your skin, your touch was so soft, and you made me feel so strong, as though we flowed together. All day I kept thinking I'd imagined it, that I—" She shook her head. "Was it a dream, Riley? Wishful thinking on my part?"

"No. It was real." Riley remembered the feel of Jayne's smooth body beneath hers and warmth flooded her body again. "It was very real." She slipped Jayne's shirt from her shoulder, exposing one upturned breast. "Let me show you," she said softly.

With a broken sigh Riley teased Jayne's nipple with her tongue tip. Desire raged inside her and she took a steadying breath. "Please. Tell me we have time for this," she begged Jayne throatily and Jayne bit off a groan.

"Actually," she said, her body responding to Riley's hands moving on her skin. "I was thinking I just might play hooky again today. Want to join me?"

Riley's lips nuzzled Jayne's ear. "Hooky? Mmm. So where do you want to go?"

Jayne smothered another moan. "I think, perhaps, upstairs."

Riley stood up, gently pulling Jayne with her. "What a magnificent idea." She slid her hands up under Jayne's loosened shirt to cup her breasts and Jayne threw back her head, her body arching against Riley.

Riley fought to control the wanting that threatened to overcome her. "But only on one condition," she added. "That you take the phone off the hook."

Jayne laughed softly, the sound playing over Riley like the rustle of smooth silk. "It's a deal," she whispered and led Riley toward the steps.

"How do I look?" Jayne ran her hands nervously over her straight navy skirt, checked the buttons down the front of her short-sleeved, tailored shirt. "Is this too casual?"

"You look wonderful. Stop fussing." Riley lay back against the pillows as she watched Jayne dress.

"Yes, but—"

"Jayne, you'd look fantastic in a Hessian sack."

She glanced at Riley and laughed. "Now that would be something of a fashion statement. But seriously, Riley, should I wear the navy slacks instead?"

"Darling, you look fine. Beautiful. No, make that stunning."

"Oh, Riley. I'm meeting your parents for the first time. I want to make a good impression."

"My parents won't care what you wear. They just want to meet *you*. And get your assurance that you'll treat me right," Riley added with a teasing grin.

Jayne looked across the bedroom at Riley and her eyes softened. "Should I tell them my intentions are honorable? That I want to spend the rest of my life with you?" She moved over to the bed and took Riley's hand. "That I'll cherish you, love you with all my heart."

Riley sat up, wrapped her arms around Jayne's waist, breathed the oh-so-familiar scent of her. "That should do for starters," she said softly as she undid the zip on Jayne's skirt and started to tug it down over her hips.

"Riley! Your parents."

Riley quickly unbuttoned Jayne's shirt and buried her face against the smooth skin of Jayne's midriff.

"Then Maggie and Dad will be here," Jayne said without a great deal of conviction.

Riley chuckled softly and slipped Jayne's shirt off her shoulders, tossing the garment on the bed. Her fingers played up the curving indentation of Jayne's spine until they reached the clasp of her bra. She quickly undid it and let her hands slide around to cup Jayne's breasts. Holding Jayne's gaze she slowly drew one erect peak into her mouth.

"They'll be here and we won't be ready." Jayne's back arched toward Riley's questing mouth. "Riley," she whispered on a moan, as she stepped out of her skirt.

Fire surged through Riley as her lips trailed downward, over Jayne's stomach. Her fingers slid beneath the elastic waistband of her undies and she drew them slowly down so her lips could continue their erotic path.

"They'll be here in half an hour," Jayne murmured brokenly.

"Then let's not waste time," Riley said softly, her fingers finding Jayne's secret spot.

"Oh, Riley, that's—" Jayne's hands clutched at Riley's shoulders and she moaned again. "Don't stop," she said urgently as she gently pushed Riley back onto the bed and moved over her.